P9-CFP-898

MOTHER COUNTRY

Also by Jacinda Townsend

Saint Monkey

WITHDRAWN

MOTHER COUNTRY

A NOVEL

Jacinda Townsend

Graywolf Press

Copyright © 2022 by Jacinda Townsend

This publication is made possible, in part, by the voters of Minnesota through a Minnesota State Arts Board Operating Support grant, thanks to a legislative appropriation from the arts and cultural heritage fund. Significant support has also been provided by the National Endowment for the Arts, the McKnight Foundation, the Lannan Foundation, the Amazon Literary Partnership, and other generous contributions from foundations, corporations, and individuals. To these organizations and individuals we offer our heartfelt thanks.

Published by Graywolf Press
212 Third Avenue North, Suite 485
Minneapolis, Minnesota 55401

All rights reserved.

www.graywolfpress.org

Published in the United States of America

ISBN 978-1-64445-087-1 (paperback)
ISBN 978-1-64445-175-5 (ebook)

2 4 6 8 9 7 5 3 1
First Graywolf Printing, 2022

Library of Congress Control Number: 2021945926

Cover design and art: Kimberly Glyder

To Rhianna Sade and Fadzai Iman,
who taught me how to love.

People are born. They are a life. They belong to nobody.

—David Gibb, father of Kilauren Gibb, who was put up for
adoption by Joni Mitchell in 1965 and reunited with her birth
mother at the age of thirty-two

MOTHER COUNTRY

PART I

DRY SEASON

I. Essaouira

And what, after all, to make of a choice? She'd chosen to return to Morocco with a man she'd wed just two years prior, a man she felt she could never know from Adam, a perennially constipated wind engineer named Vladimir who still shocked her in the mornings with his routine of gargling loudly before spitting. And now here Shannon was in calm, cool Essaouira, that frat boy of Moroccan cities, with all the riads, all the hotels, all the municipal buildings painted blue and white to mirror the water and sand opening out into the Atlantic.

After the roasted air and sandstone red of Marrakech, the breezy days and cold nights of Essaouira were a relief. Their hotel stood beachfront, with a view of the distant island of Mogador and its time-crumbled slave prison. Daytimes, when Vlad was away overseeing his powered turbines, she walked the streets behind the hotel. She wore sunglasses so no pickpocket could register her wonder, and put on the harried pace of the Moroccan women she saw running errands all around her.

Unescorted, she found flowering bushes in people's front yards, and a film of grit that blew from the graveled public lots to coat her hair. A mole, decomposing in stages until its fourth day dead, when what she found in its place were maggots, writhing in a dark, murky pudding of sand. She found an école privée for children, with a mural of dolphins and squid painted on its face. She took long lunches of fish tajine with glass after glass of red wine, and wiped her lips clean with wet napkins. The waiters exercised patience with her French. And everywhere, everywhere rode the persistent sound of wind, howling through the door cracks like lost souls.

She'd been collected at the Marrakech airport the Friday before in a private car, a newish Mercedes that hermetically sealed the extension of her American existence. Without Vlad running interference, she took in the traffic lights of Morocco, posted on actual poles, the bulbs within them old and heat dimmed, on the verge of not working at all. An ambulance had passed with its lights flashing, but no one, including her driver, stopped or even slowed to salute the urgency. In a roundabout near the city center, she saw an unhelmeted child sitting on the back of a motorcycle, holding fast to her father's back as he leaned into his turn. Morocco was at once psychedelic and ancient, like a collage of retro-painted postage stamps, every surface and every crowd turned seven different colors at once.

Even more stunning than the exquisite tiles of old palaces and the snake charmers with their cobras had been the taxi drivers, who seemed some new superspecies of human, a bridge from Homo sapiens to whatever would come next. They were hyperattenuated to the small movements of tourists and capable of replying in whatever language they'd been offered. She'd made the mistake, at the Djmaa-el-Fna, of entering the first parked taxi she'd found on the street, but when the driver started his engine, five other drivers came to beat on the hood of his car and shout obscenities: there was a queue, and in accepting her fare, he hadn't respected it. She didn't understand much in this country, but she understood the drivers—there was no other group of people so willing to have their asses beat over two American dollars.

In Essaouira, by contrast, she walked every sunblessed evening to Orson Welles Square, where people congregated and listened to the gnaoua drummers, and to the Scala, where the gulls soared overhead sighting fish in the market, then through the medina's covered walkway and up to the turret overlooking the Atlantic. She and Vlad took dinner at a different restaurant every night, and Vlad wrapped scraps of fish in his napkin to scatter to the stray cats and dogs they'd pass on their walk home. Sometimes, she walked to Bab Doukkala and took the long way back to the hotel, past what seemed to be the town liquor store and its accompanying prostitute, decked out in a woolen coat and high heels; a distinctive lime-green bicycle parked outside, one that belonged to the bearded Belgian she'd met her first day walking the beach. Maybe every small Moroccan town had one, she thought. An expat alcoholic.

Vlad was one of two American engineers on the project, the other being a younger woman named Jitka Stehnova, who'd been in a car wreck five years earlier and had her entire face reconstructed to a supermodel-level of chiseling. Jitka regularly wore black leather pants to work, Vlad told her. He spoke of her often, in tones of hushed admiration, and Shannon was glad for him, that he had someone to speak English with during his long weeks in Morocco.

Away from the demands of managing his speech in the company of people who could interpret its English-language undertone of dork, he relaxed into a sexier, less cowed version of himself. At night, he ripped the buttons off her shirt. He growled; she giggled. It felt, to her, like another beginning. Like the foreign film version of their marriage.

She asked about Jitka, whether she might like to join them for dinner some evening, but Vlad said she would not.

"But who is she going to speak English to?" Shannon asked.

"She's from Poland. English isn't even her second language."

"But she doesn't know anyone here."

Vlad chuckled once, mirthlessly. "She's doing fine for herself. Jitka's not the lonely type."

And so Vlad was high up in the hills of Diabat with his surveys, and she was riding down the main street in a petite blue taxi that seemed to be held together by one metal bar bolted to the inside of both front doors. She could feel the axle turning under her very feet. *God*, she thought, *what a country*. It was raining, so she walked through the covered part of the medina, passing stall after stall of dried leaves and herbal cures. They were stuffed in bushel baskets, with three-by-five cardboard signs explaining their uses. In every shop stood concoctions of Viagra, mostly misspelled as "Viagara." *Viagra Fort, Viagara pour les Femmes, Viagara pour Grimper les Rideaux.* She thought to buy some for Vlad as a joke, but she knew without the signs, she'd just be offering him raw herbs in a paper sack; the joke would be lost.

She was walking past a fabric store, eyeing a yard of purple cloth with gold thread running through, when she saw her—a little girl of about three, in blue jeans and a powder-pink spring jacket. Her curly hair fell to her shoulders in two braids that were sealed off with bright green rubber bands. Though she looked clean and kempt, she seemed alone. Shannon stood for a long time watching her, but no adult called or even poked their head out of a storefront.

She felt her heart step up its pace and realized the little girl was somehow familiar, though she couldn't possibly have known her. Africa was the Motherland, after all, and the proof was here in this small girl who could have come from her very own barren body. Shannon felt she was peering across time when she asked, "Qu'est-ce que tu t'appelles?"

8

The girl backed up to stand against the wall of the souk, refusing her any information, and Shannon wanted to believe it was because she didn't speak French—so many Moroccans did not—and so Shannon asked, in the small bit of dialect she'd gathered, "Asmitek?"

But still, the child denied her. She turned her body into the brick wall until she was facing it.

When she turned back, coyly, Shannon waved. "It's okay," she said, in English. "I'm just wanting to say hello." She watched, as the girl turned first one foot and then the other sideways in infant bashfulness. She scuffed the toes of her little shoes against the cobblestones.

"Where is your mommy?" Shannon whispered. "Where is she?"

And how, after all, to judge a choice? In two years with her solid, stable breadwinner, Shannon had forgotten the horror of going to the ATM and being denied. But in this quarter-developed country, of all places, she found herself again insolvent, the caisse automatique telling her there was no money to be had. It wasn't that Vlad had drained his bank account, or even that this bank was temporarily not talking to their bank in the United States, or that Vlad had forgotten to notify Fifth Third that they were out of the country, as had been the case when she'd tried a juice stall during her layover at the airport in Madrid. No. It was simply that she'd come up behind a long line of French tourists descended from a bus that waited for them along the brick sidewalk, and somewhere in that line of people, the machine had dispensed the last of its Moroccan currency.

She set out for the medina, crossing the sidewalk to the face of the Attijariwafa, but the man who'd been last in line was throwing his hands up in despair. The machine spat his card out of the slot, and he glowered at its sunken screen, clenching both his fists as though he might reach down and punch it. The cause and effect clicked, as between two sequential illustrations of an IQ test, and for the first time in her life, she understood just how much damage the French could do to a day.

"Merde," she spat, at the world of tourists. She spat a second, softer "merde" at herself.

She had a hundred-dirham note in her pocket, a leftover from her lunchtime trip through the medina the day before, whiling away all the slow hours of being someone's wife. She walked north toward Bab Sbaa, where a woman with one leg sat planted in her wheelchair, trying for eye contact with passersby. All day, thousands of times per day, Shannon calculated, the woman motioned toward her ample stomach and then rubbed her fingers in the air to make the universal sign for money. The first day, Shannon had felt cowed into giving her one of the single-dirham pieces she had jingling around the bottom of her purse. The woman had taken it in her outstretched hand, kissed her teeth in disgust, tossed the coin to the ground. Now, Shannon passed and gave nothing. Since she had no small change, nothing save the hundred-dirham note, she said it happily, even: "Je n'ai pas d'argent."

Vlad hadn't wanted to tour the medina, not once. Shannon had led him to the fish market near the Scala, but three tables in, he stopped. "All those eyes of the innocents," he'd said, viewing the mounds and piles of dead fish. She'd convinced him he had to witness the Viagra baskets, but it had been dinnertime, with all the locals out, and when they got to the bottleneck just inside Bab Doukkala, he stopped her by the shoulder and turned her back toward the exit. "All those pickpockets," he'd said, "walking shoulder to shoulder. Is there anything we really need in there? 'Cause I look at all those people and know I ain't lost one

10

thing in no Essaouira medina." He promised they'd go down to Agadir one weekend, to the real beach, where wind never blew. He'd booked a guide with a 4x4, he said.

Now she found the eggcup house Vlad had mentioned, and the fabric store next door, where she inquired discreetly and was sold an eighth of champion-quality Moroccan kif. She left the shop and walked the cobblestone streets, managing the constant wobble beneath the soles of her sandals. Above her, the sun had disappeared, and clouds swept by fierce winds at a rate of twenty, thirty miles an hour, fast as a parade. The sun shone through the clouds momentarily, and she found dust motes glistening in the air, but just as quickly the light was gone, the only visible world the one of medina commerce.

She passed a whittler, inhaling the clean scent of worked thuya wood, and then stopped to take in the fanciful plates outside a ceramics shop: goldenrod discs anthropomorphized into suns with eyes and noses, infinity-sign fish swimming in lines around the edges. She walked with neither aim nor direction, but soon came across the same little girl, in the same pink jacket as the day before. Today her hair rose free of its braids, in a bush of curls around her head. Still, she seemed to belong to no one.

Shannon bent until she was eye level, and carefully used the phrase she'd absorbed over the course of two Moroccan visits. "As-salaam alaikum."

The girl clenched her fingers open and shut: a wave.

"Come with me," Shannon said in English, taking her hand. She could almost hear the fast beating of her own heart, and she had to stop to make herself think, for she recognized the feeling: a cat, stalking birds. She didn't want to feel this bald, this rapacious, but the desire she bore was beyond her strength, as though her resistance had been drowned in all the Clomid and progesterone she'd injected into her own veins. She turned warm, and drifted temporarily to the side of herself, outside any lingering sense of morality. She'd wanted too much in this long year of not being pregnant; she'd desired too hard. She was as afraid of losing Vlad as she was of being permanently childless, and she was less afraid of losing herself as she was of losing either thing. "La glace?" she asked the girl.

But when the girl grinned and nodded her head yes, greed stepped itself back into the inner chamber of her heart. This was someone else's child, she reminded it, and she held her arm out to the girl in a manner slightly stiffer: this was someone else's child, whom she was just taking for ice cream. The girl clenched her teeth against her lip in a show of delight Shannon had never seen on anyone, anywhere, ever.

Holding the girl's hand, Shannon retraced her path, out to the Orson Welles Square and the Dolce Freddo, where she got lime for herself and, at the girl's pointed request, one boule of raspberry. Since they didn't share language, all was accomplished through pointing—the flavor, the refusal of the two napkins Shannon offered. They sat at an outdoor table eating, the girl hauling a spoonful to her mouth and then mashing it around, neither licking nor siphoning off cream but letting it melt on its own time.

"Qu'est-ce que tu t'appelles?" Shannon asked again, hopefully. But the girl understood nothing, so she pointed to her own chest, like Tarzan. "Shannon," she said, hoping it might get her somewhere. She pointed to the girl's chest, but she just stared longingly at Shannon, all the while her mouth still pressed around her spoon.

Shannon's mother had notified her of her grandmother's death at a Baskin-Robbins. "Your mimi, she has passed on," her mother said, though no water breached her eyes until the day of the funeral, at which Mrs. Cavanagh had given the eulogy. She'd stood at the church podium, rigid as a pole despite her shaking

voice, talking about how her mother had always meant the absolute best for her. Shannon was six years old and had not seen
her grandmother in eight months. What she mostly remembered was Mimi's small house in her tiny town near the Missouri
state line, the curlicues on the wrought iron columns that sup-
ported her porch. She remembered what her own mother would
say every time she caught her sliding down the stair banister, or
tracking mud in the house, or not wearing socks in the winter:
"My mother would have beaten me with a lampcord."

Shannon's grandmother had raised three children—Shannon's
mother, an uncle who also lived in Louisville but never visited, and an aunt who'd flown in to the funeral from the far-
thest reaches of Southern California and caught a return flight
back the very next day. "Sometimes, she caught us with the belt
buckle," Shannon's mother had said during the eulogy, to polite
laughter from the church. "But she always meant us well. She
raised us to succeed, all by ourselves."

"Finit?" Shannon asked the child of no French. The girl somehow understood and nodded, and Shannon walked her back to
the alley where she'd found her. The sun had moved an hour or
so higher in the sky. Still, no one stood ready to whisk the little
girl back into their arms; no one called her name. It infuriated
Shannon. Her childhood neighbor, Heather Berry, had gotten
a brand-new bicycle for Christmas one year but would leave it
lying around other people's yards. Shannon had ridden it one
day to a nearby park shelter, left it there, and never said a word,
not even as she heard Heather crying down the street, looking
for her bike. She hadn't stolen anything since, not even so much
as a drugstore mascara, and now she flinched at the memory of
her one attempt at theft.

She stood with the little girl in the alley, checking the colored soap bottles in Savons Mogador. A giant bronzed hand of

Fatimah lodged at the tail of the shop's sign, but its middle finger had been taken by vandals. Shannon wondered if, without this crucial piece, the hand still held its protective properties.

"Au revoir," she told the girl, and she tried to walk away without looking back, but she did. Several times. Until she had to make a turn through a covered walkway, and she lost sight, and then made a U-turn and doubled back through the walkway, only to emerge back into sunlight and her view of the child, to whom she'd assigned the name Mardi, for the day of the week she'd first seen her. Rain edged the day, and as she neared the fabric shop, the grit of the street swirled around her ankles, stuck itself between the soles of her feet and her sandals.

The following day, she again found the girl in the alley. "Glace?" she asked. "Encore une fois?"

Again, the girl nodded yes, though the look of pleasure on her face shifted a tick from gratitude to expectation, and Shannon wondered what would happen if she came and got the girl every day for the rest of the week she still had in Morocco, whether the routine would get old for both of them. Again, she watched the girl mash her mouth down on the spoon until all the raspberry cream had melted and run down her throat, and then, perhaps because it was a day that looked so much like rain, and she couldn't bear to imagine Mardi standing out in such weather, she took her small hand and walked her right through the narrow passageway from Orson Welles Square to Bab Sbaa. Down the brick sidewalk and past the possibly still-empty ATM, across the street, and down the boardwalk. As they walked alongside the ocean, the girl looked longingly backward, but Shannon pushed on, with one hand shielding her face against the wind-blown sand.

"Froid?" she asked, though she knew the girl couldn't answer. She moved Mardi from the right side of herself to her left so that she could block the wind that wanted to eat the little girl alive, pulling her close, as a mother bird might shield a chick with its wing.

And nothing in life had yet proposed this solution; there was no draped helix within which Shannon would become the perfect mother she herself never had. It was neither breaking a circle nor filling the hole in its middle. But when she held the soft palm of this child's hand and felt how she herself had never been enough for her mother, she realized she wanted to try.

They'd moved from a stone-cobbled walk to a brick-cobbled one, and the rain fell so hard, the droplets bounced off the ground. The rhythm of precipitation rose; it drummed the corrugated tin roof of the spaghetti diner and leaked in 4/4 time from the corner of the boarded-up ice cream kiosk. Shannon had thought that one day, when her mother was finished with the harrying work of parenting, she might become frivolous. They'd go shopping together just to go shopping. Stop and get their nails done. Eat gelato in a mall coffee shop. But it hadn't happened. Katherine Cavanagh had taken the hole in her heart, dug it wider, and poured in the cement of bridge club and gardening. A good part of her mother would simply never happen. And for that, Shannon was furious.

Against the force of wind, she guided Mardi back to the boardwalk, hurrying to the corner where the Hotel Atlas sat like a ship waiting to take them both in. They passed the reception desk, and Shannon pressed the elevator button. She felt someone's gaze, but when she looked over her shoulder, both the man and the woman at reception were busy, the man lost in counting small slips of paper, licking them with his forefinger to separate them, the woman typing, peering down at the keyboard. Neither of them was looking at Shannon.

Finally, the elevator arrived and she entered with Mardi, who was hesitant enough to have to be pushed slightly into the machine's cavernous belly, but who looked on with wonder at the reflective chrome panels as the doors closed. She stared mostly at herself, measuring the way her reflection moved its hand when she moved hers. When the machine started its ascent, she scrambled to hold Shannon's leg.

"It's okay," Shannon told her, as she again draped a hand over the girl's shoulder. "It's okay," she said again, as they exited the elevator to the quiet hotel carpeting. "It's okay," she said, as she removed the soiled clothes; as she washed Mardi's baby-fatted legs with a washcloth in the hotel bathtub; as she threw away the girl's underwear, so eaten with holes.

"It's okay," she told Mardi, as the girl sat in the middle of the bed in one of Shannon's t-shirts, laughing at cartoons. "It's okay," she said, from across the room, where she texted Vlad to warn him about what he'd find when he got home, but her spoken assurance was half drowned by the heavy rain just outside the window, and the drone of rai music from the room's small radio clock. Mardi, under the covers already, closed her eyes at last into sleep, drowning the other half.

Shannon buried her head in her own used bath towel, trying to pick up the molecular-level settling that might tell her what kind of mother she could be, but the towel gave off an aroma of high-end bath salts, crystalline and harsh. She stepped back, as if slapped.

"My mother raised us for a hard world," Mrs. Cavanagh had said at the end of the eulogy. She moved aside from the microphone. Bowed her head. "She raised us to know that sometimes," she said, directing her eyes toward a wall behind all their heads, "you're just going to have to take care of yourself."

II. The Sahara

And what, after all, to make of a choice, when capital-C Choice is no more than a bassline that disappears in fierce wind? When Allah has predetermined the groove of a life, no different from a ripple in thick sand? What to make of this small girl's teenaged mother, shortly before the small girl is even conceived? She was then a tall, thin fourteen-year-old with two long, dark braids roping down the back of her mulaffa.

She made her way five kilometers north, through the capriciousness of a desert that had removed her from slavery but left her two days wandering. In the heat of noon, she sheltered under an outcropping of rock; in the evening, she made a left turn at a sparse grove of trees and then doubled back to make a right. At night she followed the stars, taking Najam Shamal as a sort of celestial uncle. When she came upon a circle of tents that smelled like dangerous people, she avoided it altogether; at another camp, she begged for millet and rolled a bucket down a freestanding government well. She was grateful for freedom, happy to be choosing the routes of her small life. She wondered what her choices might mean, when set against the vast Sahara that meant to render her helpless.

After seventy days and seventy nights, the desert spit her out at Foum-Zguid. Seventy days of the sun's baking and seventy nights of the moon's frosting, and the skin on her arms had become hardened and dark, like a scorpion's shell. Time had been easy enough to mark in the desert, where Earth turned itself along a horizon clean of all but the stars and planets, but she'd not been able to count all the noisily landscaped days before then.

She rode one afternoon on the hot backside of a pineapple truck she hid under at Tamassoumit, and she lent her body for nearly a week to the driver of a white minivan full of tire treads. He took her from Zouérat to the northern edge of the Sahara, all the while smelling of the oil-covered tires he'd pressed into his chest while loading his van. At the border crossing, he pushed her down to the floor of the truck and spread a newspaper over her head; the gendarme asked him for his papers, and she did not breathe. When on top of her later that night, the driver dribbled palm wine from his mustache onto her lips. She was sweet like tkaout, he said, and he wanted to keep her. She ran from him in the night while he dreamed amid the smell of aging rubber.

The next dawn she stopped at a camp on a small lake east of Mijek, but it was a mistake—because she was three shades darker than they, the people there thought they, too, owned her, and though she was not asked to give her body to a man, the tribe asked her to do its most brutal work. The wash water she used to sweep away cooking ashes roughened her knuckles, and the dunes she galloped over to herd goats hardened her calves. At night, Mina Tahore, a woman from the chief's family, gave her dried camel ears. In a foam cup she'd stolen from the tireseller, Souria saved milk from the nanny goats.

Four weeks she counted, using a sawed-off pipe to groove the days into her mud floor, and on the morning beginning the second month, the ground shook beneath the khaima where she slept with seven younger slaves. The girls had thrown the floor themselves, pouring water on the sandy dirt and then smoothing

it with sticks, the seven younger girls pounding while Souria sang
and clapped time behind them, but now, as the ground trembled
ever so slightly, the floor that had been such a kind bed, so cool in
the desert heat, cracked alongside one of the girls' sleeping pal-
lets. The crack, as gently slender as a hair on someone's head,
grew long between two of the sleeping girls, and those two, like
the others, did not wake. Even in their sleep, the slaves knew it
was Saturday.

While the others slept, Souria looked out to find the tribe
enjoying their weekly holiday. Under the camp's lone mature
palm tree sat a group of men arguing, jabbing their arms into
the air over their tea kettle, and the brightly covered women with
their folds of young children had already begun to crisscross the
camp, navigating the intricate flight paths of Saturday visitation.
A morning wind blew a sheet of sand into the air, and Souria
wrapped her blue scarf around her forehead and pressed its tail
against her nose to block sand that blew at her in drifts.

A column of peace, then, until she felt the second tremor, a
clipclipclipclip that nipped under her feet as though the desert itself were waking. Souria lost her balance and fell, in a stunned
clump of herself, to the ground, where she watched as the hair-
line crack in the mud grew longer, past the sleeping girls' feet
and out through the bottom of the tent. Outside of the tent, the
tribe watched as its precious turquoise lake churned purple. The
sand all around them did not move, but people here and there fell
exactly as Souria had, as the layer of ground beneath the visible
world shifted more violently.

The tribe hushed itself in awe as poisonous gas darkened
the lake, whose surface rippled there and here with the hot di-
oxide bubbling from its depths; they were quiet enough to hear
the earth far beneath them making a hissing sound, as though it
were being cooked in a steel pan. Over this lull of popping earth,

a baby fussed; a chicken barked; an old woman began reciting al Fatihah. Souria began to walk backward, away from her own khaima, away from the camp of people encased in their own fear. This lake, this lake so pure and blue that it had called out invitation to her even before she found it, this beloved lake now swept glammy-eyed fish to its shore. The tribe watched for the ten minutes it took the lake to turn vermilion and then indigo, and then, as suddenly as if a djinn had commanded it to, the lake roiled a bloodred cloud from its depths. The tribe raised their heads and pointed. Souria stepped up her backward canter.

Because she knew, instinctively, that the cloud bore some molecular code of death, she pressed her scarf all the way over her eyes. But a young woman's screams made her drop the free edge in time to watch, from her distance, the people falling in shifts, their arms and heads loosening as though suddenly stuffed with feathers. It was a scene so powerful that she knew she'd retain it in every cell of her body. Men, chicken, women, goats, camels— all the living things of the camp—felled to the ground without so much as a chance to protest.

The clicking under her feet stopped, the wind hushed to a rumor, and a lone figure struggled toward her. He'd been emptying his bowels at the camp's edge, she could see, for he still held the palm leaf he'd taken to clean his ass—he'd not breathed the poison, either; though the violence of the event had somehow crippled him, they'd both survived. "An-najda!" he called, as he hobbled forward on the goldening sand. He shook his palm leaf at her.

His tagelmust hung in blue strips from his head, unraveling until Souria could no longer see his eyes. But the walk— tight like a bird's with a barely perceptible limp crimping the longer leg—she knew even in struggle. It was Sidi Ould Tissim, the knife sharpener, who'd slapped her across the face on Milad un-Nabi because she hadn't hauled enough water for all six of her goats. "Dark girls have no sense," he'd said, hitting her with such force she actually fell backward. Now he came to her, on his hands and knees, clutching his shirt, trying to rip it off his chest. It was his heart taking him, she saw—his heart, stabbed through with shock.

She leaned over to unravel his tagelmust, to unwind the respect he'd worn atop his head all the years of the adult life. "Help me," he rasped. He dropped the leaf and tugged at her mulaffa. The deep creases in the corners of his eyes crinkled to tell the great pain he felt. "An-najda."

"Let the devil help you," she answered in her own language, and she spat into the middle of his face.

"Arju," he coughed, before entering a clearing of language as broken and nonsensical as an infant's. He died with his eyes open.

She watched a long time, until it seemed that in death, Sidi Ould Tissim was looking not at her but through her, to her future, to her husband and her children and her children's children and her own rotting bones, until the wind died completely and she ran back to the camp. Hundreds of people, and she the only one left. Hundreds of thousands of ouguiya, perhaps. She searched the bodies of the dead, patting down jackets, rowing through pockets, lifting bosoms. She found that the well-dressed had little money on their person, but those in rags had carried every ouguiya they owned with them through the day. She'd been a slave eighteen months and not touched a man, though men had touched her. Now, she searched the men under the palm tree and found, in the shortest one's sandal, two thousand ouguiya. She restored his shoes so he could walk about freely in the world to come, but she left his kettle whistling steam into the hot noon sun.

She entered the chief's khaima and found Mina Mint Tahore

lying facedown across a mat, her two waist-long braids free, in death, of their headscarf. Souria bent and raised one of them, feeling its heft. She stroked its split ends, looked around, and made decisions. The chief had a battery-powered television set, but of course she could not take such a thing with her. She lay down, toe against toe, beside Mina and discovered, by measuring the distance, that Mina was but a few inches shorter, and she felt instantly sorry, because Souria knew what it was to spend one's whole girlhood as a giant. She removed her own mulaffa and ripped it to rags; she stripped the fine purple silk from Mina's body and suited herself. Searching from tent to tent she worked quickly, for she feared the powers of the dead. Pots still boiled on the fires, and water ran slowly from cracks in wooden bath pails, as though the inanimate objects were simply props waiting for another cast of characters. A lone buzzard circled high above the camp, but no flies lighted on the bodies. They'd been killed, too.

The sun moved, the shadows grew, and what had been the wind became the light communal noise of the dead becoming deader. Final breaths expelled as gases played inside lungs. Final shits taken as intestines released all that had sustained them. In one tent, a dead man sat straight up, his nerve endings responding to the hour's drop in temperature. Souria hadn't heard him move behind her, and almost dropped the money she'd taken as she ran past him out of the tent. She had a knowledge of death that came from seasons of animal slaughter, and all around her, she knew, the joints of the dead stiffened: she could almost hear them, as the creaking fortification of so many masts. She searched, and with each ouguiya, each franc coin, each newer pair of sandals to replace the new pair she'd slipped on before it, time wove itself into one long ribbon of overdue fortune.

Finished, she wrapped everything in her old blue scarf, secured it under Mina Mint Tahore's mulaffa, and ran back the way she'd come, aiming to leave the camp. When she happened upon Tissim Ould Sidi, already half covered with sand, she kicked his body supine and searched his pockets, finding only scraps of paper decorated with the trails of loops and dots she could not read. She shoved one scrap into her pocket in order to remember the look of cruel people's handwriting, and she reached into the bulge at the waistband of his pants, where she found a small cloth wrapped around thirty ouguiya. "Bastard," she whispered, "trying to hide so little." She spat on him twice more and ran. Past the camp's perimeter, into the desert, and away from Venus, which had just appeared on the afternoon sky. She'd always been running, she felt, and she'd always be running; until the end, since the beginning. As the sun fell behind the high dunes, lizards scattered out of her path, dragging their long green tails into holes in the sand.

The desert was quiet enough that she could hear the disturbance of an engine struggling noisily against its own disrepair, its giant wheels displacing the roots of fragile plants. "Mâshâ' Allah!" she shouted. She ran faster and faster toward the noise, faster than she'd run even in games as a small child, so fast that her thighs and stomach burned and her heart ached in her rib cage. Between herself and the engine rose a row of dunes burning orange with the day's departure, and arranged by the wind in such an orderly fashion that they looked like teeth in a mouth. She dug herself up the lowest dune and heard that the jeep had turned into the curve of trail closest to her.

The wind returned, and for the first time since she'd been kidnapped and sold into slavery, she remembered her mother, Fatou, now seven years dead. Souria thought of the lovely time of evening that came every night during her mother's final summer, the first that Fatou had trusted her to walk the half mile to their garden plot and its palms full of dates. "Be back before I miss you," Fatou would say. "Even in the garden, night is never kind." Her mother had lived only to cook and birth, it seemed, and she'd then been carrying her ninth pregnancy, the late child, who would pass through life only through his mother's death. The quiet, sweet-smelling baby brother had died after a week for lack of mother's milk. After Fatou's unstoppable bleeding, after her baby brother's swollen stomach and weak cries faded into fatal silence, the women of the village wrapped first the bigger, and then the smaller body in white cloth, and buried them deep under the sand. Her father had been unable to tend to all six of his living sons and daughters, and there were so many people in the desert who'd known—the people of their tribe, and the people of the other tribe, who'd come south that time of year for their crops. In this hundredth night of her thirteenth year, carrying apricots back from the garden plot, Souria had been pulled from the side of the road and onto the back of a truck.

Even all these months later, the vision of her father searching for her made the tears rise in her throat, but when they did, they just ran again upon that hard place, the place packed down and made firm by soreness after rapes and hunger after beatings. And there was a tectonic layer just under the hard place, one that told her that fathers sometimes sold their children when the children could no longer be fed. But this layer of her doubt, even when it warmed and melted, rarely found a vent through which to escape. The hard place kept it down, and absorbed and held her tears, now, and made her keep climbing the sand with one hand held ahead of her for balance, made her scramble down the other side of the dune into the jeep's headlights. The hard place freed her to wave and keep waving after the jeep slowed to a stop, made her stand spraddle-legged against the jeep's grill, as she'd seen angry men do in her village before a fight. She frowned at the driver even as he said his salaams, because she couldn't believe that after three firmly packed years, Allah was finally answering a prayer.

"I need to ride," she said. Through the bugstained windshield, she could see that the driver's eyes were moist and kind, not like the eyes of the people she'd been with in the months just passed. She was so close to the driver that she could see his eyes dart behind her as he searched for a solution to the puzzle of this lone, overdressed girl running out of the dunes.

"Are you real or jinnayah?"

She laughed, though the tears rose again. Though he wore European clothes, he spoke Hassaniya. "I'm a real girl. With real money. I'll pay you for a ride."

He nodded, and she edged around the hood to the passenger side, finally noticing a cigarette placed in the jeep's grill, butt-end out, a joke suggesting that the jeep itself was smoking. "Mawvalkoum," she said, as she fastened herself in. The driver closed his eyes and drew his breath at how hard she slammed his door, but she couldn't find words to apologize to someone to whom she was so grateful.

She was asleep by the time they met asphalt, and the man didn't wake her until the middle of the night, at Smara, when he touched her arm gently and asked if she needed to relieve herself.

On the contrary, she was parched: her insides were rags left out too long in the sun. She shook her head no. She felt that if she spoke, something in her would burst open and drown them both. He got out of the jeep and urinated, and Souria watched the back of his head, crowned by the headlights' glare. He pulled out a cigarette and lighted it, and by the time he returned, Souria was back in her dreams.

The next day he taught her how to drive the jeep, though he winced every time she missed the clutch. Through the windows, the sun roasted them both to chestnut, and over the course of six northbound hours, the desert left its inch-thick coating of dust on the dash. The sand turned Souria's jet-black hair to goaty brown, and the dead woman's mulaffa was still purple only in its creases. Souria's right hand, the one she'd used to grip the back of the truck at Tamassoumit, ached terribly when she shifted gears. But she was relieved to be able to let the man have a turn at sleep. He was as kind as his eyes had suggested, though he'd told her over a dinner of mouton and rice that he acted as a villain in a running show in his city. The effort of language was exhausting, and for days, through mountain passes whose summits made the engine slope and whose downward runs made Souria's stomach flutter, they failed to ask each other's names. Through sand seas and gendarme posts and a deep road rut they took ten minutes to dig out of, he asked of neither her present nor her past. Only as they approached Foum-Zguid did he ask whether she intended to ride with him all the way to the coast, to Casablanca.

"No," she said, without thinking, for the fearful little scarab in her head told her to. "I need to go home." She had woken up that morning to the sight of more mountain gorges than she'd ever imagined possible, and she knew that she no longer knew this land. Running away from Venus should have led her home, but she'd gone too far north, and now she was two thousand kilometers from Bou Naga, the last place her tribe had settled.

"Where will you go?" he asked. "And who will you go to?"

Souria stared at him. Took in the kind eyes and the dusty curls. She turned to the windshield.

"You have nowhere to go, do you," he said, not asking. She knew that he thought she was looking at the road ahead, when really, she was only studying a beetle whose back half had been smeared across the glass. "You running from the police?" he asked. "Like a dog? Well, you seem like a good girl . . ."

She thought he would debate with himself like this forever,

with each word burning a pinhole in her mind where the rays of disquiet could shine through. She took his hand and placed it in her silken lap.

"I'll help you," he continued, as though to himself. "I'm heading east on the next good road, and then I can take you to Casa. In Casablanca, you'll find a new life."

She no longer had the words to say such a thing as thank you. When he took his hand away from hers to shift gears, she took it back. She trapped his hand like a bird and held it to her chest. Slid it down the front of herself and pushed it into the space between her legs. The purple silk puckered in her lap, and she helped the man along by gathering the hem up with her free hand. She let his hand go finger by finger, until she had only the index, which she began to direct.

"You're just a girl," he said, though he didn't take his hand back until he needed it to shift gears.

"I have enough money to feed myself anywhere," she said. "The next town, leave me."

She smiled when they lucked upon the center of Foum-Zguid, and a patisserie that served pain chocolat, which she had never eaten. While she sipped mint tea and looked across the road at the white mosque with its red lettering speaking the way to God, the man asked around and found a caravan heading west. Souria took another round of tea with him and they waited. They waited until the buildings had ceased throwing shadows, and she could no longer make out the distinct shapes of the letters on the mosque. The sky lost its purples and oranges, and the trail of a passing jetliner gleamed moonlit against the cobalt ceiling.

In time, camels began to complain as the drivers kicked them to standing. The men pitched blankets to one another. "Ana mojoud!" yelled the leader, and Souria stood up from her table.

"What is your name?" she asked the kind man who had driven

her so, so far. He had driven her from slavery to freedom, a distance she hadn't known to imagine.

"Hassan."

"I'll always remember." It was as close as she could let herself come to thank you. She found herself unable to walk, and it wasn't the scared little animal in her head that nailed her to the spot in the little café on the mountains. It was Souria herself who could not move, who was so afraid and so tired.

"You can still ride with me if you want," said Hassan. He offered her two shirts he'd taken out of his jeep. "For the night. For the cold. You'll have both of them."

And the shirts, their distinct colors blending into one dark mass in the growing evening, told her what she needed to do. She bowed to Hassan, took his clothing, and ran off into the middle of the caravan, where, after some negotiation with the man atop the herd's leader, she mounted one of the last sitting camels. She dug her sore right hand into his fur and gripped the harness with her left hand just as the leader, wrapped against the cold with a striped gandoura, yelled for the pack to begin. Her own dromedary smelled like a latrine. He groaned and bayed at the hooves of his brethren marching all around him, but he refused to rise. Souria looked with terror at Hassan, who was standing stolid in the way of permanent goodbye. She kicked her camel's side, and the animal turned its giant neck. It hissed; it spat. Only when the very last animal passed, when she saw the stub of its tail and the waste falling out of its hindquarters, did her own camel rise to begin the long journey.

She tried to look back at Hassan, but her camel was moving fast and unsteadily on its stalky legs to catch up with the rest of the herd, and she felt herself sliding perilously forward. Her memory, then, would never get its fill. She'd remember Hassan only in parts—the sand-ridden hair, the thin arms.

Venus shone behind her and the North Star shone overhead. The cold air sunk its teeth right through her clothes and into her lungs. She was farther north than she even knew existed. It was Muharram the twenty-first, and though she'd long since lost track, it was the night of her fifteenth birthday.

III. Louisville

And what, after all, to make of a choice, when the great universe removes all others in an instant? When God snuffs out the promise of a life as if it were a cupcake candle? What to make of Shannon—shortly before Mardi is even conceived—a clinically depressed twenty-eight-year-old with a credit score of 590 and forty-seven dollars in her bank account? What to make of the front end of her fourth-owner, seventeen-year-old car, its metallized plastic crumpled like a wad of paper, its razor-thin front rotors warped beyond recognition? Shannon's head, wedged at an angle three degrees away from permanent paralysis? Her knee, its crèche of pain now sealed permanently into her nervous system?

But she wasn't dead. She knew because she was hungry.

Trough-empty hungry as she hadn't been in years, as if a small rodent were lodged just under her stomach, chewing its lining and emptying its contents with sharp little teeth. The hunger was such undoing that it threatened to unmake her altogether, and she wanted to stuff things back in—her Aunt Dixie's best green bean casserole; a slice of pizza she'd had once at a county fair; the popcorn with wholly believable butter that she used to have in high school, on the upscale end of Bardstown Road, at Louisville's lone arthouse movie theater.

Around her, all seemed pitch black, and she felt her eyelashes, shellacked with blood, pressed together like the bristles of a brush. She opened her eyes. Blinked twice. Thin shards of light penetrated reality, and all was not black, she realized: she simply could no longer see. She blinked again, and again the shards came—buried coals of light, scoping into focus like the first ticks of dawn. The world announcing itself in minute fractions. Which meant, effectively, she could not see. Full shadows no longer reached her, because now, she was shadow.

She couldn't see even inches ahead of her own face, but she could still smell. On her clothes, she could smell Vlad, his hair, its coating of cigarettes. Davidoffs, he smelled like. Karelias. Du Mauriers. He smelled like money, like the kind of thing she herself did not have. Just hours ago, she'd been on a second date with him, a dinner meant to transform their friendship into something shadier. He'd shown up with his whinnying laugh, his thick glasses magnifying the rosy circles of constipation under his eyes. He was cursed with the eyelashes of a pretty girl, and through them he fixed her with a look, the look of a small child who's managed to trap an insect under glass. He wore a bomber jacket that made him look, with his big leafy ears and fade, even more like a teddy bear.

She'd met him online, so she'd spent the first date trading real names, gauging actual height and weight. This second date, she waited a polite thirty-five minutes and two gimlets before pulling out the Barbara Walters. How did a brother come by the first name Vladimir, she asked, in what she hoped sounded like a tone of genuine wonder, and he told her how his father had been an engineer for Yugoslav Railways.

She had an entire system of questions then, since Vladimir seemed Perfectly Crafted American, the kind of Midwesterner bred from at least ten generations of previous Midwesterners, poring over his drink in the most intense manner available, sitting not erect but slightly hunched, in the manner of all nervous American men on blind dates.

"You grew up there, in Yugoslavia?" she asked.

"It's not Yugoslavia anymore," he said puffily, as if this weren't layman's knowledge. "Where I was born is now Macedonia." She watched him across the table, watched him put up an arm and pull an imaginary stop cord. "Toot toot," he said, because he was almost as drunk as she was. She giggled, not with him but at him, though Vladimir, she could already see, was never going to know the difference. "But I grew up mostly in Germany," he said. "We fled. The war."

Which war? Shannon wondered, but thought it crass to ask. She signaled the waitress with a nod of her head, ordered a third gimlet so she could make it politely through the final hour.

"The Makedonski Zeleznici," he slurred drunkenly, as she toasted. "Rusting shipwreck on wheels. May you never have to ride."

Shannon leaned over as she sipped, and so did Vlad, such that she caught a scent from his jacket, which he hadn't bothered to remove. Murattis. Stokkebyes. Sobranie Black Russians. She wondered if he smoked them with other women. She imagined him, with a thin slip of an Instagram influencer, rolling tiny leaves in rice paper. She found herself getting jealous.

Now Shannon couldn't hear her own breathing, and she was taking on the sinking knowledge that she could no longer hear anything, that somewhere inside her skull, the brain-to-ear mechanism had been shattered. But she felt, in her chest, the knocking of a shifting gear. She felt, between her skin and the car seat's upholstery, vibrations like water popping in oil. She hadn't heard her mother's voice in so long, and maybe she never would again, though she wondered, dimly, whether if she survived, she might feel voices instead of hearing them, whether voices she didn't love would send terrible vibrations running through her skin.

And she held pain everywhere. In the square of her back, and between her scapula and her clavicle, weighed a mountain of torment. The left side of her neck: one long column of hurt. She felt blood running down her face, viscous as glue; needles of injury pressing into her scalp. A burning tide rolled into her stomach, spreading to her intestines her liver her kidneys her—

She was a pincushion. She tried to raise her chin to take air, but the pinch at the base of her spine stopped her. The proper use of her body, she bet, wasn't something the women at the mall spa would be able to massage back into her life. God would never let her try anything again. The most she could do now was hope. Stay very still. And hope.

But as she was hoping, wondering how she might live in this new shell of a body, whether she'd ever go on a third date with Vlad or anyone else, darkness came. The shards of light disappeared altogether. They vanished even as the back of her tongue involuntarily moved itself to say no, please, please do not close me in. The darkness came and shut her down, first the torn ligament of her shoulder and then the deep zippered gash along her left cheekbone and then the boiling pool gathering in her innards. The darkness drowned her vision and then her thoughts, and it was frightening and merciful all at once. Chthonic.

She couldn't connect to the past or the future—conscious thought had lodged itself in one limited, discrete spot on the space-time continuum. But she could smell, as if it were petrichor, the moment of the tire's coming, as if dropped from the sky, its bounding onto the hood of her car. *Trop de gimlets*, she thought, but the thought hadn't come as fast as the tire, whose rebound off the hood of the car wedged it right through the windshield. The cosmic *boom* knocked through Shannon's brain now like a pinball circuit, as if it had happened over the course of hours rather than half a second—the black rubber advancing toward her, the slide of the car into the median, the 180 her Toyota did in the newly cut highway grass, the crunch of metal as it smacked into the face of an oncoming tractor trailer and ricocheted into the outcropping of shale. Glass on her shirt, then. Square grains of it on her eyelids. Granules in her mouth, in the pockets of her cheeks. She'd heard her own sharp, unsurprised breath, and the world had left her. She couldn't know for how long.

Now, in present, in this inadequate cache of time, she heard weeping. It was the most defeated sound she'd ever heard, the repeat of a machine part about to perform its last. "My God, my God," said the weeper, and Shannon heard that it was her mother, her accent returned to its native West Virginia for this production of grief.

"Mom," she said.

She thought she said. But her mouth no longer worked.

"Mom," she said again, and her brain at last connected to a muscle in her speech mechanism, so that a noise did emerge, and she could hear, even with her dead inner ear, that this noise had meant something. "Mom, my face hurts," she said, but her words were a spread of water trapped under glass. Shannon felt her mother's hand atop her own, air-conditioned flesh so cold she would have pulled it away, had she still control of her own body.

She'd solidified against both of her parents since she was held back in the fifth grade and they'd smoothed disdain over her all summer, as if illness were her fault, as if the cresol spill that third-degree burned her backside and plumbed out her hair in tufts was her own little eleven-year-old doing.

She'd been fleeing a Saturday afternoon of ennui, her mother at the head of the dining room table, shelling peanuts with her bare hands, squeezing the pocked and withered shells as though they'd hurt her feelings. Her father sat at the table's foot, as far away from her mother as possible, using a silver vise to crack walnuts. Shannon had run downstairs and walked past them, right out of the kitchen, through the breezeway, and out the side door. Down her small street of rust-bricked houses and into the forest beyond. She followed the trail but came across nothing special—no fallen trees, no coupling deer—until she got to the end, a clearing where the railroad tracks lay. There, just ahead, the boxy compartment of a train car had rent itself apart in halves. She saw the knobby limbs of a shrub spread out from beneath the metal and imagined the world of marvels that had been crushed. The small, unsuspecting animals now dead, anthills flattened back against the soil.

The grass looked wet beneath her feet, but she sat down to watch. The brown car was marked all over with the Archer Daniels Midland logo, but she couldn't see what had been inside. A lone bulb had been caged in metal on the car's ceiling; now, the cage bent outward so that the bulb poked out into sunlight, its filaments glowing orange.

"You can't be sitting here," someone said from behind her. She turned to find a man, tall and lanky, dressed in a yellow reflective vest. He'd just taken a piss, she supposed, because he zipped his fly. He put his hands on his hips, said, "Them's chemicals you're sitting in."

She got up to run, but he looked her up and down, took in the moisture all over her shorts.

"Shit, kid," he said. "Where's your parents?"

She'd had a hospital stay then, blisters covering her backside, a respirator strapped to her face. The first time she'd seen her father weep. The first time she witnessed her mother with her hands bowed in front of her face, praying. And Shannon's own first terrible decision: she wasn't allowed any more, not ever. But she'd make more faulty steps that year, more and more user errors, until the end, in June, when her mother took Shannon's final, failing report card and folded it into a little triangle that she flung into the fireplace. It hit the dark bricks with a satisfying thud.

It stayed there for months, through the summer and fall, until her father lighted the first winter fire. She was there, sitting silently on the steps where he could not see her. He unfolded the card—she heard him. "Waste of a child," she heard him say, before folding it in fourths and throwing it back in.

She coughed, intentionally, then heard the snap of her father's forty-seven-year-old knees as he rose to look over the banister.

"Dad. I'm not stupid. It was just a lot this year."

"I know, bird. I'm sorry. I didn't know you were sitting there."

But she knew the word *sorry* relieved only the person on the lighter end of a sorrow. And she'd always suspected she couldn't trust him—could not, in fact, trust either of them. The weekend of her first school play, her mother had skipped town. Not for a necessary trip, but for a regular weekend at Lake Barkley with her college girlfriends, an annual gathering they could have taken any other time. Her father had been left in charge, and Shannon remembered the cold eggs she'd gotten as she was already putting her jacket on for the bus stop; she remembered dressing up in her costume after she got home from school only to sit there waiting for him, waiting and waiting, the papier-mâché apple bowing itself around her body so that she had to sit on the edge of the sofa. He'd forgotten, he said, when he finally walked through the door at a quarter after six, when there was no use going—she'd missed her entrance.

But he had his way of ignoring her, too, when he was right in the room with her. He'd taken her to the pediatrician for her earache, but the doctor had examined her pelvic area, claiming he might as well do the regular routine while she was there. Her father frowned slightly, then turned himself back into the news magazine he'd taken from lobby. She'd indict him later, in her mind, when she remembered Dr. Cannon's heavy breathing. That was in the fourth grade.

When she heard her father say it at the end of fifth—*waste of a child*—she decided to break apart from her parents forever, the frustration being that she knew she had seven more years to live with them. It would be less like the snap of a branch from a tree than like the excision of yolk from an egg.

She looked for love in other children at school. Her teachers. Unleashed puppies she met on the street. The only person who fractionally loved her seemed to be her neighbor, Mrs. Kleese, but since Ms. K had dementia, she couldn't trust that either. Then again, sometimes she thought that was just it—to perfectly love someone, you needed a disease of the mind, a lack of filter that would supply all the conditions. Ms. K was an eighty-three-year-old woman who lived in a house full of mice and boxes and spoiled food, and Shannon never told her parents about the visits. At the door, Ms. K always kissed her on the cheek; they were wet, sloppy kisses that air-dried slowly as Shannon walked home.

After the cresol, her body tried to solve itself with a tic: anytime she sat, her legs flapped open and closed like the wings of a butterfly, and she couldn't stop it. *Flutter flutter flutter*; her central nervous system took over. It was worse at school, the boys staring at her as if this scissoring of legs meant she was open for other things. When she did it in public, at restaurants, or movie theaters, her father gave her a pitying look.

"Mrs. Cavanagh," she heard someone say now, and when her mother's hand slid off her own, she tried to open her eyes, but she couldn't. "We're going to try nerve stimulation. Get some localized response to pain. You can stay in the room, or leave—no matter."

Shannon felt, on her skin, her mother's slick, oily whimpers. Her developing sense of echolocation told her that the rod of her mother's spine had bent all the way forward, so that her face hovered inches above Shannon's own. "Oh dear God," she said. "I can't watch."

Shannon tried to shut her eyes, but they were already closed. She willed herself back to the underworld, but Hades refused to row.

She regained sight her second week in the hospital; she could see, as if through planum glass, the outline of her mother, tapping into her phone, but the stubborn little snail of her tongue still refused to uncurl itself into words. She still had no gross motor skills. Still peed via catheter, and shat—involuntarily and explosively—into a diaper. But she could move her fingers to write notes, small missives about things she needed, and the times at which thirst and hunger arrived. *Brain like thick mud*, she wrote. Once they understood her deeper understanding, the doctors spoke back in response, in a mash of clinical and lay language that indicated she had a traumatic brain injury.

The good news: it would heal. And save for its two shattered vertebrae, her spinal column was intact. She would, they wrote, recover the ability to walk, dance, and piss.

Some bad news: her face was ruined. Her mother had shown her with a chrome-handled hand mirror, her mother's head dropped in shame as she held it apart from Shannon's face. It was a long, puckered thing, the wound, running the length of her right cheekbone. They'd sutured it together quickly, with old-fashioned staples, and in the mirror, she saw the little bite marks where the staples had been removed. Twelve of them, in two neat little rows of six, just like the little French girls in *Madeline*.

She imagined a third date with Vlad and his money, his telling her it was okay, her face was fine, he was just glad she was still alive. Maybe he'd even say something sweet and winning, something like *scars are beautiful because they're proof you survived*. A bit of virtue signaling before he ghosted her altogether. Maybe he'd even take one of her unruined hands in his own, expecting the sweaty palm he'd shaken on that first date, but he'd be getting a different hand now, a cold, dry palm. He'd be getting a woman who'd brushed up against mortality and returned with prophecy.

She thought how unfair, because it was a car wreck, and the scar could have shown up in some other, less devastating fashion, but apparently the scar had had aspirations just like everyone else. It could have settled for being a crick in her neck, a bruise on her forehead. It could have left her completely untouched; it could have been the cute chipmunk running across the road at the moment of impact, forever lodged in her cerebrum to sadden her. The scar could have announced itself as a crushing case of PTSD that would leave her white-knuckled every time she got behind the wheel of a car.

But no. The scar needed her. It had seen how optimistic she was, and for no good reason—her parents had been awful to her, just as their parents had been awful to them, and even her maternal great-grandmother had been an unmaternal icebox of a woman, and so on and so forth, up a line all the way to Eve, every damn thing every mother's fault. Not one of these women had left her cheating husband, pursued that machinist's job at the factory, or left the state in a loaded-down station wagon, destining herself and her progeny for freedom. These women had

stewed in their trauma, passing it down through the generations like the seeds of an heirloom tomato, and Shannon, who
had become the scar's aim and target, simply did not deserve any
better—this scar needed her, like a glob of molten glass it would
blow into spiritual shape.

She'd grown up unscarred and—she was realizing too late—
beautiful. Now, she'd have to grow further, as a woman the world
devalued on sight.

When her head hit the windshield, the wound spread into
something deep in her flesh; it lay bare things she hadn't even
known about herself. People would look at her now and think the
worst, that she'd been in a knife fight, or that she'd survived the
explosion from a house fire that was somehow her own, drug-
addled fault. It was simply human nature, to look at other people
and presume the worst. And so, the scar had ripped into her because as a host, she was the best. It had zippered Shannon's face
clean open because it wanted attention, and her face was the most
efficient way.

Some worse news: the second MRI had picked up a ball of bone
in her uterus. It was just a mellow stone, the surgeon said, the size
of a sweet pea. It was causing no harm, resting there in her body,
but it would stop any children who tried to take root in her. It
was easy enough to remove at the same time they repaired her
spleen, so she needed to decide, right now, without even being
able to say it aloud, whether she'd like to propagate the species.

And because it came to her instantly, like a cat springing onto
a shelf in her mind, that it was probably the early chemical ex-
posure, that the cresol residue was that powerful, that it would
never stop snuffing out the possibilities of her life, she wrote
this note: *Likelihood of bone growing back?*

"Good question," said the surgeon. "We can't know."

Good question. She was so wise to ask. A smart girl after all. What she wrote back to him was entirely, dearly true: *I'm not sure I need to be reproduced.*

He chuckled, thinking she didn't mean it. He was going to push her into having the stone removed, she saw. There was money and pride in it for him. He would save her; he would get paid. But Shannon wasn't joking. She fancied the end of her miserable line being her.

If it hadn't been too long to write, if it had been socially acceptable to tell a stranger her deepest resentments, if she'd thought the doctor cared, she would have explained to him that this second week in the hospital, she'd begun to hear her mother's voice. "Shannon," she'd said the day before, her speech pressed into Shannon's consciousness as if conjured from the back of a dark arts store in the French Quarter. "Shannon, it's not natural not to talk to your mother for ten years. I am the person. Who loves you. The most on this earth." Vision had almost completely returned to Shannon's retina, and she could see sunset streaming across her mother's brown hair, revealing all its auburn strands. The almond skin of her face had turned blotchy and red. She'd left no room for argument, and Shannon was trapped there, her eyes closed as if she were still deaf, no way to call a nurse, who might click her mother off down the hall.

What she'd wanted to tell her mother was that there was no way to be certain anyone at all ever loved anyone else. Love was like Santa Claus, or the Tooth Fairy, or Godot—highly conceptual, subject to individual interpretation. Love was like a Catholic reliquary: its authenticity could never be assured, yet people held it sacred, regularly offering their devotions. She wanted to tell her mother that under measures both subjective and objective, she didn't love her so much as she saw her as proof of her competence. A project. The houseplant she'd finally kept alive.

Shannon could not, however, say any of that. All she could do was make a sound half-whimper, half-breath, and continue listening, even as a nurse came into her room and drew blood for surgery prep.

"I love you," her mother continued, in a tense whisper strained by her outsized insistence. "I live for you."

She'd always spoken that way, in refrain and platitude, pausing for effect after each clause, like a Baptist minister. "I talked to your father," she said. "You know your father and I are divorced now?" She left audial space to heighten the drama. "The year you went to college, I filed. I could not take Marshall even one second longer than I had to."

She'd continued, her voice a grade of peace Shannon had never previously heard, and she wondered if her mother had taken up yoga, procured shrooms, discovered Jesus. "But your father and I will come together now," she said, the end of her phrase turning up in whisper, "for our one and only baby."

When she got up to go to the hospital cafeteria, Shannon rolled her eyes as far as her strained muscles would allow. She lay there, swallowing bile, until she fell asleep. Her dreams crashed into one another, splicing one long montage of angry. She woke again and again: someone had just thrown a plate, screamed at her kindergarten teacher, tossed sand into the eyes of a kitten. She woke because her mother was speaking into her phone, telling someone, "Getting her ladyparts fixed might not be such a great decision. I mean, you should see this thing on her back."

It was a tattoo Shannon had gotten freshman year of college, right after her first set of final exams. She'd wanted a tiny tramp stamp, but the artist had protested, told her that in order to get the detail she wanted, it would have to be bigger, and so she'd ended up with a huge phoenix, its wings spread from hip to hip, one of its talons dipping into her left ass cheek. She could turn far enough to see three-quarters of it if she stood, naked, in front of her bathroom mirror: every time she looked, she felt like a porn star. One more of a set of questionable decisions. In high school, she'd chosen terrible friends. Girls who insisted she do worse than they did on math tests, boys who made her take them in her mouth under the bleachers at football games.

By her midtwenties, the crawling rot of her self-esteem had gone more upscale: the coworker who made her go shopping in a boutique too much for her salary, the married man who took her all the way to Paris to fuck her. She wanted to tell her mother that this had all been mostly her fault—even the razor-thin rotors that had no doubt contributed to the car accident were an indication of self-neglect, that and a transference of abuse. But before she knew it, she was in the surgical staging room with no pen handy. No pad. No one to ask, because they'd closed the plastic screen all the way around her and her mother.

"They're going to fix her," her mother was saying, still to the phone. "But she has no business being anyone's mother. No business at all."

IV. Louisville

The University of Kentucky's Financial Aid Office has been notified that the current status of your student loan(s) is DEFAULT. **Who sends the default notification?** *Notification comes from any of the agencies that track student loan history—*

Shannon found herself unable to breathe. When excised from its envelope and unfolded, the letter wouldn't let her. They were adding a 25 percent collection fee to her student loan balance, the letter said; she now owed $112,520.37, due immediately. She tried to reread—the individual letters blurred, danced within their words. She looked at the blank wall and saw the projected film of her future, now dashed against rocks. She looked back down at the letter, smoothed it on the table, then picked it up again to tear it to bits, tiny bits of confetti she might throw at a parade.

A celebration for the class she'd taken on Karl Marx, and Werner Sombart's theory of late-stage capitalism. How much had the class cost? At the time, she hadn't paid any attention—just paid her bursar bill with the loan check. Maybe, if she had divided up a semester's tuition, she would have figured out that one class cost a cool four thousand? How much would she be paying for that class now, these ten years later? Eight thousand?

Ten thousand? Shouldn't she have been taught simple division and subtraction instead? Isn't that what adulthood turned out to be—division? Subtraction? What would Werner Sombart say?

She'd started off flying right, making payments until the day she was fired from her temp job, at which point all of life had seemed pointless. "We're just waiting for you to make something of yourself," her mother said, as Shannon floated through her perfect state of unemployment. *Make something of yourself*, Shannon heard in her head every time she brushed her hair before an interview. *Make. Something.* "Wait'll you have kids," her mother said, ominously. "You'll want all your financial ducks in a row."

Unemployment had lasted for two fatal months, during which she drove up her credit card balance to an unsustainable amount, and after she got another temp assignment, she was still haunted by the day she'd gotten that first notice of termination from the agency—her direct report at the insurance company hadn't had the gumption to tell her himself. She'd forked a sausage into the skillet and then rolled a joint, forgetting the stove until the smoke alarm began its terrible Morse code of shrill. She ran back into the kitchen to find the oil all round her food turned to sludge, and she tossed the burnt sausage in the trash. The dead meal was a metaphor for her life, she thought. And poverty made you think in clichés.

Now, she took the tiny bits of Sallie Mae's letter, put them into her mouth, and swallowed them in one fierce, mulchy gulp. She tried to breathe while thoughts of her future exploded in her head. What remained were days of penury. She'd cart her cheap groceries onto public transportation in a metal basket. She'd shuffle into court in a tunic from Wal-Mart, listen to the judge sentence her to debtor's prison. Blood streamed out of one nostril and down onto her lips. She pressed the heel of her hand against the side of her nose to stanch the flow, and tried to breathe through the other side.

How does default happen? Default happens when a student fails to repay a loan according to the terms agreed upon when he/she signs a promissory note or makes payment arrangements with the lender—

The rest of what she'd bought with $45,000 of borrowed money turned $112,520.37 became flotsam drifting through her consciousness. It wasn't, she remembered, all for an education, not of the formal sort. There were cans of cheap ravioli, tanks full of gas from the Circle K, dollar-store wine glasses she displayed on the dusty bookshelf the college provided. And she'd stood facing herself in a mirror one night in 2005, wearing a little black dress she'd ordered from J. Crew. She turned to the side and checked the mirror girl's cinched waist; she touched her own waist—they were the same. The same scalloped hem as in the mirror, the same silken overlay on each shoulder strap. The young woman in the mirror looked like someone Ralph DeBurgh could fall in love with, and so also, she supposed, did she.

When her telephone rang, she left her dorm room and found the noise of cicadas filling the spring evening, and a slight chill that made her more excited than cold. She found Ralph DeBurgh, sprung from his fraternity house and sitting on a brick wall, waiting for her with a bouquet of lavender roses. She'd take them home later, put them in a Mason jar, look up the meaning of his color choice. She'd wonder aloud whether he knew what they were said to indicate: love at first sight.

It didn't matter how the date had ended because this was how the dress was ending now: it had been $80, now turned—if she did her math correctly—$200. In the back of her mouth, a cavity made itself known with a pulsing ache. People didn't understand how you could work all your life and still die with rotten molars, but here it was. She thought of the letter again, its clinical *This is to notify you*, as if the recipient wouldn't know. An awful gurgling sound from her stomach prompted her to pick up her cell phone.

Accidentally, in her stress, she dropped it on the floor, and it went skittering across her kitchen. She bent to pick it up and the lack of oxygen kicked her brain; hyperventilation made her lie prone while dialing. She looked up and saw a thick upholstery thread hanging from one of her old dining room chairs, swinging down like a kind of tail. Again, her stomach made a terrible noise, but it wasn't the glob of paper she'd swallowed. It was the shits she felt coming on.

On her phone she made a search for Sallie Mae, but when she scrolled down to its 800 number, she couldn't dial. She couldn't, she couldn't, and then finally, when she thought about herself standing before a judge, she did. She heard the smile in the female robot's voice as it offered a menu of choices, a kind of spoken-word essay about what Sallie Mae might do for her, which she knew was nothing. She cradled the phone, felt it shaking in her hand. The robot asked her a second time to dial 9 for a regurgitation of choice. She hung up.

*In order to get out of default, you must complete **ONE** of the five options:*

- *Repay or satisfy the loan in full;*
- *Make six agreed-upon monthly payments over a six-month period. Your payment must be approved in advance by the Department of Education. You must continue to make timely monthly payments to maintain your eligibility, or else it will be permanently lost until the debt is resolved entirely. You may qualify for this program only once;*

- *Consolidate your loan through the Direct Loan Program;*
- *Rehabilitate your loan through a loan rehabilitation program; or*
- *If your loan status is listed as default and you have paid the loan in full, request a Default Resolution Letter to submit as verification.*

She had no plans to tell her father, yet he called. "Your grandmother got a letter from Sallie Mae," he said.

"I'm in default."

"I know. This has upset her. Take care of it."

"What did the letter say?" she asked, but he'd hung up in a fury, her father had. Neither of her parents understood that this wasn't the same country they'd young-adulted in. You could never just hand over $112,520.37 to make a piece of paper go away, the same way you couldn't hand over the initial $45,000 when you were twenty-two years old and temping for $12 an hour. You could never secure a mortgage for the $275,000 that would net you a very average house in a very average neighborhood, and it didn't matter, because on $12 an hour, you'd never save the $20,000 down payment.

But when she saw women her age not living in her shitty apartment complex on Brownsboro Road but turning off ahead of her into the newer housing developments, when she saw them at the coffee shop wearing upscale leather shoes and unpacking chic strollers from Range Rovers, she knew they'd come from a different place to begin with. No student loans. Wealthy husbands, helpful parents: places Shannon had never been. A baby was the ultimate American symbol of success. And one more thing she'd never have.

V. Mauritania

In Tazenakht, where the caravan stopped, Souria found a large, kind family of sheep farmers who needed help butchering. They were Amazigh, could not communicate with her, and did not try. They spoke encouragement to her in their own language, and, when she at last sliced cleanly through a tendon with a single stroke of the blade, gave her a chorus of approval.

The mother of the family was short, thin, and nervous. She chewed gum all day, and every few hours she'd walk to a small, dying tree on the property to affix her used gum to its bark. The tree was covered with pink and green dots, such that when the woman stood next to it, Souria could see how the gum started at the height of her ankles and ended just above the crown of her head. Souria wondered whether the gum was killing the tree, or if the woman had chosen to torment a tree that was already ill.

The father of the family had exactly seven teeth, all of them in the bottom of his mouth. He had one good eye and one wandering eye that sometimes rolled to focus on her, and when she had occasion to look at him, when she handed him a pair of ears, or the slick liver pulled from a goat's insides, she made a point of looking at the poor, unloved eye, the one the rest of the world never watched.

The father, perceiving an understanding Souria didn't actually have, spoke to her in his language, sometimes gesticulating wildly and even blooming to anger ahead of the thesis of his one-sided conversations. "Ash katfker," he'd say in conclusion, then spit, as though she'd responded. Souria listened, and sometimes even grunted in agreement. The mother and the father had eight children between them, and the older children helped with the slaughter while the younger three climbed in the argan trees. At night, they roasted goat meat over a desert fire. The younger children sang, and the mother stood on her knees in the middle of their circle and danced gedra. Between key changes the father pressed on with his vitriol, though everyone else ignored her.

She stayed the two days until the town market, where she inserted herself in the line for a bus heading north. The bus turned curves and passed along mountains, and she grew so angry with nausea that when at last the bus pulled in to its gate at Bab Doukkala and stopped, she shouldered her way past an old grandfather to disembark first. He yelled at her in his language and kept yelling, until a middle-aged woman who'd been standing along the brown brick wall of the gare came over to tell him to stop. Released from his noise, Souria looked over the woman's shoulder and saw the wide concrete path, the people zooming by on mopeds, buses and cars belching smoke as they shifted gears. The city was more frightening than Souria had thought it might be. It was a colossus.

She'd been to a city before. According to the way other people believed these things worked, she had not. But once she'd left camp with her father and her two brothers in Hassan Ould Diallo's jeep, and she'd laughed as they released her older brother's roan goat from its thick ropes and then chased her across the desert. In the jeep, driving twenty kilometers an hour, they wore the goat down, slowing when she slowed, sometimes stopping the jeep to give her hope, then speeding up again behind her just as she caught wind. After three-quarters of an hour the goat stopped, wide-eyed and braying, her knees buckled in exhaustion beneath her belly.

Souria's younger brother, the one not leaving the tribe for the city, got out of the jeep and roped the goat back into imprisonment, this time with her fore and rear legs tied together on a wood post. He shoved her, face first, into the back of Hassan Ould Diallo's jeep, where they'd put down a matted tarp to absorb her excretions. She never stopped braying, and Souria brayed back at her in her small girl's voice, setting the inhabitants of the jeep to laughter. The goat brayed all the way to the black-topped national road, to the place where the bus to Nouakchott stops to take in its people. They stopped there and got out of the jeep, the small breeze blowing Souria's hair out behind her, the desert heat rippling the air in front of them so that when they got out of the jeep they looked, to the people of Aguilâl Faï, as if they might be a mirage. Hassan Ould Diallo stood with his arms folded, her father beside him. Souria stood between her older brothers. She was the only girl in the line of five, and she'd been allowed to go because she was only six years old, and not much needed in the camp.

She watched her brother set the stick over his shoulder and carry his groaning goat to the bus. He set her in the sand so that he could climb the ladder on the rear of the bus, then reached out for someone to hand her from below. He set her atop the bus with the bags of rice and the plastic suitcases, much faded from so many trips in the desert sun. He climbed back down, and got on the bus. Souria watched him stare sadly out the window at all of them as the bus pulled away, but he didn't wave, and she didn't know whether he was looking at them or at the fierce noonday sun. She watched her brother carrying himself to the capital city, she imagined his ride there and his disembarkation from the bus, and so she felt, by extension, that she herself had been to Nouakchott too. Her brother would tell people later that he'd been there for a year, when it was really eight months, Rabi al-Thani to Dhu'l-Hijja, at which point he returned to the camp, penniless and broken by the city. But no one quibbled when he spoke of his year.

The city in which she'd arrived, though, was not going to allow the spirit-world company of her brother. She could feel it, even as the woman from the wall brought her a can of Fanta and motioned for her to drink—this city was a monster.

"Ismi Zahrae Elouafiq," the woman said, and Souria gathered that this was the woman's name. "Asmitek?"

"Souria."

She tried to say little more than that. The woman pressed her, but it was easy to hold silence because Souria mostly did not understand her, and the woman had to pull her words out with slow tones and wild hand gestures. Souria told her about only a fraction of her money—"ten thousand ouguiya," she admitted—and Zahrae narrowed her eyes. She was two or even three times Souria's age, and when she raised her eyebrows, her forehead became a curtain of wrinkles.

Zahrae had approached her with the confidence of someone who herself had made many journeys. But when Souria told her own, Zahrae did not know Bou Naga, or Zouérat. She didn't even know Foum-Zguid, which was in her own country, and so Souria supposed that the journeys the woman had made were mostly within her own soul.

"Nouakchott," she told Zahrae, to make her understand the giant puzzle piece of Mauritania. "My country," she told Zahrae. "My country's money."

On the ride up, passengers had closed the curtains of the

bus windows, so Souria hadn't felt the heat of la canicule until the ride was finished and she was joining the clotted stream of people easing themselves and their parcels out the high, narrow door. Now, as she stood facing Zahrae, the hot street burned the soles of her feet through her sandals, and sweat ran in runnels down the nape of her neck, stinging the rash that had grown in stages as she'd crossed the desert.

"Your face is wide," the woman said. She placed a hand on each of Souria's cheeks to make her know what she was saying. She removed her right hand and put it on her stomach, rolled it in a semicircle. "Are you pregnant?" she asked, then laughed one harsh *ha* that sounded like tree bark. Souria did not know what she'd asked, and the woman quickly gave satisfaction up to the division of dialect. Souria felt her hair curling at the roots. She couldn't find one woman in a full mulaffa, and some women hadn't even covered their hair. Most of these uncovered had their hair clipped or tied modestly to the backs of their heads, but she saw plenty of hair left hanging, brazenly, down the young girls' backs, where it swung, long and thick, as they walked. Two girls crossing the street wore short-sleeved blouses and pants that cut off at the knees. The wet heat of Marrakech, she supposed, was such that they'd lost their heads to the devil.

Zahrae took Souria's arm and hurried her down the wide, busy street leading away from the station, away from the exhaust of aging buses and the smell of rotting melon and the hissing calls of the drivers with their taxis spraypainted gold. Away from the fear Souria had been feeling since she stepped off the Allal Transport and into the searing heat of the medina. She'd seen through the bus windows that Marrakech was a big city, with so many streets radiating from its center that you could never know them all, not even in a lifetime. One of those streets, she hoped, could be home.

"Yalla," Zahrae told her, and grabbed her by the elbow.

Zahrae walked her back to Bab Doukkala, where they entered through the imposing brick archway and wound their way through the narrow medina streets. Unlike the packed sand roads of her country, these streets were level and even, the stones worn smooth by all the people, horses, and motorcycles all around her, the tranquillity of a country that hummed itself to work every morning without kidnapping young girls. She was dizzied by all that happened in the space of one city block: A man snipped beef off a shank and into a pan with a pair of metal scissors; an elderly woman with the tattoos of the Berber begged at the entrance to a mosque. A Frenchman exited a shop with the lower half of a female mannequin, its naked legs blazing white, and a gaggle of small boys played soccer in the alley, returning curses to the cyclists who stopped and tapped their horns when the ball rolled before their wheels.

At last Zahrae brought them to the small steel door of a riad made of crumbling concrete, and she took from her pocket a ring of keys. "You have a place in the house," she said as she opened the door, "because Marrakech is no place for a girl all alone."

Just inside the entry was a stairway, but they passed it to enter a small kitchen, lit on one side from the sun through a courtyard window, where the woman removed her shoes and Souria did the same. They took a left, then, into a tiny room whose threshold Souria had to duck under to enter. In the far corner, a small, cubed television sat on the floor. "This place is my family's," Zahrae said. "You are welcome."

Souria understood nothing, but put a hand on her heart and nodded thanks. Zahrae bent to turn one of the greasy floor cushions, revealing a fresh side that only looked dirtier. "Sit," she said, or at least Souria thought she said, because she threw her small hand out at the cushions for emphasis, and then Zahrae dropped her market bags and crossed back into the kitchen.

Sitting, Souria could see through the doorway to the second and third floors of the riad, where other families lived, and she could see into the bathroom, where stood the little metal bucket for showering, and a new, nylon-bristled hand brush on the basin of the sink. The miracle of a hole in the floor where the family toileted inside the house, away from heat and flies and scorpions, and even a cracked plastic splashguard where they could situate their feet as they squatted.

"I do want to hear the story of a young girl all alone in a bus yard," Zahrae yelled to her, "but I need to cook the evening meal. My children and my children's children will soon be home. I have a son and a daughter older than you. And a son your age. He'll be happy to meet you."

Souria understood *evening*. She understood *children*, and *children of children*. Her travels hadn't been wholly unsavory: she understood *happy*.

When Zahrae reached for the wall and removed a pot from a nail, Souria felt that she should rise from her cushion and help cook, or at least keep the woman company while she chopped carrots and poured couscous. But she was so tired, the thought of even this small act of etiquette exhausted her. She stretched her legs across one end of the red, phoenix-patterned raffia mats that completely covered the floor, ignoring the crumbs she felt on her bare feet. She fell into an empty, healing sleep, one without any dreams that she'd remember. Each time one of Zahrae's family entered the house she'd wake, without opening her eyes, to digest the person's voice, testing it for kindness. She slept, then pretended to sleep, drifting in and out of space.

"She must be tired," one of the daughters said as they

sat all around her in the small parlor, eating their couscous. "Mauritania. A long way."

"Don't wake her," said Zahrae. "I think she's seen trouble."

Two children—possibly three—jumped over her legs in a game. Someone got up and turned on the television, and she fell back asleep. Quiet came eventually and with it a shocking wakefulness. She assumed that the family had retreated to other parts of the house, but when she opened her eyes, she found a boy her age standing over her, appraising her as if she were a delicate relic. His face spread wide like Zahrae's, his features and coloring so much his mother's it was as if she'd hatched him. Souria closed her eyes and willed herself back to sleep, but the memory of a certain fear kept her awake, and when she opened her eyes again he was still there, staring. "Like the most beautiful doll," he said, but it was more Dharija than she understood, and she shut her eyes again. Her travels in the desert were a long twilight before resting, and here was the dream, she thought, though she didn't know yet whether the dream would be pleasant or disagreeable. But this boy sitting here staring at her—she already knew he'd be a part of it.

VI. Marrakech

Shannon's first trip to Morocco shaped a new sensory layer atop reality: even on the fifth floor of Le Chevet, she could smell charred sugar. Vlad complained, wondered where it was burning and who was burning it. He closed the window. Asked aloud why his firm had put them up in a barely lit alley in the center of the medina. Shannon found the smell far and away better than the murderous smoke coming off the kebabs they'd had at Beyrut, or the cumin-flecked couscous they'd found in one of the European-style shopping malls. Each night, like the tourists they were, she and Vlad found a different open-air food stall in the Djmaa-el-Fna, where they could eat and watch the sun set on the two thousand partying Marrakchis all around them. Hawkers tossed neon aerobies into the darkening sky. Shannon watched them rise, spinning a hundred feet into space, only to return to earth and lose their spin in the milling crowd. The burnt sugar from the street below their hotel, the molecules of it in her nose, were but a microcosm of the Marrakchi psychedelia all around them. The smell was everywhere, even after he closed the window, and it left Shannon a bit lost—she was one small American in a tiny riad, situated on one narrow alley, in one desert-covered country, on one planet. But it was a nice lost, like being found was just around the corner in some dusty recess of the medina.

Memory was a wily snake that got her nowhere and every-where all at the same time. On the one hand, she wanted this to be fun, but she kept remembering that Vlad hadn't had to do all this, certainly not for some wreck-ruined woman who had to make her face back into a whole with Dermablend every morn-ing. Despite his satellite-dish ears and the high-pitched whine with which he notched the word *vraiment*, he was a solid man with a solid job and a solid face, and who was she? This vaca-tion was the nicest thing anyone had ever done for her. It was so damn unobligatory that when he asked, she'd wept.

He hadn't seen her tears because he hadn't been in the room with her—he'd proposed the trip via telephone. Her second week out of the hospital, he'd sent a two-line text, shaming her for not having responded to any of his other two-line texts. She'd been lying on her back under hot-pink bedsheets, in the canopy bed she'd slept in as a girl. At home. Not at home, but in the house where she was raised. The house that could never be home, the two-story Tudor that now, postdivorce, belonged cleanly and singly to her mother. The cool slab of her phone was facedown on her belly, and when it buzzed against her skin, she picked it up.

If you didn't have fun I understand, Vlad was saying, though it was obvious from this, his third unanswered dispatch, that he didn't understand at all. He was taking it personally. From a first date, this man wanted closure. It was a bad sign.

She closed her eyes against this electronic affront. She'd been, the moment before the accident, a Humana temp in the process of solving every one of life's gluey mousetraps. She'd just paid off the smallest of her loans. Brought her credit score up to a re-spectable 672. Now, she'd resigned from her job, and she had no idea how high was the bill for surgically rearranging her insides twice. She was twenty-eight years old, and living with her mom.

Shannon's mother had "cleaned" her bedroom, meaning she'd

thrown out all Shannon's favorite clothes and stripped the walls of everything she'd prized—the poster she'd bought at a Violent Femmes concert, the satin-finish photographs she and her friends had staged on the empty playground of an elementary school. Her mother had discarded the empty wasp's nest she'd found in the woods behind their house, and the graphically realistic sculpture of a heart that her first boyfriend had made her in art class. In her bedroom's reincarnation, her dresser held the participation trophies she'd won on the 4-H basketball team that had been her father's bad idea. On the wall opposite her bed, where she'd have to stare at it all day, her mother had hung a gilt-framed print of her as a flower girl at her aunt's wedding. Dropping petals on the runner had been terrifying for Shannon, and in the photo, she could still see the salty remains of tears, streaked wax down her cheeks. Her mother had wedged, in a frame on her nightstand, the certificate she'd won at the all-school spelling bee, along with a vase full of artificial daisies that perfectly matched the ones on the border she'd scalloped along the top of the wall. Shannon's room was now a museum, dedicated to the holocaust of her childhood.

In the aftermath of the wreck, trapped upstairs like Rapunzel in her tower, Shannon had begun an obsessive affair with tuna salad. She'd asked her mother to bring her half a Panera sandwich, then a whole. When she was able to make it steadily downstairs, Shannon reverse-engineered the sandwich's contents: tuna, mayo, relish, onions. She'd avoided tuna in the past because of its mercury levels, but she didn't mind, anymore, the thought of going stupid, or dying; on the contrary, her next grocery list included a request for Atlantic albacore because it had the highest mercury content of all. In bed, under the covers, eating these sloppy, sea-poisoned sandwiches, she felt closer to her lifetime of underachievement. She started eating them for breakfast. She started to stink. She asked her mother for gum. She felt more clarity of mind, which surprised her, but she also felt consistently oily.

She'd been turning over, like a turnip deep in soil, the requirements of her life going forward. She had ninety-nine problems, she figured, and she didn't need Vladimir Grenfell to be one. So when he broke into her sleep again, two hours later, with a third line of text, she flipped the phone over, saw his name, thought *Jesus, buddy.* Flipped the phone back over on her belly, where she could feel its activity-heated screen pressing into the scar from her second surgery.

I leave for Morocco next Saturday, he'd said. *If I don't hear from you by then I'll forever hold my piece.*

The word was *peace*, she wanted to text back, but she gave him benefit of her doubt—busy, employed man that he was, he was probably using voice-to-text. And to be fair, he knew nothing of her accident, nothing about the 1.5 seconds that had crushed her vertebrae and ended her soul. If all you have is what you are, all she was now was pain. Men always wanted to presume you weren't returning their calls because you were lost at the bottom of an ocean, but this time, this man was almost correct.

But since one of the rules of her life going forward was to seek out ways to change her karma, she found herself texting him back. *My life has changed*, she typed, *as, I'm sure, has yours. The body's cells regenerate every second, right? Much to tell you. In person, please.*

There was a beat when she wondered how she'd go on a date when she still couldn't walk. She punched herself in bed, rolled into an L, dropped her feet to the floor, and stood for three difficult seconds before taking a step. She wondered what she'd look like going to meet Vlad, how she'd even get from her car to the inside of a restaurant. But then it didn't matter what she looked like, how gracelessly and tunelessly she might be walking, when her mission was goodbye. She was thinking all this when he texted her back. *Why not come to Morocco with me.*

The tears came; she felt the condensation of them on the bridge of her nose. She texted back. *Why not.* She remembered the savage way Vlad had cut into his steak. Macedonski Zeleznici. Do widzenia. Here was a man who'd been born knowing how to escape. *Ahoy, pirate,* she thought, *show me your ways.* She'd need health insurance, going forward. This man could be her personal Underground Railroad.

It was the end of the American economy. The end of her mother's final hold over her, the end of the earth's temperate climate. If all went well in Morocco, maybe she'd watch the glaciers melt with this man. She'd go to Morocco with him so that when the time came, she wouldn't drown.

She'd never witnessed a bat midflight in the United States, not in all her twenty-eight years of American living, but in Morocco, they were everywhere. At sunset the trees released them, so many of them launching their black bodies against the orange sky that they looked like a confetti spill. They filled the horizon, flocking toward underpasses and escarpments and interior moldings like the one here in the lobby of Le Chevet, where two of them now took turns flying from wall to lighter-blue wall. They liked long hair, the lobby attendant told her, so Shannon banded hers up in a bun on the back of her head, though she didn't actually fear them: the bats, like everything else, were a miracle.

A translucent-skinned adolescent boy—maybe French, maybe minority-British, maybe Lebanese—leaped up to smack the ledge with his hand every time the bats landed. In response they'd take off again, two inmates tortured into performance. But they did not fly in tandem. One by lonely one, they'd zoom across the hotel lobby, much to Shannon's delight.

In the daytime, she stayed in the hotel watching Arabic-language television. Men in white robes dancing with canes and sabers, piped in via satellite from Oman. A British children's cartoon, voice-dubbed in Arabic. American music videos on the channel from Beirut: Aguilera, Madonna, Britney, all with Arabic-script advertisement running beneath the feet of the backup dancers, on a ticker at the bottom of the screen. When she tired of listening to a language she'd never understand, she left her room and let the concierge flag her a taxi to the Djmaa-el-Fna, where she'd wind her lost way through the narrow-laned medina, grazing slowly on the uneven brick, minding each precious step through the narrow doorways, appreciating, then, every single additional footfall she would make on this planet. The tar of the street stuck to her sneaker, it was so hot in this country. It made her ecstatic.

Now was la canicule, she was told. One hundred twenty degrees in the daytime, a cool ninety-five at night. Le Chevet did not air-condition its lobby, but its inner chamber had no windows—by blocking the sunlight, the inner sanctum kept itself cool. A small standing fountain filled with live rose petals sat in the middle of the lobby; she got up and dipped her finger in the water, received a shocking, baptismal chill. She'd spent a previous hot French-language summer in a nonclimatisé apartment in the twelfth arrondissement, but it was nothing like this, this psychedelic collection of colors, this tapestry of African odors. And she had only thirty-seven dollars in her bank account; she'd checked, the last time the riad had solid internet connection. She closed her eyes against the disbelief that she was actually here, on African soil, living any of this.

She sat back down in one of the lobby's coppery chairs,

waiting for Vlad to come downstairs after his evening call to Windsolver, which he jokingly called the Mothership. He'd warned her that his days would be long, and now she saw the actuality of it—2:30 in Louisville was 7:30 in Marrakech, and they could not have dinner until 2:30 in Louisville a finit. After the call, he'd come down to the lobby and allow her to lead him out to the spotlit, Olympic-sized swimming pool where they'd jump in and play Marco Polo as quietly as possible; one could, Vlad told her, be an ugly American without being a loud one. She'd listen to him laugh, marveling that he no longer annoyed her, that she'd somehow gotten used to the skinny, awkward pipestem of him. All humans have disproportionately matched eyes, she'd read somewhere, and under the intense Marrakchi sun, she'd found Vlad's runt: the left one. The one that, when he looked into the glare, refused to open itself fully. In Africa, she found this runt endearing. In Africa, when he pressed into her back to signal that he wanted sex, he seemed almost on the verge of handsome.

They'd done this same thing every night they'd been in Marrakech—ordered burgers and frites poolside, then gone swimming for the long, slow, forty-five minutes of their grilling. In water, Shannon discovered, her body performed its best muscle memory. She was five years old again in a neighborhood pool; she was ten at winter day camp; sixteen and jumping off a dock while holding hands with a thin, pimpled boy. Even Vlad noticed her body regaining its power. He seemed to enjoy assisting her; at the airport, he hadn't let her so much as wheel her own luggage down the concourse. "You poor thing," he'd say, when she winced from the sharp pain that came anytime she bent over too far, turned her neck too quickly. *You. Poor. Thing.* He watched, seemingly pleased now, as she swam the entire length of the pool without stopping. "You're on your way to wholeness," he said, like a war medic. It was the kind of thing neither of her parents would ever have said. It was the kind of thing that sounded, faintly, like love.

They hid under evening-darkened water, calling out the word *perpetual* each time one found the other. It meant nothing—it was just a random word Vlad chose—but she was grateful it wasn't Polish or German, because she didn't yet trust Vlad not to pick a word that would make her look stupid when he measured her against himself. *Perpetual!* she shouted, when she saw his head at her heel, his black hair wavy in the distortion of the moving water. *Perpetual*, he said, when he shot up. When he found her, she didn't smile. When she found him, he did.

"Why'd your family move back to the States?" she asked him one of those nights when the swimming, the grilling, and the eating had passed. They were back upstairs, toweling dry, sloughing off skin cells. She hadn't thought to pack a bathrobe, and now she was naked, wholly disarmed, in the little fifth-floor room. Vlad killed the lights so they could leave the window open—the absolute darkness, he explained, would stop any view from outside. They'd brought ice cream back from the pool—mango with flecks of candy like Pop Rocks. With the rim of the cold cup, Vlad traced the outline of her lips, then kissed her. He set the cup on the nightstand beside them, and its aroma strengthened and gathered in the room's heat.

"The railroad moved my father to Sarajevo is why," said Vlad. He zagged a towel around his head in a fury, rubbing first the crown, then the back, then each thinning temple. Even his hair had grown higher in the week they'd been in Morocco. He was a mammal in his natural habitat. "But that's not all of it," he said, coming closer, leaning his face in so close to hers that she could no longer look at both his eyes.

The sun had burned the bridge of her nose to something

skinned and raw, and as Vlad stayed close and continued talking, he dabbed it with his wet towel, then patted her cheeks. The cool of the fabric felt profound, like a calm lake that Vlad would pour into her. He kissed her. She felt the whiff of air on her ankle as he dropped the towel to the floor; he put his hand in the groove of her jaw, forcing her mouth wider so that she could take in more of his. He pulled his face away, said in a low voice, "The whole of it is that we were there in the Bijeljina massacre."

In the languid way he said *Bijeljina*, she heard the manipulation: he was a man who could get off only after telling a story. He laid her down gently on the bed, hovered over her. "We watched Sarajevo fall," he said. He slid his hand up her thigh and back down again, and she closed her eyes in order to concentrate. "You'd hear a rifle's report, and then something clattering in the street—maybe housekeys, maybe a canister of water—and then you'd be alone in your thoughts, your mind racing in the night, hoping it was a bag of rice you'd heard fall, knowing it wasn't." He kissed her again, fondled her breasts. "Our parents would wait to argue until sunrise," he said, "because they knew we kids didn't sleep the nights either."

His chest was still wet, and Shannon traced the pattern that moisture had left there, a question mark of black hair. "We had American passports," he said, moving on top of her, "and we could have left, but my father said when it was your day it was your day, and that was true in America or Herzegovina or anywhere on the earth."

"What happened?" Shannon said. In anticipation of his entering her, she tried to turn herself under his body, found out she could not—her stubborn spine. "I mean, you lived. You're here. I see that you lived."

"I did and I didn't," Vlad said. He pushed himself inside her, then stayed very still, though he spoke in a voice that shorted itself of breath. "We waited with everyone else. Dad went to the market when the UN came, and he ran behind the trucks."

He pulled out. "Which seemed even crazier," he said, then pushed himself back in. "You stopped caring whether it was your day.

"At first there were the ambulances"—"you heard the sirens at all times"—"when everything in the world broke, you heard them no more"—"and that was worse."

He put his hand on her chest, in the flatness between her breasts; he metered the rise of her breath, its fall. Moonlight shone through the window, and Shannon saw that his face had gone sodden. "We had a cat," he told her, when he'd caught some of his breath, "and it went blind while we were holed up inside. It was like the cat knew what was happening out there, how the city was dying."

Shannon giggled. "How do you know when a cat goes blind?"

"He started to run into things. His eyes were blue, and then they were the color of clouds. He'd creep up on me and just stare, but not into my eyes. He was staring at my shoulder, or the base of my neck. He couldn't see where I was anymore. He couldn't see me seeing him."

He moved inside her again, then broke, then lay beside her, his breath a soft, contented zag. The ice cream had reconstituted itself, and in the moonlight, Shannon watched as Vlad put his glasses back on, took the whiskey sour on the nightstand, and poured that in the ice cream. He offered the mixture to her, but it hadn't made a float, and she refused. He put the glass back on the nightstand and when he turned back into her, she could feel that he was still hard.

"I watched a man run across the street with a bag of bread," he said, "and then *boom*, he was down. It's not like in the movies.

This man, he screamed, and he screamed, and he screamed until he stopped screaming."

Vlad got atop her and pushed himself inside her again, but this time it was like being stabbed, and before long she felt him go limp, roll off. "You asked did we get out?" he asked. "We did. One night they cut the water in our building, and my mom started crying in the middle of the kitchen and told my dad to stop pretending he was a cowboy. She said we were Black people caught up in some Whitefolk bullshit, and it was all his fault. I guess the way to make a man change his mind is to make him feel stupid, because we were gone two days later. We took our nice American passports and we left."

The memory of escape seemed to put him to sleep, and when she heard him snoring, she removed his glasses from his face and folded them neatly for the nightstand. Their room faced poolside, but she could hear the traffic perpendicular, and she heard the shouting as a motorcycle revved itself too fast down the alley; she imagined the people shoving themselves out of harm's way. She rolled to her back and began counting the cracks in the ceiling. The cat was real, but Vlad hadn't seen a man die. She knew from the intense way he'd stared at her when he told it—he'd said it so he could come.

She hardly knew him. It mattered little to her, either way.

Outside the breath of the city rose and fell, the chirr of the Vespas like the insects that, in early spring, reclaimed her parents' very American backyard. As night fell and the street lay emptier, the human sounds thinned, until she found only the reverb of one lonely motor, its desperation echoing against the closed metal doors of the medina.

There was the time Shannon thought of as B.W.—Before the Wreck. She'd been temping then, in an actuarial department that offered her two poorly perforated checks per month, but the truly beautiful part of the gig was big, soft Enrico Bolognino, a runner in the company mailroom who met her most Fridays with his duffle bag full of foil-wrapped weed. She could never be 100 percent certain he'd be selling, but she'd text him her work extension and he'd drop a note from the mailroom saying Y or N, and she'd meet him on the vacant, mysteriously unlocked nineteenth floor, where he passed out everyone's purchases as if he were Santa Claus.

The Friday before the wreck, she'd bought. Enrico traded a baggie for two twenties, then unwrapped one of his own bags, licked a paper he got from the side pocket of his duffle, expertly rolled himself a joint. The aroma of product was overwhelming, and Shannon remembered the newspaper that morning at Starbucks, how it said Venus was then transiting the sun. It was visible in Hong Kong, she'd read. Through one of the nineteenth floor's curiously open windows, she heard the straining of an acoustic guitar floating up from the street, a man singing "Wild Horses." Singing it badly.

"Can I touch your boobs?" Enrico said as he got out his lighter.

"What?"

He sparked up, took a drag, held out the spliff. "I'll give you this free, you let me touch."

She waved it away. "They're just boobs. You've got them too. Touch your own."

He pulled out the collar of his shirt and looked down. "Not the same," he said. "Come on then, just a look. I've never been with a woman of color."

"Idiot. Your mom's a woman of color."

She'd turned around and left for the elevator, refusing to look at his face, because she knew when she did, she'd find there the kind of unbridled hubris that would ruin the transaction. But she missed that life, the ashtray with its roach clip that she kept on the soap tray in her bathtub, the way the sun shone through her frosted bathroom window and fixed her in the stoned, stunned glow of a Saturday afternoon.

Here in Africa, sunlight was nothing but intense. It never relaxed into clouds; it never softened into anything that might qualify as early summer. Something to do with the earth's axis, she thought, or a scarcity of precipitation. The sun had burned her cheeks but lit the edges of the sandstone buildings to brightness. It dappled the exterior of the central train station such that when she passed in a taxi, the building appeared to be moving. It had elucidated her view of Vlad, this running sunlight—it brought him into stark relief. He was more confident here, outside the States. He knew how to queue up at la poste and weigh his own vegetables at the Aswak Assalam. He knew how to order the natives around.

She understood him more deeply now; she understood the ways in which he miscommunicated himself to his own countrymen. He was like a Vietnam vet who kept asking for additional tours of duty, and it was no doubt why he'd chosen this line of work. Windmill engineering would land you on all the earth's most desolate plains, hide you in its rockiest, least inhabitable cliffs. Vlad didn't fit, in the States. Being consistently American wasn't his superpower.

Here he was again, at 7:30, disembarking from the lobby elevator, his shirt opened down to its third button. "Shall we?" he said, extending an elbow. It had begun to bother her, this subtle bit of offered help. It bothered her that she still, to some extent, needed it, but it irked her all the more that Vlad enjoyed feeling sorry for her, that he was so attracted to trauma, and she had so much of it to offer. She understood now why blind people preferred to walk across the street unassisted.

At the pool, he removed his shirt, ran his hand down an imaginary necktie. He ordered drinks and food, pulled two chaise lounges together so they could be close without touching. "Want a sip?" Vlad asked when the waiter, knees bent, set down his martini.

It was a fancy one, an affogato, cocoa and Kahlúa with curlicues of ice cream floating on its surface. In the pool restaurant's terracotta-tinted martini glass, with one spherical cube of ice still swirling around the perimeter, the drink looked like Jupiter as seen from space. She thought to tell that to him, but she didn't; she knew already that he was the type of man who would never see anything save liquor in a glass of liquor. She sipped. Felt nothing.

The privations she'd suffered postaccident had rendered her sensorily halved, yes, but also, she wished for the smoky magnificence of weed. Weed, it turned out, was the only thing that cut through the wrenching pain of her lower back, and After the Wreck, A.W., she'd sought out her old high school dealer. Keva was still, to her relief, dealing. Shannon would sit in her mother's garden in the morning, blowing smoke rings among the roses; evenings, when her mother got back from work, she'd drive to the Jefferson Memorial Forest, spark up, smoke on federal land. She'd regard the sky above her, her mind drifting free as she classed the clouds—cumulus, stratus, cirrus.

Product had been too dangerous to put in her international luggage, and she thought Morocco would be such a psychedelic experience she wouldn't need her mind additionally blown, but now she knew she'd been wrong: by the end of any Moroccan day, she was drowning in an ocean of pain. Also, what paired

70

best with zellij and oud, she knew now, was weed. Only and exactly weed. She bet Vlad knew where to get it.

"You like to smoke?" she asked him.

"Regular cigs? Sure."

"Other stuff."

"Never," he said, looking away from her to the bar. They stood on the deck of the pool, waiting to feel like jumping. Outside, the circuit of medina traffic grew louder. A herd of goats passed outside the hotel, a chorus of bleats.

"Oh well," she said.

"But I like to do this," he said. He took her chin in his hand and kissed her.

It was the last thing she wanted.

But it always began like that, she thought. Drinks. A slobbery kiss. Even in Africa. The universe wasn't transformation; it was consistency.

And it would always end in tragedy: Screaming outside some man's apartment building. Sobbing in the passenger seat of a speeding car. Watching the steady, hypnotic light of an empty voicemail cache. With Vlad, it wouldn't matter. He'd lied about a dead man. She could never take him seriously.

VII. Mauritania/Marrakech

Souria's father had met the rose-lipped woman by accident, in the part of the year when the tribe left Bou Naga. When the rains came, the people stayed: acheb sprung from the desert, its leaves opening like a million quenched tongues. The animals grew fat, and the young people entered into marriages. But each year, when the sand dried, it baked hotter than it had the year before. The Sahara was growing old, stretching its bitterness farther into Senegal on the one side and Algeria on the other, and though the people of Souria's tribe knew neither distance, they felt the desert's passing from their outermost skin to the marrow of their bones. The hassiyat they dug for water had to sound ever deeper. In dry season, they took their starving animals farther south, all the way to the land near Gorgol el Abiod.

The season he met the rose-lipped woman, her father had taken his herd and a small part of his family—Souria, her little brother, Hafs, and her older brother, Khair. In the daytime they walked, shouting at their animals, and at night, they quietly settled on the richer land of others, letting the animals drink and eat freely. It wasn't stealing, her father told them, not like the landowners thought. Allah had given first rights to the desert to the people who lived at its center: it belonged to the people who lived near Bou Naga, and to no one else.

There was Qadir Ould M'Barack, who had bragged about the new way, of crossing to the Sahel under government rules, paying for well water and rice. But he returned from that crossing a ruined man. His sheep starved on the piste to Senegal, her mother told her; one of his sons fell ill and died that same day, on the side of the route, in a pile of his own waste. Some people, her mother said, seeing that they have very little, fall in line trying to hold on to it. Others understand that, having so little left to lose, they might as well live freely.

And it was in this liberty that their family stayed alive—Souria, her father, her brothers, one camel, seventeen sheep, and two cows, all making the crossing, until the day Hafs found the edge of the amber-brown soil near the valley and told them he was tired. They found an untended hassi whose opening was almost buried in silt, and they set up camp in the dangerous light of afternoon sun, ignoring their own rules about camouflage.

The following day, Souria woke to a disastrous cold. She gathered her thick mulaffa around her, the stiff black one she'd worn to Tabaski, and she went to draw water and make wudu. Even in Bou Naga, she woke earlier than the rest of her family to leave the tent and say prayers. The solitude of the desert cheered her, and she wanted to see the small animals that, at that empty hour, would sit still and stare, the lizards returning her curiosity with the steady focus of their ancient eyes.

Some mornings, Allah broke the silence by putting his voice in her mind. But in her father's camp that day, on the route to Gorgol el Abiod, there was the report of a gunshot, a *ping* that left dust ricocheting from the dent it made in the sand. The bullet had landed twenty feet from where she was sitting; she'd felt its impact in her buttocks. The wind carried away the dust and she watched, calmly: the gunman could have hit her if he'd wanted, but he had not.

"Thief," came a voice. "Thieves."

She watched as he crossed the sand, holding his small gun now at his side, and she found the reluctance in his posture. He passed the gun from hand to hand as if it were hard to hold, as if its metal were burning into his fingers. She turned her head to the left to see that her father had come out of his sleeping place under the escarpment, as had Khair and Hafs.

Souria turned back to the man and, still sitting, held up her hands. He was a Moor, and etiquette dictated that she not look him in the eyes, but she spoke to him. "We will leave now. Please."

Still, he approached. By raising her eyes slightly, still without looking directly into his, she could see how red his nose was, how purplish his lips had grown in the cold. He switched the gun between hands again, tightened the collar of his dr'aa against the cold. Only in his neck did Souria find his years: the skin there had worn older than the skin on his face.

When he got to where she was sitting, he pulled her to standing and grabbed her into his body. He turned her around so that she could see her father and her brothers looking on, their hands hanging at their sides in a paralysis of anger. "Thieves," the man yelled. "What if I took this one here?" Then he lowered his voice so only she could hear. "How old are you?" he asked.

"Ten."

He spat over her shoulder, on the ground in front of her feet, in disgust. He'd wanted a bigger animal as trophy. "And that man is your father?"

"He is."

"He is a thief," the man whispered.

It was a fine thing to give away a man's honor, Souria thought, so long as you saved his life. "He is," she said then. "Indeed, my father is."

A beetle burrowed into a hole near her foot. The sun shifted one gear, from orange to goldenrod. A cloud passed over the turning earth. And then, a miracle, as the man shouted over her shoulder, "You are the people of Sidi Ould Coulibaly?"

"Yes," her father yelled back. The whole of the five of them knew this to be a lie. One of her father's sheep bleated, as though even the animals knew.

"You are lucky to have come now," the man said, "because today is his funeral. Come."

Her father turned back to her brothers to instruct them about the sheep. He joined Souria and the man, who began to tell them the story of Sidi Ould Coulibaly. He himself was a shepherd, he told them, on this—Coulibaly's—land. Coulibaly had been arguing with death for some months, ever since the day he discovered that the scarab-sized mole on his arm had turned ugly and full of seeds. He'd taken a boning knife and cut into his own flesh, thinking simply to raze the mole he'd always thought so ugly in the first place, but when he scraped it off in one painful sweep, he saw, beneath the blood that came, that the cancer ran deep, down layers of flesh. He cut into himself again, deeper, and again deeper, thinking to scoop free this whole mistake in his being. The shepherd had been there, he said, and he watched Coulibaly hold a deep breath and dig a crater in his own flesh that would, for the short rest of his life, need to be covered with a thick bandage.

When Coulibaly leaned to say sunnah, he took care not to let his butchered arm scrape the mats. When his harvest came in fuller than usual, he bought a new set of clothes for the rainy season, not knowing they'd be his last. The mistake had mixed with his body, flowing through his blood to the glands at the side of his neck, to the lining of his stomach. Like an invading clan he could never beat.

The rose-lipped woman was sweet high-ebony, beautiful and

round-bottomed, and she was Sidi's wife. Except that she couldn't be his wife, because she was slave to the Toukbal family. But it was Tumtum who'd been Sidi's for all the nights of seven years; Tumtum who in the beginning of his illness managed his swollen, ruined arm; Tumtum who stayed in his house at the end and cleaned his bedcovers and cried with him. In the last day of his dying, it had been Tumtum who sang prayers until her voice was as the rough grains of the desert, Tumtum who begged Allah to forgive Sidi's sins. Everyone else passed through Sidi's house in resigned calm. Tumtum had never been able to give Sidi children, but the village had known her as Sidi's only happiness. The surprise was that Tumtum had felt the same way. "Sad like a broken radio," the shepherd told them now.

Souria wondered if there weren't enough mourners in the village, because the shepherd invited her father to sit with the men under their tent, while he sent Souria in the direction of the women, who gathered around Tumtum and sang prayers as she squatted in the center of their circle, waiting for the men who would take turns carrying Sidi's washed, shrouded body to his grave. Souria was loosening her third tooth with her tongue. She'd never before seen human death.

Souria watched Tumtum as she walked behind the Moors who carried her husband's body; she looked for tears, but Tumtum did not cry. Instead, she looked to the left and to the right of herself, and then off into the reddening afternoon sky, as if an invisible presence were watching. As the men approached the grave, Tumtum hung back with the rest of the women, but when they lowered Sidi into the bottom chamber of soil, she cried out and ran to its edge. "Bury me too," she begged, and she crouched alongside the grave and began to lower her legs.

Souria's father came to the lip of the tomb and grabbed her around her middle. The men sang louder; the women behind

Souria began ululating so loudly that Souria pulled her mulaffa tighter around her ears. "Enough," said a man. He crouched in Tumtum's face. "You know what you were to him, you black dog? A hole. A hole with arms and legs."

Souria's father was still holding Tumtum around her waist, but he let go of her then. Tumtum bowed her head and cried, at last.

The men shoveled the dirt over Sidi and lay branches on his grave, and all the women walked back to the village to kill their chickens and pound their millet, but Tumtum stayed, crying, at the edge of the grave, in Souria's father's arms. Souria felt that the woman had courted insult by showing her emotions so openly, and so perhaps deserved it.

But she didn't think Tumtum cried for the insult. She wasn't even sure Tumtum was crying because Sidi was gone. Because Souria found her own throat echoing pain, she found that she wanted to cry too. She wanted to cry because of the secret of the tooth that had come loose as the women were singing, and she wanted to cry because people never saw you as you were so much as the way they thought you were. The world couldn't function any other way.

And then, the second miracle of the day, the second saving, because Souria's father took Tumtum's hand and spoke to her. "We need another to help us herd the animals," he said. "You will come."

And so she traveled on the route with the Maoulouds. So far from Bou Naga, Souria longed for her mother's meals. But the rose-lipped woman traded for nutmeg, milked the camel, and made zrig. When she returned with the Maoulouds to Bou Naga, she drew their water, washed their camel hides, swept sand from the floor of the family's tent. The women of their quarter of the village talked, wondering that Souria's father had taken another wife of unknown people. Souria's mother held her head high and smiled at the well, and the women stopped asking their underhanded questions.

People grew angry, her mother told her, when you did not want the things they wanted in life. But when you took on other people's desires, tending them was too heavy a chore.

Allah had delivered her from the tribe at Mijek and all the way across the desert to a stone-roofed, stair-laddered dwelling inside a wall of bricks. People sometimes did not pray in Zahrae's house, but they seemed to prosper nonetheless. A bulb hung on a wire from the kitchen ceiling, but the wiring might not have worked, or the bulb itself might have been shot, for they ate in darkness. Souria had not removed her mulaffa altogether, but she'd slept free of her headscarf, and woken up in the middle of the night to give her hair a hundred strokes with a brush she found in the washroom. It had been quiet indoors, in this city house—no goats bleating in the distance, or men outside playing cards through the night. Not even a lizard scurrying behind the walls, here—just silence, broken only by a persistent drip of water in the kitchen.

In that silence, she'd been able to look in the washroom mirror and see herself—really see herself—for the first time in months. Her face seemed narrower, in the stillness, than it had in Mauritania, her mouth hardened with wisdom. Even as she threw her head forward so she could brush the hair at the nape of her neck, even as she washed the hairbrush and spanked it clean so none of the Elouafiqs would see all the dust of the desert that she'd left in its bristles, she felt a solidity in her spine that hadn't been there before. She couldn't know how many inches, but she'd grown. Now, with Zahrae next to her at the table, with her plate full of khobz and her silky cream pajamas, Souria watched the sun make its horizon. Light broke into the kitchen, refracting through glass to project blazing right angles on the wall, washing the frames of the chairs with illuminated hope. .

"Your hair," Zahrae said, leaning over so she could stroke it all the way to its curly ends. She leaned closer and took a river of it in her hand. "Beautiful," she said. "Zwina hadi."

Zahrae's own hair was cut short, stopping at her chin, and gray a few inches out of her scalp. She changed into street clothes while Souria covered her head and went to the dirty raffia mats of the parlor to say fajr. She was hurrying to finish when Zahrae came to lean against the doorway. "Let's go," she whispered, so that Souria had to finish her dua while rising to stand.

Stepping outside the riad, Souria had the sensation of being compressed: one saw only the narrow city alley with its bricked streets and its many thick doors closed into the wall. Straight up was sky, and the clouds reflecting the aspen pink of the rising sun, and the birds singing sweetly on roofs. It was a new day in life. The canicule was already hot under her clothes, and Souria wondered if, as long as you still carried the memory of having lived a thing, you'd ever get past having lived it. Even as a woman rode by on a motorbike calling *As-salamalaikum* and Souria watched the dust rise from under her tires, she held cautious doubts about her freedom.

She and Zahrae walked inches from the curb, dodging traffic, until they arrived at the Attijariwafa just outside the medina. Orange and yellow stripes screamed along the top of the gray building, and just above its glass front door were written two kinds of script. She'd seen Arabic writing before, but now she found another kind of writing, like pictures. Squares and triangles and circles. Compact and blocky. The new world was one for people who could read.

She wondered if she'd made a mistake not going to Algiers

with Hassan. Or maybe she should have ignored his jeep altogether, prayed harder for the favor of Allah, and waited for someone going south. She could have hitched back to Bou Naga, where her father had perhaps waited for her even after the rest of the tribe had moved on to a better season on better land. Her eldest sister might be waiting there to braid oil into her hair, and her middle brother might be waiting to knuckle the back of her head and run away, giggling. She could have taken all the tribe's gold pieces, all that jewelry, and made her family the richest in all of Mauritania. Bought them goats for seasons upon seasons.

Zahrae took Souria into the bank, where the chill of the air-conditioning pressed upon her a first, virginal knowledge of luxury, and the smell in the air was of nothing—no souring food, no cigarette smoke, no body odor save the faint scent of sweat from her own bosom. In the desert, everything had smelled of such power; even the sand, blowing straight into her eyes and up her nose, had worn a warm, flat smell of infinity. In the camp at Mijek, the mere thought of certain foods had made her want to vomit; tea was no longer soothing, and eggs were out of the question. Bread was heavenly, a smell of foreignness and spare time for leavening, a smell of rich people's communion. She'd begged for bread in the camp at Mijek—mostly, Mina Tahore told her no.

In the Attijariwafa, the line to the teller already stood three people deep. While she and Zahrae waited, she watched out the bank's front door, where a man in uniform emptied garbage from a marked city bin onto the sidewalk. He emptied all the rubbish, bit by dirty bit, pausing only to wipe sweat from his brow. He worked hard at dirtying the street, then walked away. No one called after him or otherwise seemed to mind what he had done. The new world, Souria thought, stood on its head.

Her final week in the desert she'd felt it inching up her throat, always, all hours of the day. But in the streets of the new world, the rotting food and burning plastic pulled it higher, this tide of trouble in her stomach. Zahrae had pulled her past the bustling crowds of the square and deep into the medina, where Souria was now leaning against a brick storefront, vomiting up every last bit of the rice and kebab the woman had bought on her way out of the Attijariwafa.

Her nose had turned traitor. It betrayed her body and broke her composure. This time, it was the smell of watery coffee that entered her lungs as she passed the French people's corner café. She felt the hydraulic clench of her stomach, which she could not ever, now, control. And she stayed back from the store Zahrae had entered. Souria closed her scarf around the lower half of her face, feigning a modesty that women did not seem to observe in the new world, and she waved Zahrae on. She turned herself to the wall so no one could see but her—the rice, the fibers of meat, the chickpeas, all lying now in a pool of her own yellowish bile. In the desert, she'd savored the smells her body dispensed. The sweat of her arms proved she was alive; the musky stickiness in her underwear proved she'd not been injured beyond repair. But this, the smell of her own partially digested food, proved something ravaging and consuming, an illness she could not control, a thing that might finally end her.

In the jeweler's Zahrae argued, then laughed, then argued again, striking a bargain. Back in the bank, at the teller window, she'd taken fifty of Souria's dirham. She hadn't asked, even, just taken all of Souria's new money out of the teller's hand. "Khamsin," she said, holding the three bills up for Souria to see. She collected those bills for herself before handing over the remainder of the money, and Souria had felt the flame of outrage beginning all over again. But when she looked to the teller's face, she found no judgment, and no fairness—the teller simply looked tired. The teller gestured for the next person in line to bring his transaction, and Souria snuffed the flame. She had so many more ouguiya on her person, after all, many more that Zahrae would never find. When she ran out, when she'd gotten used to the new world and its language, she would return alone to this bank.

She was still leaning, steadying herself against the wall with a hand on its brick. She was calculating the price that the new world put on its hospitality, gauging the cleansed feeling in her stomach, when she felt something on her shoulder. A hand. "Do you need help?" came the words, but it was a language Souria had not yet heard in the new world, a language so far from Hassaniya that she knew she could never absorb it. All she heard were sounds—large, slow, open hills of words.

"Assistance?" the woman said, and these were different sounds still. French, but not French. The woman wasn't from this new world, but from a world even beyond. She wore new clothes—blue jeans that Souria saw would be so soft, dare she touch them, and a black shirt whose satiny ruffles scalloped along her collarbone. She had a scar on one side of her face that might have ruined her, except that even it told of a life in that world beyond, where even the worst things that could happen to a body were fixable.

"Assistance?" the woman repeated. Her teeth were even, set in the prettiest ridge of symmetry, and so white, white as animal bones left in the sun. Her skin was the same dark color as Souria's but she had the most piercing dark eyes, and Souria thought that in another world, a world beyond the new country, she and the woman might live in the same tribe.

But she felt herself shaking her head no. She knew without language what the woman was asking, and she also knew it not to be possible. The woman could never help. Souria could never help the woman help her, even as she saw it would make the woman infinitely pleased. This woman, her world was too far beyond.

VIII. Marrakech

The route of the medina had finally stamped itself onto Shannon's memory, but even with this neural map she felt, in the days she walked the alleys, an emptiness that shifted her center. People spoke French, but they did not want to speak it to her. The actual life of the country happened in Dharija, words of which fled her ears, uncomprehended. Only small transactions of ordering food and buying ceramics were available. Outside of these, her plug did not fit into anyone else's outlet. The merchants in the small shops of the souk smiled when they saw her American money coming. Some of them accosted her with loud, exaggerated English; they opened their mouths wide for the vowels. They grinned in the easy way they thought they'd seen Americans smile on the television, and they patted her on the shoulder, even as she stepped away from them.

Connection, she could have only with Vlad. Nights, after he finished his meetings, she unleashed the whole of the English language upon him. They talked politics. They storied their childhoods. Together they sang show tunes they both knew— "Tomorrow," from *Annie*, "Maria," from *West Side Story*—verse to chorus, chorus to verse. Vlad was a terrible singer. She clung to him anyway, for the reflected shred of herself.

He ministered to the deficit in her mobility, bringing her

dinner from the hotel restaurant when pain kept her from making the trip downstairs. With a firm, steadying hand on her waist, he helped her step over the high gate to the hotel bathtub. At night, as she was falling asleep, she found him tucking the bedcovers under her chin. He seemed to enjoy this kind of project management.

He liked feeling sorry for her, she thought, then just as quickly unthought it: it would be an unworkable idea between them, going forward. But when he tested the bathwater before helping her in, when he balanced its temperature with more cold water from the tap, she had to stop herself from laughing. For once in her life, she needed someone. For once in her life, she'd found someone who enjoyed being needed. It made her feel even more alienated from herself, from her previous bodily wholeness.

By the time she came across the girl standing outside the jeweler's, she knew what it meant, to be standing outside oneself in a different country. The girl was clearly an immigrant: you could see it in the dark, smooth ale of her skin; in her sandals, whose thongs were unraveling; and in the long, purple scarf the girl had intricately wrapped around herself in a code only her fellow countrymen could have understood.

"Do you need help?" Shannon asked, then realized she'd asked it in English. The girl was Shannon's same skin color, was all, and her broad nose had tapped some syrup of kinship. She'd been leaning against the brick wall, but when Shannon spoke, she stood to her full height, and what Shannon found in the girl's sharp, green eyes was the shock of her wanting some connective tissue from this encounter: the shred of herself was more desperate, even, than this girl who had landed so far from home. The girl shook her head no, in the kindest way possible. She looked, slowly, at Shannon's clothes, and Shannon grew embarrassed at her own riches. Shannon watched the girl stop and focus on her facial scar. She was looking at Shannon's face, watching carefully for her own future losses.

"Assistance?" Shannon asked, on the off chance the girl understood French, but she just continued to stare at Shannon's scar.

Finally, an older woman came out of the store. She eyed Shannon suspiciously, with untamed, furrowed eyebrows, and made sure to bump her as she linked her arm through the girl's and walked her away, down the alley. Shannon hoped the girl would turn back to look at her one last time, but she and the woman passed the man in the toy soldier uniform, whom all the children were saluting, and the girl did not turn. They continued down the alley, past a woman in a miniskirt and sunglasses, shaking her hair out of its roller mold. Shannon watched and kept watching, so oblivious to her own life that she didn't notice the smoking man until she smelled his cigarette. He'd been walking toward her, and the closer he got, the more she saw that he seemed to have been punched, repeatedly, in the face. He was close enough that she could hear him muttering, and as he passed her, he threw his smoke to the street. It was familiar; it was weed; she breathed deeply. She watched mist rise from the blunt's lit end, watched the paper, soiled with the blood of the man's busted lip.

Vlad had asked her to this country after one date. He'd found Rapunzel in a tower and decided to climb up and effect rescue. But here in this new world, where no one else could, or would, talk to her, she just felt further trapped.

PART II

RAINY SEASON

IX. Marrakech

Affliction, Shannon found, was a tricky thing. It wasn't a splinter from a wooden chair, or the prick of a cactus she'd brushed against in an arboretum. Affliction, stretched toward permanency, upended her mind, hollowed her sanity. The hours she lay in bed, pain tacked across her body, grew into a jealous lover who would not let her eat. She fell asleep; pain fingered her neck and pinched her into wakefulness. She tried to think, to remember anything at all neutral, to invite joy—the pain surged forth to say no. *All that will fill the deep cave of you from now on is me, me, me.*

Pain chiseled her life into its smallest form, and in Morocco, she was trapped in this airspace with no weed, which she didn't dare ask Vlad to buy. She lacked the wherewithal to make discoveries at the pharmacies, which Vlad told her didn't require prescriptions; she didn't have the energy to walk the three blocks down Rue Mohammed VI, even if codeine was exactly what would take her mind off the hurt. She didn't have the spoons to order up pommes frites from the poolside restaurant. All she could do was prop her ruined back against three stacked pillows and watch television.

She cycled through memories of what life was like before all this pain, how she'd drunkenly pushed a grocery cart through Kroger at two in the morning, how she'd smelled the dreamy coconut of her own shampoo in her college study carrel. All those years of sensory neutrality, sliced clean by one second of highway. She could walk, now, and she could hear. She was going to be fine. But fine didn't mean whole, not by a long shot. She'd wear pain on her body for the rest of her life; her lost physical future was a hurdle of grief.

French nouns from le lycée returned to her lexicon here and there—not enough of them that she could comprehend the news announcer's agenda, but enough to keep her distracted for the half hour of his hawkeyed analysis. When Shannon stopped the process of translating his words into her English, when she lost her train of thought and drifted into passive listening, pain grew again to its full height; she sipped club soda to stanch the nausea.

And who, in any case, did she need to stay alive for? In the night, Vlad came to her with little regard for what she may or may not have been feeling. Encountering her stiffness, he arranged her like an old-fashioned doll, bending her knees slightly, telling her to relax, as if that had ever been her problem.

She'd let him do all the work precisely because she didn't want to talk about it, because feeling him slide the palm of his hand around the back of her neck, having him cup her left breast, was a different enough physical sensation that it blocked her nerve channels. She enjoyed the irony of his thick, waxy condom, the secret of the stone-emptied pit in her uterus that made prophylaxis entirely unnecessary. The joke was on Vlad, his big leafy ears, the way he said *holy shit* every time he came. But her postaccident body craved sex. Like the bud of a carnivorous plant, she found herself hungry for simple touch.

It was entirely possible, she thought, that she was like this before the accident.

It was possible she'd been this way for a long time.

It was possible that before the accident, she'd also been in pain, a pain so constant, so much a part of her fiber, that it had gone undetected. It was entirely possible that the fancy, high-register pinch she felt now at the base of her neck and spine was psychosomatic, not real so much as inescapable. It was possible she was still her parents' poor, dumb daughter, a rabbit trapped in a cage, her ears sticking up beyond the metal bars to listen for that which might save her.

Their fifth night in Morocco, Vlad said he'd been married before. He'd been worked over by some Eurotrash golddigger, he said. A Latvian exchange student he met his senior year of college. He'd made bad choices too—he told her over Friday couscous at Dar VI. "Her name was Nastasia," he said, "but everyone in our dorm called her Nasty."

Shannon wondered how that didn't tell him something. She chewed her harissa-laced carrots as he told her about his divorce, which took three months, or one-eighth of the two years they were married; Vlad spoke constantly in math, quantifying what he dared not measure.

Shannon pressed her napkin to her mouth as Vlad told her he gave Nasty half his retirement. He handed over half the equity in his house, he told her, and Shannon trained her eyes directly on his. She had no health insurance and $147,000 in medical bills she'd never be able to pay; her student loan balance brought the weight on her head to a cool $258,000. She wondered how anyone could be so stupid as to take their financial freedom and halve it with an ESL speaker they met at an ice cream social. To keep from smiling at his stupidity, Shannon took a sip of her wine. It was red. From Argentina. It floated to the top of her brain and shattered the ice there.

"How many years ago was all this?" she asked.

"Five," he said, holding up his splayed palm, his five stumpy fingers. "I've been free five years."

"Think you'll ever do it again?"

Vlad pulled his hand back to his lap and looked at her again, as if she were a lab specimen, fixed this time under the restaurant's surprisingly bright fluorescent lights, turned up because the evening's high wind would not allow candles. At the table to their left, a British couple had chain-smoked through each phase of their meal; just before the waiter came and cleared the second course, Shannon had watched the woman grind her cigarette into the hatch-patterned rim of her salad plate. The table to their right was a group of young Moroccan men, all in black leather jackets, watching a soccer match on one of their phones. Every time the team scored, the three of them hooted in unison.

Vlad bit his lip. Gave her one of his most losing smiles. "I think I might," he said, and her stomach filled with a fear bisected by hope. Her job was long gone. She had no health insurance. One hundred forty-seven thousand dollars was a deadly amount of money. She was a foster child hoping for adoption.

Back at the hotel she lay in bed with her telephone and its new international SIM card, scrolling to the impersonal boilerplate of the subject line: *RESULTS*. She opened the email, downloaded the document, rowed back through the software of her phone to open it. It was long, full of medicalese and further recommendations, but what it all meant was that the stone had regrown itself; power had rescinded itself from her womb. Results, they'd called it, as if one of them had dumped alchemy into a wash and waited for the mix to change color. *RESULTS*: her womanly walk on this earth had fallen into an icy crevasse.

Vlad sat on a hotel chair, still in his navy-blue suit, paging through leaves of architectural drawings. Creases still lined the shoulders of his jacket. An hour earlier, he'd lain beside her and showed her how he could knot cherry stems with his tongue, but now he was sober, sunk in his engineering. He'd lost a little weight since they'd been in Morocco, and now his eyes floated in his face. He'd crossed his legs in concentration, in the manspready way of his right shoe hanging over the cliff of his left knee.

Reading the report felt like wrecking her car all over again. She heard the sick crunch in her head, felt the crack of the windshield in her inner ear. She'd never have children, she knew. She'd not thought of it until it was taken away from her but now, she found, the most regrettable pattern of a life was fashioned out of its empty squares. She imagined children, their eyes, their taking turns on playground slides and hunting for Easter eggs, their falling from the bicycles as they learned to ride, and then she imagined someone coming to erase the children, like a film effect on tape. She was dressing her soul in hazmat gear to get through.

Vlad suddenly looked up at her, and she felt a pronouncement coming, but he only smiled faintly and looked back to his sketches.

"I already miss the food," she said.

He rubbed the beard he'd started growing during their week in Marrakech, but he did not respond. She'd claimed food, where she might have claimed tajine. Harissa. She was too generic. She'd failed a test on the Macedonski Zeleznici.

"Do you eat like this at home?" she asked.

"Ha!" he pealed, a short burst of a laugh like a bicycle horn. "In my refrigerator right now are three Healthy Choice boxes, one questionable head of cabbage, and some definitely sour milk. It's a bachelor's fridge. There's a six-ounce steak I'll defrost tomorrow."

Shannon understood: He ate out every night. He had the money. "What will you pretend to eat now?" she asked.

He looked back up at her curiously, as if she were an x he needed to solve for y. "Don't need to eat," he said. "You've filled me up with pastille, good wine, and the hope that I'll be seeing you again soon."

"Of course you will," she said. "No doubt."

The next day, they went to Menara Airport and boarded their KLM. They shoved their jackets into the overhead compartment and buckled in for the six-hour ride, and when Vlad proposed to her, low in her ear, under the roar of the turbine, it was nothing like it was in the movies. "You'll marry me, right?" he told her. She heard it as she felt sounds under the weight of the accident, as a series of clicks and hums that moved her skin rather than her brain. What he said, she heard as one with the engine, a joined vibration.

She laughed nervously, because she'd been genuinely surprised. "Yes," she said eventually. It hadn't even been an idea she'd had.

But it worked. It worked well. He'd be the first solid, adult decision she'd ever made.

X. Marrakech

The music spread royally. Cradled the trouble in Souria's mind.
Settled first in her right ear and then in her left, swirled like the
smoke in the base of a water pipe, rattled her brain as though fighting itself to sit in one ear. It wasn't funneled through a loudspeaker:
on the soles of her feet, she could feel the vibrations. The new in-
strument was large enough to rock every alley in the quarter.

The sound was something grown solid and heavy, anchored
to earth. She stood in the doorway of the Elouafiq parlor and listened. Adwan, Zahrae's son, sat forward on a cushion with his
wrists crossed atop his lap, each of his palms stretched over an
opposing knee. His skin was as a quail's egg, his neck and the insides of his arms mottled with lightness. Or perhaps the lightness was the true color of Adwan, and the rest of him, the warm
darkness of his face and the backs of his hands, were the errors
of pigment. He pushed his glasses back up his nose and stared at
her, and she felt ashamed of the secret thing happening inside
her own body.

"That noise?" she asked.

"An organ," he said. To further explain, he stretched his arms
forward and moved his fingers as if across keys.

Still, she did not understand. In the desert, she'd never seen
such.

Adwan spoke to her only in two-word sentences, but he helped her mop the floor with a towel in the evenings after dinner, and he walked her around the medina, showing her where to buy cooking oil, soap, and the vegetables the family needed. She didn't yet know all the words for gratitude in the new dialect, so she was relieved to be able to express it in housekeeping. Her third day with the family, Adwan had taken her to a nearby abattoir and told her something in Dharija. When she hunched her shoulders to show she hadn't understood, he pointed discreetly at the shop and sliced his hand horizontally to indicate *no*. He took her to another abattoir and made the same motion with his hand, and then to another. Finally, at the fourth shop, he nodded and smiled, and it was in this way that she understood that the meat there was the freshest.

Her fourth day in the house, Adwan taught her phrases. *Which way is the spiceseller? The price for fish is too high. I feel like a drink of tea.* Then, he taught her words that stood by themselves. *Hot. Arm. Twenty. Elephant.* On this, her fifth day, he talked to her about music. Rai. Gnaoua. Cheb Mami. The organ. He clapped his hands over her ears. "Too loud," he said.

She shrugged. She rather liked it. The baby in her womb moved. The baby liked it too.

"Made by le français," he said.

She didn't understand.

"Like in a Christian temple."

The organist came to a crescendo of minor chords that made an empty vase rattle against the floor. Adwan came to the doorway and slid his hands to rest on the sides of Souria's face and she dropped her head in what she hoped looked like modesty. In fact, she was deeply embarrassed. For Adwan. For his feelings. Deep in her belly, fish swam. Her lungs felt awash in the vibration of the organ; the music reconstituted the very beating of her heart. She didn't feel attracted to Adwan so much as connected to him, but the connection, in this new land of her immediate future, felt essential.

Since arriving in Marrakech, she'd been invariably perched on the edge of tears. While hanging the family's laundry, she saw a cat on a neighboring roof, eating the remains of a pigeon, and found herself weeping. She walked to the Djmaa-el-Fna at night to watch the bands and dancers and storytellers. She stood at the edge of one of the circles as a man wheeled a cart of false teeth past and found emotion congealing itself in her nose. She was perpetually moved here in Marrakech, though she didn't understand why now, when life was so easy, she was gating back tears.

The second day, after hearing all that had happened to her in the desert, Zahrae had held Souria's hand and cried. "I have three children and two grandchildren and a dead husband, and I've always wished for help," she said. "You have a place in my house. You need never leave."

Souria hadn't told Zahrae about the tireseller. She didn't want Zahrae to think she was fast.

While the family was away in the day times, Souria let herself out of the riad with Zahrae's key and fed a dying dog she'd first seen from an upstairs window. She threw it chicken bones stripped to the tendon, as well as fish bellies that one of the upstairs tenants had forgotten to refrigerate. With a bread knife, she sawed off a quarter of a tin can and set out water, meaning to slake the dog's thirst for the world it knew. She fed the dying dog until it was no longer dying, until, after a few days, it had energy and presence of mind enough to limp away down the alley and disappear, leaving only a dark oval of dried blood on the corner bricks where it had lain.

Inside the riad, she watched the programs on the Elouafiqs' television. The soap opera actors spoke such rapid Arabic that she had to infer the drama from the hammered pitches of their voices and the liquid zooms of the cameras to closeup. If she changed the channel, she found young Arab men in the bleached-white thawbs of the Saudis, standing in lines of chorus. Nodding canes. Tossing sabers. Sometimes the satellite failed, and the television would die, save for the blocky, inscrutable letters in the middle of the screen. It was a relief, then, when Adwan came home for the lunch hour. He'd fix the television and then sit in the kitchen and watch her prepare the meal.

The seventh day, Adwan taught her how to make different tenses of the verbs of his dialect. After the lesson she went down to the kitchen to cut chicken for a tajine, and she was pleased, while pulling off a severed wing, to find that she could now say that she existed, and would continue to exist further.

He taught her the past tense of *take*, *khadat*, and in past tense she remembered the night, in her country, when she'd gone walking to the garden. She remembered having ignored the fear that rushed to the base of her throat at the sound of an approaching truck, and how she'd straightened up, instead, to her full six feet, to prove she was brave. She'd screamed when Ousmane's nephew grabbed her by the waist and pulled her into the battered truck, she'd kicked so hard into air and against the truck that she thought she heard herself dent its side, but by then it was too late: he'd pinned her against the cab window with all his weight, and the driver, whom she could not see, was driving her away. They were hustling her away from her village in the black, shadowless night, and only the tire treads in the sand would tell it.

The tire tracks rolled out away from her, deep and rutted, making shadows in the bright light from the truck's busted rear window, but by morning, she knew, the sand would have blown out of form, and no one would ever know where she had gone.

They'd think the djinnah had materialized from the smoke of the desert to collect her.

Adwan put his lips to hers, and the warm moisture of his kiss stirred an anger she hadn't felt since the camp at Mijek. She leaned into her consciousness and fell. He had no idea who she was. She would work hard to speak his pronouns and discern his beef, but he'd never know the first window of her mind.

He had no capacity for deceit, which she liked. As a child, she'd once seen a man eating scorpions out of a bowl, but when she got closer, she found that he'd severed the little curled tails and set them aside in a row on the sand: the scorpions in the bowl were only crawling through their own blue blood, wriggling themselves to an inevitable death. The scorpion eater kept a straight face even as Souria got close, and though he eyed her for her own reaction as he held one of the insects ready to drop into his mouth, he held no concern either way. Zahrae was like this man, but Adwan was not. He wore, always, the blank, wondering stare of someone whose relationship with the world hadn't yet completely unfolded.

Now, Adwan pulled back to study her face, like a child stacking blocks in order to test the propulsive force of knocking them down. She broke free of him and ran, tying her headscarf tighter on her head, to the fresh air of the alley and the medina beyond.

The full moon was high in the night but behind drifting clouds, covered in tissue paper. Souria heard Adwan climb the stairs to the square hole that led from the third floor to the roof. She heard him calling her, but she wouldn't look. She heard him climb through the hole and say his salaams, but she wouldn't talk. Though she was not yet at home in his language, she could hear the permanent youth in his head that came through in his voice, and it was so clear to her, the thing she must do to satisfy all those Elouafiqs: Adwan, who wanted her, and Zahrae, who knew her son could have no other woman he wanted. When he went downstairs to take his cold dinner, she stayed on the roof, saying sunnah, until a tiny drop of rain lit on her nose. The heat would break, she thought. The rain would fall and the roofs and the streets and the doors of every riad in the quarter would come clean. She wiped moisture from the bridge of her nose and climbed downstairs, and for the first time since Zahrae had found her sitting in the central bus station, she washed her hair with the Elouafiqs' metal bath bucket.

In the exact middle of the night, when the windowsashes were closed and the riad had already stood through three hours of quiet, Adwan came to her. He stood for several minutes in the Elouafiq parlor, where she slept alone on her pallet of sheets, and then he slowly removed his pants, tossed them lazily on the television stand. In the moonlight coming from the courtyard, she could see that the skin on his thighs and groin was as mottled as the skin on his neck and hands. Before bed, she'd eaten a slice of goat cheese, and she still had the milky taste on the back of her tongue when he kissed her. Her hair hadn't yet dried completely, and when he pressed himself down on top of her, she felt the moisture of the sheets against the back of her neck. He wasn't like the tireseller. He was slow. Curious. Shaking with wonder.

He came to know her first with his hands. He lay them along the divide between her breasts and moved them along the length of her legs, and for the long moments of it she held this revelation, that this same body that she'd been living in for fifteen years could for someone else be a new land, undiscovered. Despite his trembling, he caressed her feet and put two fingers in the warm place between her thighs.

He came then to know her with his mouth. He licked the small circumference of her nipples and moved his bottom lip along her neck. He held her clean hair in his mouth. With his tongue, he put pressure on the strange-feeling center of her navel.

As rain pelted the riad's corrugated roof, Adwan came to know her with the rest of himself, the same piercing, sudden way the tireseller had. She moved her pelvis to make herself more comfortable, but by the time she'd registered the thought that he was far gentler than the tireseller, he'd already finished, and he kissed her cheek, and she made a noise, a soft moan that even she herself did not understand. As rain pebbled against the windows, he removed himself from her and, with his penis, marked a trail on her belly that he did not know already housed other seed. Adwan had so little understanding of the world, she decided, looking at him, that he'd never come to suspicions. She decided then that the baby, when it came, would be named Hassan, after the man who had rescued her from rougher men.

The next morning, she woke earlier than eleven, though so little sunlight came through the courtyard that it might have been dawn. It was late enough that the Elouafiqs were gone, but the mists of the previous night's rains still hung in the air of the riad and chilled the courtyard. She sat at the top of the stairs washing vegetables in one plastic bowl and cutting them over another. She dropped a squash and watched it bounce without bursting into all its seedy pieces. It landed, whole, and rolled unevenly to a stop. Just ripe enough to live. In all its future tenses.

XI. Louisville

Shannon had had no friends in the third grade because she was the only Black girl in her class. Third-grade September, a month into the start of school, she'd asked her mother for permission to go home with a classmate named Ayla Teague, who lived two blocks away. The houses on Ayla's street were smaller and less dignified than the houses on Shannon's; the perimeter of the neighborhood held its older construction. Postwar tract homes. Houses for Americans who'd expected, from the coming boom, too little. Instead of a garage, Ayla's house had a sad, cluttered carport. Her porch was a tiny square, and the front of her house sat distressingly close to the sidewalk. The wooden head of her doorframe looked rotten, ominously so, as if it might, at any time, come crashing down onto her life.

The hottest part of autumn had come to rest over Louisville— Indian summer, her mother called it, but her father said no, it was hotter than that. Slave summer, he said. He turned down the thermostat and closed all the windows. Down Ayla's street, a woman in a yellow sundress was walking a puppy. Her body was shaped like her dog's, both of them with short necks and stomachs bowed toward stoutness. Each of them sauntering forward with light steps, as though they were pleased with a mystery the rest of the world could not see.

When she got to Ayla's stoop, her mother appeared, stiff as buckram. "Well, where did this child come from?" she asked.

"It's Shannon," Ayla said.

Her mother peered down through the screen door, then opened it and bent over from the waist, her face so close to Shannon's that she could smell the coffee on the woman's breath. "I thought with a name like that, she'd be White," the woman said. "I assumed you had sense enough to have White friends at that school."

Ayla shrugged her shoulders in a loose, unconcerned way, but looked down in embarrassment at the toe of her shoe. She turned her foot inside it so that to Shannon, looking from outside, the shoe became a wriggling worm.

A feeling came bleeding over Shannon, an inky supposition that home might be a safe place to do the unraveling. Without saying goodbye, she walked northwest. She walked tall down Ayla's street because she knew it was the only way to even partially win, but when she turned the corner she ran, pumping her legs such that by the time she got the length of the two blocks and into her own cul-de-sac, she'd sapped herself of useful oxygen. She leaned over, hands on knees, and reclaimed her breath, and then came the worse feeling, that home wasn't home either, her parents not people she could talk to so much as people with whom the universe had mysteriously deposited her. Into this feeling of cosmic homelessness, she nonetheless walked into her own front door. She told her mother nothing, because Mrs. Cavanagh hadn't been wild about her going to some strange White person's house in the first place, and here Shannon had gone and proved her right.

At school, she stopped talking to Ayla. She still sat in the same foursquare of adjoined desks but made careful practice of avoiding Ayla's eyes while doing seatwork. Ayla's breathing, which she'd never before noticed, was so loud in her ear that she wanted it to stop. When Ayla was deep in concentration, she pumped her breath in stops and starts that made her sound like a garbage truck, and when she wrote in cursive, she smacked her tongue against her teeth. If she accidentally ended up behind her in the lunch line, Shannon drifted away, got herself milk out of the refrigerated bin, replaced her spot farther back in the line.

All the other friend groups had already gelled, though since Ayla was White, she had an easier time fitting the pipe joint of herself into established social plumbing. Shannon was a different caste. She sat by herself at lunch, at the end of the table. At recess, she played alone. She found a patch of continually replenishing four-leaf clover about which she told no one; she'd save that good luck for herself, all those Whitegirls in her class be damned.

Now, with Vlad, it was a bit the same: she was a scavenger, feeding off the half-rack that Nasty had left behind. Shannon had health insurance now, because she was married. She still had her $147,000 medical bill and her $112,000 default—they were the dirtiest secrets she kept—but her nose-diving credit score no longer mattered. She had a rent-free roof over her head, and dental coverage with Aetna. She was driving Vlad's old BMW, the one with the loud, squeaky front-end suspension and the fatally cracked oil pan, but it was the newest car she'd ever owned. Before they got married, Vlad had planned to sell it. When she punched the button for the air-conditioning and found actual relief blowing on her face where previously she'd found intermittent blasts of hot air, she felt like a million of the best bucks.

She was still buying weed, but not because she had to— courtesy Windsolver's Rx program, she had Oxycontin. She grinned at the gleam of her own newly cleaned teeth in her Beemer's rearview mirror; she tossed her expensive haircolor that was courtesy of Vlad's AmEx. When she got to the boutique bakery and swiped his bankcard for the two gourmet cupcakes she'd eat after smoking, she'd issue jeremiads about being too happy. She'd think about how just a few months earlier she'd shopped at yard sales, scavenging the broken, mold-dottered pieces of other people's lives.

She felt herself scavenging, too, for Vlad's admiration. Vlad rarely spoke of Nastasia, not of her having lived in their house or slept in their bed or eaten his organic food at their kitchen counter. She knew that he'd divorced in 2012, after buying the house in 2010. Nasty had lived there two years, Shannon computed, but it hadn't initially made her feel any way, really, because Vlad had had the good taste to clear every last bit of her out of his house. She kept expecting to come across a photo album on the dusty part of the bookshelf, or a pair of panties accidentally fallen and forgotten in the space behind the dryer, or a pink-handled razor in the back of a bathroom drawer. Nasty seemed to have packed up and vanished without physical trace. But her absence somehow eventually made her stronger. Like a poltergeist in their house. A mystery of negative space.

Shannon would sneak out of the house to buy weed while Vlad was at work, and before he returned in the evening—seven at the earliest through commuter traffic—she'd sit in the garage, inside his airtight BMW. She'd take her papers and hash and cupcakes, and she'd smoke and eat. There came a day when, just as she'd sparked up, a rectangle of light opened into the garage, and the door ground upward. Vlad was early. Shannon unlocked her glove compartment and smashed her joint against the inside of its little rhomboid door panel. She closed it in, hoping it was fully extinguished, hoping to hermetically seal in the smell of skunk. Through her own car window, she watched him pull in. He smiled at her, as if she were more than she was.

He got out of the car, with the vintage periwinkle suitcase meant to signify him as a hipster, scissored through the inadequate amount of space Shannon had left between the front end of her car and the garage wall. "Are you ever coming in?" he asked, opening the door to the kitchen.

"In a bit," she said. "My back's hurting," she lied. "Sitting here with the lumbar support."

She let him close the door, and she pulled out her joint and relit. She rolled down her window and blew smoke into the closed garage. He'd smell it. They were legally joined now. She barely cared.

By the time she got herself inside, she found him buttering a slice of focaccia, taking the knife across it so angrily he made a hole in the bread. She stared at his downcast eyes, willing him to look at her and acknowledge what had just happened, the open secret of it, but he kept his eyes on the bread, tearing it now with his hands. She watched him chew, and finally, he looked up at her. "You want kids?" he asked. The afternoon, she saw, was moving toward emotional poverty. The stone in her belly. One more secret.

She smiled. Said, "Don't you want to wait until you've had a midlife crisis?"

"Midlife crisis? I'm not the type."

"Sure you are. All males are constantly in a state of midlife crisis." She crossed the kitchen and pressed her shoulder to his, praying he couldn't smell how heavily the weed was riding her clothes. "Fast cars, fast women—that's just maleness. What you do at age forty is a heightened state."

"Well," he said. He wouldn't drop the question. She saw that.

"Why now?" she asked. "I mean, are you not happy with the way things are?"

"Sure I am. But people have kids, you know. Eventually, everyone does."

"Everyone?"

"The normal people. The people who make the future."

The acoustics of the kitchen were such that words never echoed, and what Vlad said came right out of his mouth and into her ear, where it lodged in her consciousness. She'd known about the bone in her uterus for six months, but it was theoretical. Vlad's words had jammed her blood, congealed it into fear. She was Anne Boleyn now. It'd be off with her head.

She'd never in her life come up against this emotion, not even in the crunched folds of her old car, where she'd thought she was dying. This was different. It was the end of a dream she hadn't even known she'd had, the primal need to recreate, the urge that had solidified in the moments after the words "normal people" flew out of Vlad's mouth. She couldn't pop out puppies. She couldn't do the job of a simple park squirrel.

She imagined life spooling pitifully ahead of her, the rest of the world pumping out its crying infants, women all around her raising their babies and sending them off on a yellow bus to kindergarten while she watched, like a kid at a pool party where everyone else could swim. She'd tend her own gray hair. Sit in the nursing home alone, looking out the window. She'd grow up an old woman yet unseasoned. In evolutionary terms, it would be a waste that she'd ever been born.

Vlad closed his eyes and took a deep breath. Finished his bread, put the knife and butter away without offering her any. "I'm sorry," he said, stroking her arm. "We just got married. Why are we talking about this?"

They'd just gotten married, he said. Hell, they'd just *met*.

When she turned out the table lamp that night, he pulled her back onto the mattress with him, so that her head was resting in the crook between his arm and his chest. "Well then," he said, "what can we possibly do?" He pushed her t-shirt up, then took off his own, and then his underwear, and she watched the chiaroscuro his skin made in the sodium vapor light coming in through the window. She caught the fleeting outline of his erect penis in the harsh glow of the full moon and willed her own interest in the act. She'd accidentally left the window open, but even against the fall breeze she found the sex, post–baby talk, disappointed her.

The next morning, against the sound of the birds screaming in the coming dawn, they reprised and repeated. "What else are we doing?" Vlad said as he rolled off her to take a shower. He thought they'd made a baby, she realized. Or would soon make one. Tonight. Tomorrow. Next week.

Downstairs, she slid the patio door open to the exact width of her body and sat herself down on the steps of his pool. The sun hadn't yet cleared the trees, and darkness closed her off from the visual dimension of the world. From the pond outside Vlad's privacy fence came the loud croaking of frogs. Crickets made their neat, steady chirrups. The whole world was still trying to mate, despite the waning year. Shannon sat, listening to the occasional gulp of the filter.

Through the patio door screen, she heard Vlad put his landline voicemail on speaker while he rattled silverware out of a drawer and poured his coffee. In a discomfiting monotone, a woman said *This is a message from the Kentucky Victim Offenders' Program. Thomas Watkins has been released today. The owner of this telephone number has asked to be notified.* The woman paused, turned suddenly cheery: *God bless, and have a nice day!*

"Who's Thomas Watkins?" she yelled through the door.

Vlad's voice drizzled with fatigue. "Why would I know?"

"Well, they're calling you."

"Who knows how long he's been in. I haven't had this number the whole time I've lived here. Only a few years."

"Oh." Shannon looked to the striations of sun beginning across Vlad's pool, the sunlight gathering in its bottom. All the cells and DNA helixes accidentally expelled from her body. Leagues of them. "You had another number before? In this house?"

"I had it changed so I'd stop getting her calls. Hell, if I hadn't had the number changed, I'd think maybe Thomas Watkins belonged to her."

"Oh."

It was the closest he'd come to speaking ill of Nastasia, ever, and the mere intimation of shade made her ghost fade slightly, as if it had entered a dead zone on a television screen. A baby would disappear her altogether. A baby would fill up every bit of that negative space. No exorcism required.

Marriage: Studio Album Version
You help your husband pack for his weeklong business stay in Morocco. Helping is, perhaps, not the word that fits: his actual question—"Do you mind filling my suitcase?"—indicates that he's made you king. It astonishes you that one soul should trust another with so intimate a task as planning a wardrobe, but Vlad has left you the honor, and you guess this is what marriage will be—growing closer and closer until, like dogs, you begin to smell alike. Chase each other's tails.

You don't want to disappoint. You pack a pre-threaded needle, a small tube of Neosporin, a trial-scented bottle of Listerine for his carry-on. You fasten his less substantial clothes—socks, underwear, neckties—into the compartment of the suitcase that zips closed. His pants, shirts, and jackets are less susceptible to TSA molestation— you fold them into the part of the suitcase that battens with a fastener. He thanks you, genuinely thanks you, for the bottle of Cade you bought him with his own money. He's been living alone all these years without catastrophe, you know. But when you ask him to come check everything over, and he hugs you to himself, puts his nose into your curls, and tells you you're the reason he feels finished, you hear in his voice an atomic split of truth.

You get out of the car to kiss him goodbye at the airport, but after you do, he lingers there in the starting snow. He rolls his suitcase slowly to the revolving door, his head drooping in thought, and then he stops, turns around, and yells your name. He runs back to the car, leaving the suitcase all by its lonesome on the Departing Flights porch, where the rapidly thickening snow will dampen it. He comes to your door and kisses you again, bunches your hair up under his nose. People watch as they hurry themselves from their own cars to Departing Flights. An elderly woman standing with a small trunk clicks her glasses apart in the middle and lets them hang from the chain around her neck, as if to see you and Vlad better with her own eyes. She looks through the precipitation, dead at the two of you, and smiles beatifically, happy to be witnessing love before the astral heights.

It's cold in Essaouira this time of year. Accordingly, you've packed him three pairs of knitted socks.

Marriage: Live Concert Version

Vlad flies his own coffee beans to Morocco, but this time, when he gets to the hotel and commences unpacking, he'll find that his grounds have been upset in transit. Not so forcefully that the jar will have emptied, because the suitcase is full enough that the jar can't much move. He'll still have enough to use in the machine at his worksite; he'll still be able to season his cold, Moroccan mornings.

You could have sealed the jar, pressed your palm carefully around the lip of the lid to be sure, secured the bottle in Ziploc. But when you saw that the plastic hadn't cleaved perfectly to the glass, a vicious little crow in your gut made you leave it that way, slightly unsquared, even as you packed clothes all around it. You drive home from the *airport imagining the jar being jostled as it's loaded in Louisville, upended as it's transferred in Chicago. The lid comes loose, the physics of its contents happen, chaos theory becomes a thing Vlad will accept on the other end of his closed system. You imagine grounds sprinkling themselves out, working their way through the dark, airtight six hours of flight from Chicago to Marrakech, settling into Vlad's shirts. You imagine Vlad in his luxury suite, unzipping his suitcase and blaming the TSA, and you feel satisfied. Why should his life continue according to plan? Why should he get to gallivant around the world like Vasco da Gama while you're stuck in Kentucky arching your back into its lowest-pain positions? Why should he have all the power in a marriage? Why should he expect a baby exactly when he wants one?*

You already know what's going to happen, that you'll pull a baby out of a hat in order to stay in his good graces. You'll have the stone removed, you'll have yourself pumped full of hormones like a Thanksgiving turkey. And he won't care about you then, just as he doesn't now—he'll fuck you for the ten minutes it takes him to come, and then he'll roll off. He'll reproduce. Make his normal.

You've tried, these six months of your marriage, to remember the softer parts of yourself, the parts you thought might connect to a lifelong partner, but you can't. It's like trying to break into your own house.

Vlad will be off in Morocco jousting with windmills, and you'll be home worried about babies. You'll buy your weed freely, though, and you'll smoke it in his pool, in his garage, his living room, his bed, his shower—wherever the fuck you want. You'll smoke naked. You'll smoke while masturbating. You'll smoke while dumping pennies in his meticulously arranged dresser drawer and scraping them back out into the palm of your hand. You'll fling open the windows and run the air conditioner for a couple of days before he comes home— but it's your house too now. You'll remember when you were a little girl, and you lay in the grass of your backyard, watching for airplanes, and you and the sky and the grass were a single exchange.

And you'll remember that when you packed his travel razor and saw that it had gone to rust on one end, you told him you'd buy a replacement blade, and it wasn't that you'd been vicious—you'd simply forgotten. You imagine him in Morocco, watching the beach through his hotel window, nicking himself once, twice. He's a careful man, so the slices will be small—no one, save him, will notice these cuts. Still. He made you king. Left it up to you. And so they'll be tiny beads of bad blood, nicks on the smooth skin of your new marriage.

XII. Marrakech

The three youths of the quarter had come in the night, singing in Berber, waking all the houses of the alley. They'd walked to the big brown door at 78 Rue Zouika and knocked, asking for Driss, a name that did not belong to the Elouafiqs. When no person of the riad answered, the youths sang even louder. The November wind carried their voices, which crept through the doorframe, landed under the ceiling, settled in wall cracks. The embarrassment Souria felt for their low manners pounded her gut.

The next morning, before she left for her employment at a laundry in Gueliz, Zahrae shook Souria awake. The men had pissed on the street, she told her. They'd pissed on her strong brown door. "You must get up right away to clean this," she said, and Souria wondered if she heard the insult in her own voice.

But after all, it was a tone she'd grown used to hearing in both Ousmane's compound and in the camp at Mijek, so she cleared the sheets from her legs and said, in her halting Dharija, "Of course."

It was almost a comfort, then, for her to be on her hands and knees, with a rag and an old scrub brush, in the role the world had carved out for her since the night she wandered away from her mother's garden. Wiping piss from a city street, as if it mattered. In the desert, you could see the traces of ancient wadi that the Sahara had long since dried to gullies, but city piss left no such trail. It was cleaning while blind, attacking an entire area of smell.

She looked up from the odd angle of her crouching and found the mosque at the corner of Rue Mouassine—tall, imposing, monstrous. Its tower had been unused since the muezzin had wired a modern loudspeaker. Now, instead of the imam singing *Allahu akbar*, a stork roosted there, parting its beak occasionally as if to take in more air. Surveying the quarter with its small, devilish eyes when it didn't have its head folded under its wing in its own little private bird dua.

There were so many bolts on Zahrae's door, more than the highest number she could count in her language. They stretched from the base of the door, where they formed a line, to the top of the door, about ten feet off the ground, where they accented the outline of its arch. She cleaned the third bolt, changed her mind, and poured the soapy water from the bucket out onto the street. The sun would burn away the night's piss, and only Allah would know the difference.

"You must be very tired," Adwan said when she came back in the riad.

"Last night," she said. "The singing."

"Not to worry. They won't ever be back." He raised her to sitting and kissed her, in the sloppy way he hadn't yet overcome.

"I need new pants," she said, as they'd both graduated into this new space, where they expressed needs simply, without shame or pretense.

"I'll take you," he said. "But first, come to my room."

She did as she was told, even when he turned her over so that she was again on her hands and knees, as she'd been while scrubbing the street. Each lunch hour now, he asked for something new. For five dirham he'd bought a sheet of sexual diagrams from a shopkeeper in another part of the medina, and brought it home to try each of them with her. She had squatted in his lap (diagram 5); lain on her back with her long legs overshooting the mattress and her hair cascading over the edge of the bed (diagram 8); she had opened her legs and let him enter her sideways, such that she felt like a wishbone being broken apart (diagram 17). Still, Adwan was gentle, so much gentler than the tireseller, and he said nothing over the months as her abdomen grew bigger, and her breasts began to swell over the top of her brassiere.

Afterward, sometimes he'd take her to the main street for a glace, or, if she asked, he'd take her out for something she needed from a store. Now, he walked her to Rue Mouassine, where they merged with the busy traffic of the medina proper, and he put his hand in the small of her back, as he had taken to doing when they walked in the street. It was barely there, his touch, but it caused her a certain heat.

"So many people," she muttered to herself in Hassaniya, and out of some absurd instinct of self-preservation, she took the tail of her headscarf and covered the bottom half of her face. Her father had often touched Tumtum's hair when they passed in the tent. He would cup his hand under one of her curls, or he would press the palm of his hand against the crown of her head, and now, Souria wondered about her father's purpose in bringing her back with them to Bou Naga; she wondered whether Tumtum, too, had used her body as a means of finding shelter. But Tumtum had come to them with nothing, save the shifts of her clothing. Souria still had money left, and could escape the Elouafiq house just as she'd escaped Ousmane's, just as she'd left the camp at Mijek.

"Here is a shop," Adwan was saying. "This man might have something you'd like—"

But she was walking away from him, away from the heat of his hand and the pain of his earnestness and all the other troubles she'd found so far in this new country. She was colliding with this man in his black windbreaker, this woman in her flowered pink djellaba, this baby stroller caught in a rut in the street. Her father had welcomed Tumtum to a wonderful home, and she hoped the Elouafiqs' riad would be such a place, but she'd seen enough of the world to hold her doubts. She wound her way through the wind-chapped crowd and past the shops of the medina, carelessly brushing past the shopping Marrakchis, creating a maze of heated points between herself and Adwan and all the other troubles she'd found in the new country. Even with the thing inside her, she'd always be running, walking, away, away. Disappearing off the edge of the known earth. Bit by fearful bit.

She was in the riad's lone washroom, standing wet and naked, washing the sirocco from her hair, when the door opened.

Zahrae choked on air. It was the sound a large fish might make if someone took it out of water.

There was no place for a lock on the washroom door, and the mistake happened to everyone in the house. Usually, the accidental offender begged pardon and walked away, back up the stairs, embarrassed, holding their bladder for some better time. But Souria had no such place in the home, so she stood there, letting Zahrae take in the roundness of her belly. When she slammed the door closed she ran upstairs, tutting at herself, so that on each stair, she sounded like a noisy toy being shaken.

Souria stood ashamed. Ashamed to move, ashamed to towel dry. It took her feeling chilled before she put on her clean, damp clothes and went to sit in the parlor. Zahrae came back down the stairs, sat across from her, and stared. Her eyes were darker than Souria's, but they seemed to blaze under her half-closed lids. "How many months?" she asked.

In the desert, she might have calculated the time since the tireseller by the moon. Here in the city, she had no answer.

"I want you and that stranger's baby out of my house," she said. "Gather your things. Get out."

Souria didn't move because she could not move, not until Zahrae stood up and came close, an inch from her face, as though she might slap her. "Vas-y!" she screamed.

Souria scrambled then, out of a fear that had become as instinctual as breathing. Upstairs, she threw her things into a plastic duty-free bag that she'd found left by tourists in the alley. Her ouguiya, wrapped in layers of newspaper, were already the base layer of the bag, and now she put in her swak and the plastic toothbrush Adwan had showed her how to use. She pushed more and more things in the bag, and, grateful for winter, put on layers of clothes that she would not want to carry.

By the time she went back downstairs, Adwan had joined Zahrae in the kitchen, and the woman sat at the table, calmly scooping couscous into her mouth. "Tell your whore goodbye," she said. "That baby is not yours. This girl should never have slept in your bed."

Souria looked at the lines set alongside Zahrae's mouth and knew begging would not make a difference. It was her life now, this moving from place to place as though she were a tribe unto herself. She turned and started for the front door.

"Wait—" Adwan said, but she kept walking. "Souria," he said, and because it was the first time he'd ever spoken her name aloud, she stopped. He came to her and held her, whispered in her hair. "You can't go out," he said. "It's cold."

She closed her eyes. He was so inadequate, so insufficient.

"Going out?" Zahrae called in a mocking voice. "It's raining.

117

You hear that rain?" She said it as though she were holding Souria's stupidity before her on a tray. Her voice dropped to a hiss. "You get that Black man's baby out of here," she said.

Souria slipped her feet into her sandals and walked out Zahrae's front door. Rain streamed immediately down her forehead and into her eyes, soaking through her djellaba and through both of Hassan's shirts and the camisole Adwan had bought her in the souk, right through to the bare curves of her shoulders. A figure in a blue raincoat passed on a bicycle, splashing her with the muddy rain from a pothole. She tightened her headscarf so the condensation wouldn't cloud her vision, and she ran toward Rue Mouassine. A donkey clopped by, and then a man with an empty oil drum.

A fierce wind came just as she cleared the first bend of the souk proper, and then the rain cleared, and then the clouds. Only a sliver of moon like a fingernail lay in the sky, so that even with the big city's many lights, it seemed, when Souria looked up past the roofs of the alley, that the night was holding her. When the rain returned, she ran.

Rain, that vast colorless, molecular infinity so much less solid than a human body—it won. It beat Souria under the roof of the Café Tayouart, where a puddle of rainwater under her chair made it look as though she'd been unable to hold her water. She shivered, but none of the men of Allah moved to offer her their coats. She remembered how, when Tumtum first came to Bou Naga, her father would allow her to sleep closest to the fire, and she held out hope that one of the men in the café—just one, insh'allah—would be as the men in her village, or as Hassan the Algerian, or even as Adwan. But when a waiter came to her table, all pressed black pants laundered to a charcoal gray, his apron bleached so white it almost hurt to see, when he came and discovered that she could not read the laminated card of dishes and prices, let alone say what she wanted in the King's Arabic, he frowned and snatched the menu out of her hands.

Indeed, it was a nicer restaurant than she would have chosen had she not been blinded by rain, and the waiter said something she thought might have been "why leave your country if you can't live outside it?" but his accent was so different from the Elouafiqs', so much more impaled on its glottal stops. She wanted to tell him she wasn't stupid, that she understood more Arabic than she spoke, that her Hassaniya was perfect; she just did not have the words in this flavor. She knew what happened to people like her in the new country, people without papers or language—Zahrae had explained it. She could never have a visa. Could not work. Could not have money. Could not leave the country. Did not actually exist in any realm of official knowledge. Was not actually a person.

Again, she shivered, and the owner of the café, who was moviestar handsome, came from his place in the back of the restaurant and sat at her table. Rainwater had dripped from her cheekbones onto the beautiful gold-rimmed plate of her place setting. The owner calmly moved the plate aside.

"Where do you come from?" he asked, in French. "Senegal? Nigeria?"

"La Mauritanie."

He nodded. "What are you doing in my country?"

She had no answer. She couldn't explain it even to herself. Because why not go back? Why not at least try? Some nights, it was all she wanted, to be walking atop warm sand, sleeping under the millions of stars that the city of Marrakech blocked out with its hustle. But how to go back, through desert, through rape, through broken people and their sundry violences. How?

The owner slammed his flattened palm down on the table in

front of her. Had he not already moved the plate, he would have broken it. He raised his thick eyebrows. "What are you doing here in my café?" he said. "Begging?"

In the rain, the restaurant was empty, and it shouldn't have been a problem for her to sit there, this young girl taking up as little space as a basket of cloth, or a dressmaker's dummy, or a wide-angle broom; if he'd just let her, she'd get down on hands and knees with a napkin and mop up the rain she'd left; she'd wash his dishes, steam his couscous, fry his cut potatoes, put her mouth around his penis (diagram 27), let him pull her hair the way Adwan sometimes did, if he'd just let her sit here and rest.

But the next words out of his mouth were "Vas-y."

By the loose elbow of her djellaba he pulled her to standing. "Vas-y," he said again, pushing her slightly, and she exited yet another door in her long, long life of doors. The rain still fell in sheets, and she stood under the veranda to try to stay dry, but the owner came back, opened the clean glass door of Café Tayouart and screamed "Vas-y!" loud enough that the whole street could know and understand.

She was back in the rain, running. She had not known to expect this in the newer, kinder country, that the people would look at the shade of her skin and guess what kind of dog beating to give her. She was cold now, and hungry, her feet streaked with mud. But even against all that water, she had a will.

She ran from the Djmaa-el-Fna, out into the larger city where she'd never been, past Club Med and the line of drenched, resigned horses attached to their carriages, past the Koutoubia Mosque and the internet café with its sandwich board sign running wet chalk, then up the street to a quiet, residential neighborhood. This far outside the medina there hung high traffic lights, and more open spaces, and a large grove of trees that looked like a public park. Stepping off the curb, she accidentally slid out of her sandal, then stepped backward to reshoe her wet foot. Mashallah, though, the rain was easing, and so she kept jogging up the street.

She came upon a calm, bare neighborhood and turned up and down streets, hoping she wasn't simply making a big, wet circle. She had nowhere to sleep, no one to ask. She stopped running and walked, kept walking, thinking not to return to anywhere she'd known so far in her life. After a while, she realized she wasn't walking in a circle so much as through a maze, because when she reached the end of the final street, the corners of the riad gates met and blocked her in refusal. A final answer from Allah, then, a warning: *you'll never be free.* She retraced her steps until she was back on Mohammed V, and she walked back past the internet café and the Koutoubia Mosque and the horses, come back to life now, whinnying and tossing their drying manes. One polar drop of rain fell from the leaves of a tree onto the bridge of her nose, startling her with its cold.

She hadn't thought to wear socks, and now, to keep her feet warm, she walked the Djmaa-el-Fna, listening to each group of musicians, the storyteller with his carpet of shitting chickens, the imam warning of the displeasure of the malak. At the end of each performance, when a dish or a hat or a tambourine was passed to collect dirham, she scooted herself to the circle's periphery. She watched the glowing neon boomerangs tossed into space to rival the stars.

When the storyteller finally rolled up his carpet, and the singers and acrobats subtracted themselves one by one from the square, she sat on a bench in the Place de Foucauld and put her feet up under her for warmth. A small strip of her legs was bare and cold, and she shifted position, but her djellaba rose up her other leg, and an hour passed before she figured out that she could, by standing and shimmying her sweatpants down her legs until the waistline circled her hips, keep any one patch of skin from being exposed. At two in the morning, when the hoofsteps of a passing carriage woke her, she hummed herself a Peul song she sang in childhood. She heard a plastic bag blowing down the bricks of the street. She heard sandy topsoil soughing through the tree leaves. A tiny white cat approached, meowing his hunger. He stared at her, begging with little green eyes. When she shushed him, he ran across the park and crouched under a metal doorway.

Just before dawn, the call to prayer came from the Koutoubia, and the sky turned from black to silver to orange, and the fruit-sellers began wheeling their heavy green carts into the Djmaa-el-Fna. Gold taxis seeped into the medina. ALSA buses passed, and the muezzin called another prayer. It was Friday the eleventh of Du al-Qa'dah. She was halfway through her fifteenth year.

The second night, Souria took herself across the street to the royal garden park, and the third morning she woke there, smelling her own arms. The odor didn't lie on her disagreeably—it called to mind a batch of rotting corn, or a rag left too long on a bathroom floor. Still, she crossed the busy intersection, back to the medina, where she lined up outside a hammam. She had neither bucket nor soap, but she paid the attendant to lather her up and roughen her skin. She kept the duty-free bag full of ouguiya and dirham in the antechamber with her, peering through the steam to keep an eye on it, and when the attendant had finished with her, she put the bag on her naked shoulder and dressed. She went to a store in the medina and purchased a pair of long socks.

The third night, she was so tired that not even the call to morning prayer woke her—she found herself unwilling to open her eyes until the sun had risen and the birds in the trees had at last gone quiet. Harder than the cold, or the distressing pattering she heard on the bricks, or the ungiving wood benches was boredom: she had no floor to mop, or sit on, no walls against which to echo the telenovelas she used to learn Arabic. All day she spent facing the sheer purposelessness of sitting on a bench, so that it was almost a relief when the Frenchman showed up, offering her ten euros.

"Seulement les photos," he promised, but when he got her to his hotel, in a shadowed corner of the medina, he touched her as she undressed. He cupped the pregnant bump of her belly. Put his fingers in her vagina. "Bend over," he told her, demonstrating what he wanted her to do, when he realized she did not understand French. He snapped photos of her bare ass. Her breasts. He lay on the floor under her spread legs and photographed the place where he'd put his fingers. He made her stand against the glass patio door with its greasy window, with her legs spread in a V. He came over, took her jaw in his hand, and turned her head just so, so he could snap her face in profile. He pantomimed how she should hold her face, with her lips parted slightly and her head arched so that her hair hung down her back. He offered her the ten euros, but when she touched the money and raised her eyes in disbelief, he reached into his pants pocket and gave her a hundred-dirham bill. He'd done this before, it seemed. He knew the going rate.

Then there was a second Frenchman, and a second hotel, on a distant alley she'd never seen. The second man actually wanted to put himself inside her. She had given her body to enough men enough times that she knew where to take her mind while it happened; she knew how to go into that place of mind that was olive groves, or sunshine, or the warm sand yards of the khaimas in her village. Every few minutes, she came out of the inside place and into the presence of her unwillingness, but then she'd remember the dirham and remind herself to make soft noises, so he'd finish sooner. There was a third Frenchman in a different room of the second hotel. He stripped her roughly and did not pay when he'd finished. There was a Saudi who took her by taxi to an apartment, where he spanked her with a comb. An elderly Moroccan who threw a fifty-dirham bill at her and told her to beg Allah for forgiveness.

Very early on the first day of her second week in the royal garden, just after the birds had tuned up their morning song and the street sweeper started swishing his straw broom, a man came to Souria in a puffy, red, triple-down coat that was too warm for the weather. Tied lazily around his neck was a plaid scarf that hung down the front of his boubou. It was the stiff, silky kind—blue wrap with gold embroidery—that the men of her village wore, and as out of place as it was under the red European coat, it gave Souria a vague, daring hope.

"Two hundred dirham," he said, raising his eyebrows into a smile. "I hear you get fifty, but I'll give you two hundred, you come with me. You're worth two million."

Rue Mohammed V was empty enough at that hour that they didn't need to run to avoid being hit. They made a leisurely crossing, Souria walking a few feet behind the man, holding the peeling plastic of her duty-free bag to the right side of her chest, and entered the medina. She followed him down the alley at Bab Skour, and then they walked past the spiceseller's and the butcher's. They turned left at Derb Chaban, made a right down a quiet, nameless alley, and came to a large black door with brass nails. The man in the kefta knocked; the door, when opened, seemed to have moved by itself.

"In here," he said, and it was only when they'd gotten inside, when the man was sliding the heavy bolt back into its place, that Souria saw who'd let them in. The woman was naked except for a tattered blue blouse that was unbuttoned to reveal her sagging breasts. She disappeared down the hallway, and the man pointed to the narrow staircase. "Up here," he said. Paint had been worn from the concrete walls as though fireblasted away, and the stone steps seemed never to have been new. Small patches of red and blue showed through, in a repeating pattern, where someone decades gone had once cared.

She followed him into his second-floor room and he appraised her as she undressed. He rose suddenly to his full height, in the threatening way of a panther, and he came over and brought his mouth to her ear. "You can't work for yourself, pretty girl. Too pretty." And it began again. But in a new, frightening way, because he watched her face the whole time. She found herself unable, out of pure fright, to enter the empty space in her mind.

He whispered to her that he might break her neck, and she closed her eyes. He then growled at her to open them and she did, but still she went far, far inside, past the olive groves and the pretty boats of her mind, to a place safer than this room, this room where she might die, where this man was saying that he might slice her open like a goat and roast her. When he finished, he slapped her and told her to sit up straight.

"You live somewhere?" he asked.

She shook her head. He knew, anyway. She coughed and the tears came.

"You live here now, you pregnant bitch," he said. "Go clean up." He left the room, and she curled up into a ball in the middle of the soiled bed. She felt semen in her hair, which had been so clean from the hammam. She found a deep sleep that vacuumed up all her dreams, and when she woke hours later, so much later that the birds were greeting another dawn, she remembered her duty-free bag. She fished its innards, but there was no money at its bottom. No ouguiya. No dirham. Just her personal effects.

So it was all over again, her game of freedom—she had advanced half a space on the board only to have her playing pawn smashed to pieces—and she went back, deep into the hard, packed place. She tried to roll over and cry into the mattress, but her stomach muscles protested. She was nauseated, but not to the point of actually vomiting—now, perpetual discomfort merely hung there, right at the gate between her stomach and her throat. She hadn't known how terrible a body could feel.

Sometimes people left her village in Mauritania. When they came back to visit in the rainy season, occasioning goat slaughters and great feasts, they would tell their stories of the city. They seemed always to marvel at the people still living in the desert, as though everyone in the Sahara should be willing to make any deal with the devil to have a cement roof to block the sky. And walls to close themselves off from night breezes. Souria wondered why Allah was punishing her by keeping her away. She for one had always been content with her family's tent in the desert. Happy to gaze, each night, at the stars.

XIII. Louisville

Have a baby, young woman! You can't have one on your own the normal penis-through-vagina-in-an-evening-of-lust way? Then come on down and shoot yourself with Clomid, then walk around town with shooting pains in your groin while your ovaries spend two weeks blowing themselves up until they're the size of walnuts! In the shower, feel the water running over your ovaries! Feel. Your. Lady parts. Through. Your. Skin! When you sit on the roof of a building talking to your weed dealer, sense the outline of them through your now-too-tight jeans. Watch Keva glance down to take in the new roundness of your stomach: it's pooched out like there's a baby in there, but guess what—a baby's never going to come! But tell Keva nothing, young woman—infertility is your secret. Your cross to drag through the streets, all by yourself. A thousand pounds of cedar, just like Christ's.

Have a baby, young woman! Keep your infertility a state secret for just long enough that your new husband begins to doubt his own manhood. Watch him pour Jack and Coke into tumbler after bigger tumbler; realize this isn't a great game plan. Ask him finally, one of those liquor-soaked nights, whether the two of you should see a specialist. Watch him in the clinic's plush leather seat, watch his face regain its warmth as the tobacco-scented old doctor tells him that yes, his boys can swim. The problem's yours, then: watch your husband's face grow warm again, at this turn of information.

Consult with the doctor at a second, private appointment; tell him about your uterus, then tell him exactly why, verily though it's your husband who's paying for all this, you want your medical information kept from him. Listen to your phone vibrate in your cupholder on your way home; see it's your father calling; pick up and listen to him tell you how he received a certified letter in the mail from Harris and Harris, how your credit's about to be ruined, how they're about to enter a court judgment against you. Hear the serrated edge of your father's voice, the same as he used when he called you a waste of a child, the same as when your beloved old car was parked in his driveway, refusing to start, and he asked you, For fuck's sake, why can't you get a decent job and a serviceable car? Imagine the tired look on his face, the look you noted when he first visited you in your very first, West End apartment, when he locked the doors of his car not once but twice, even though you'd already waved from your second-floor window so he knew you were watching him. That look with all its reproach, the look that said he'd hoped so hard in this life, only to end up with offspring that failed to thrive.

Hear, without listening, as your father asks you what you and Vlad will do about this problem; listen to yourself telling your father that you're not going to tell Vlad.

Hear your father advise you not to keep secrets in your marriage; listen to yourself failing to catch the chortle that burbles out of your throat.

Listen to your father fall silent in the aftermath of your laughter. Listen to the anger in his voice as he tells you that his marriage to your mother wasn't a great example, listen to the implication there: that you're too stupid to have figured that out on your own. Get loud then, young woman. Call your father an out-of-touch dinosaur, and hang up.

Wonder, as you continue driving, what even happens after a court enters judgment for $150,000, and whether both Harrises show up at the judge's bench, or whether they send another lawyer whose name isn't even Harris. Wonder how one even parents with that kind of number on their head, how one then freely sings a lullaby at night, or blows silly raspberries on their toddler's belly. Realize there are no options of honesty that allow you to keep your self-respect. Realize you can't possibly tell your husband any of this. Stop wondering.

Have a baby, young woman! Go to a clinic, lie down on a table with a paper gown scratching against your sore, swollen breasts! Spread your legs and open your vagina to every blast of air in the lab. Feel the needle penetrating the innermost of your insides as the tech takes fifteen of your eggs, but don't flinch, young woman—gotta be still! Listen to your children being sucked down the aspirator—*shoop! shoop!* Hatch hopes for your gene pool, now lying as a film of jelly in a nearby plastic dish. Wonder if you'll ever meet any of these little wonders, whether any of these fifteen will ever crawl across a carpet, play the clarinet, learn to drive, cure cancer. Here comes more and more aspirating, young woman, but you can distract yourself with thoughts of Keva, who herself has lost sixty pounds since you met her— *she's* not trying to have a baby. Keva won't tell you how she lost it, whether it was exercise, or water intake, or the keto diet, and you know it's not polite to ask. Realize how this weight loss has actually been so bad for Keva's face—think about how her eyes now swim on her head in an uneasy way, a way that suggests death; how she has, now, not the eyes of a deer caught in the headlights, but the eyes of a deer caught stealing drugstore cosmetics.

As the technician finishes, as he withdraws the needle and then the tube, as the lubricating jelly drips down to pool between the skin of your buttocks and the butcher paper crinkling beneath you, think about how your new husband, whom you barely know, is in a nearby room fapping off to a magazine so that he can put all his swimming sperm into a nearby dish. Wonder why they don't in this day and age just show him porn, whether the clinic has some politics about that. Wonder if he even needs the magazine, because of late he's been speaking, in your kitchen, of Jitka Stehnova, speaking about her in such tones of hushed admiration for her mind and spirit that you now realize your new husband, even after all these years away from the adventures of his childhood, still has a fetish for Eurotrash. But never mind this predictable turn of Black male realism, young woman—let's get back to you, living the worst sci-fi movie imaginable! You're back in high school chemistry, but now you're the glass tube! You're the rinse! You're the pipette!

Have a baby, young woman! Spend two days lighting candles for your tiny eggs and Vlad's tiny sperm! Ignore your postprocedure cramps as more earthly, quotidian pain, a hassle that will mean nothing, you're told, when measured against your baby's first ethereal cry. Drive back to the lab, sans your new husband, who last night told you about the black leather pants Jitka wore to work. Repaper your breasts and respread your legs for those spermified eggs that go back in your body! Feel them siphoned into your uterus in one gloppy clump. Hope one of them implants, keep that hope keep that hope keep that hope, keep that hope through the dull ache in your crotch that comes at night when you're trying to sleep.

Push aside thoughts of just how much has happened to your insides these last ninety days, how you first had to have that knot of bone scraped, laparoscopically, from your uterus. Know that since there are no nerves there, on your insides, the pain of that is pain you're making up—you were sedated, for fuck's sake, stop being so first-world dramatic. And that tiny scar from the port hole they put through your belly, the one Jitka Stehnova doesn't have, the one that let the surgeon's microscopic robot do its work? Just be glad you had your husband's excellent health insurance, young woman. Be glad he's desperate enough for children that he coughed up the fifty-some-thousand-dollar copay on all this. Never mind your own lingering, single-lady, $140,000 medical bill now gone to collections—Vlad doesn't know about that. Doesn't care. Your more immediate problem is that Keva is on vacation in the nasty part of Florida, and you've only got however long it takes you to get pregnant plus nine months to smoke all the weed you want before you pop out this baby and turn into June Cleaver.

And that scar sure is ugly, yes, but there's no fixing it now, because this baby might not crawl up in there just right, and that ball of bone might grow back—you're a circus freak, who knows what might happen?—and then you'll be right back at square one, having your uterus rescraped, so why cosmetically fix that hole now? Just be glad square one will be paid for, again and again, so long as your husband is obsessed with reproducing himself.

Have a baby, young woman! But ignore the sharpening fact that you'll never really have one, how there was only that 34 percent chance with an IVF in the first place, how it was even less, in your case, because of your freaky, Morticia Addams uterus. Ignore the numbers, ignore the diciness of what is made to seem like marketable science when it's really just magic gum and luck, because stress throws a wrench in ovulation, young woman!

Ignore that hammering in your mind, the monologue that's detailing all your deficiencies, physical and psychological and financial, in a voice like Charlie Brown's teacher. Ignore the hormone-laced tears that mingle with your sweat and run down your face when you watch commercials for diapers or children's toys. Turn off the television when that financial services spot comes on—you know the one—the one where the bride is having her beautiful day in a garden somewhere that looks like New England, the one where her dark curls are cascading down her Puritan bare back, and some man who looks like her brother is walking her down the aisle to give her away, because, as the voiceover tells you, "Life's not guaranteed."

The commercial that tells you that after some people do the superpower reproduction thing, they even have the presence of self to put their affairs in order. Turn off the television and focus on Keva's impending move because you don't need this reminder that you can't accomplish even Step 1a of the parenting process. You don't need a commercial that tells you how to protect the progeny you'll never even have. Turn this off and focus! Is it polite to ask Keva whether she knows anyone else who sells weed? Aren't you discussing her bicurious love life and inquiring after her mother's health and pretending you're actually friends? But have a baby, young woman! You don't want to die sitting in your own piss!

Try to have a baby, young woman! But when your period comes again anyway, when you're standing in the middle of the produce section, shopping for leafy greens chock-full of folic acid because you've been feeling a bit vomity and you think you might finally be pregnant, when that telltale cramp comes that's neither a Clomid cramp nor an egg-harvesting bruise, but one of those pains that comes with a telltale stickiness in your panties? When your body lets you know that you've failed yet again? Realize that hey—you're pumped full of babymaking hormones anyway! Your figure is shot, and your stomach is a mess of portholes! Take that bagged spinach out of your cart and shove it back in the refrigerated bin arranged to look like someone's garden. Take your cart and turn right down that snack aisle, zero in on the kind of salty food that the extra estrogen makes you want: Chips! Crackers! Peanuts with extra salt! Fuck folic acid—you need your own life!

Go to ring up your ridiculous gourmet snack food and be glad for health insurance, but realize that it doesn't care whether you ever become a parent. Health insurance knows what squirrels can do but doesn't care whether you can do it too. You've failed to the tune of $50,000 this time, young woman, and we don't know whether your new husband loves you *that* much, do we? Whether he even thinks you're an entity that *should* be reproduced? Look at the gum in the stall next to you, but don't buy a pack. Know that it's just going to eventually lose its flavor. And maybe this is the way your husband is starting to feel about you, after shelling out all this cash. And maybe it's the way you're getting to feel about him, and about this whole IVF thing. You're tired of him, you realize, tired of his punky insistence that you can't just leave your tired body alone and adopt, tired of the idea that his kids have to be *his* kids, with his big fucking ears and oversized canines.

Hear the bagger ask whether you want paper or plastic, and wonder that humans ever even came up with the concept of sacks. Let's forget the bag entirely! Carry our groceries in our arms! Let's chuck this body, holding these useless ladyparts, these organs, these eggs. Let all these eggs spill across the Kroger parking lot, for fuck's sake—let all your IVF-hostile emotions make an unsweepable mess, all the fuck yous you want to give to every pregnant woman in the store, let them boil out of your pores. All the epithets you want to hurl at the woman standing at the Coinstar with three children—one sleeping in the cart, one standing beside the cart, one circling her legs, making a game of the space between her and the cart—fuck her too. Fuck her and her thrifty coinwrapping.

Carry your plastic bags (because fuck the earth, if you can't reproduce on it) out to the parking lot and see the man standing in the grassy median, his cardboard sign proclaiming, simply, the seven characters John 3:16, as if that verse has anything to do with charity or poverty or anything that might make you fish in your too-tight jeans for a dollar bill. Realize this man probably has four or five children running around somewhere, and resist the urge to ram your cart into his whiskey-soaked ass. Resist the urge to tell him hey, you know what? God's a bit of a dick. God never had to make an appointment at the IVF clinic and spread his legs open to air-conditioning in the dead of winter. God doesn't know a damn thing.

Have a baby, young woman. For God's sake, have a baby.

PART III

TOURIST SEASON

XIV. Afire

Deep into her second lunar year as a faux Moroccan, but not far into her second day moved into the little flat in Diabat, Souria found a chair tossed into an alley. The chair was so tiny, so small, exactly the size of her daughter. Its creator had hewn it out of a cheap, insubstantial wood and tossed it into the alley in a fit of violence, perhaps, for its left front leg splintered off into almost complete brokenness. But it was a stroke of luck. Souria had left Marrakech in the high-sitting passenger seat of a CTM bus with nothing save the clothes on her and Yu's backs, and then, weeks later, that second day moved into a home, she'd had a taped-together chair to put into the emptiness. A life, she figured, would grow around that chair.

And it had.

Yu sat in the now-repaired chair, at a tabletop laid with blue and yellow zellij. Eating aa'sada. Telling her dreams. "An owl found a spider," she said. "The spider was black with a red belly." She tried to convey, with her infant grammar and raised eyebrows, the gravity. The childishness of her face lagged comically behind the wisdom in her eyes. Like Souria, Yu had eyes lighter than her skin, though Yu's were darker green, the color of desert moss. "But the spider ate the owl," she explained, her eyes blazing in the rays of morning sun, "then the spider started to fly."

"Don't be afraid of this," Souria said. "They're pictures, knocking on your head."

Soon enough, Souria thought, her daughter would forget everything save the limitations of the actual, physical world, and her dreams would be rehearsals for surviving it. Instead of a spider trying to eat an owl, the owl would be trying to eat Yu.

Nasr, who owned the fabric store where she had her employment, was teaching Souria how to read Arabic. Some days, he grew impatient and slammed his notebook shut on her lack of quickness, and at night, Souria dreamed of the things that had evaded her during the day—the loops of the letter *ya* wrapping around her torso like a python, the hamza atop the alif falling like a boulder to crush her impenetrable head. Mornings, when they both arrived at the shop, she watched Nasr's mood. If he let the stray dogs of the alley jump on his coat without kicking them, or if he had on his face the safe, calm look of having made love with his wife just after fajr, Souria would ask him to teach her words. *Boulla*, she'd write. *Nathara*. Lamp. Eyeglasses.

In her Marrakchi life, she hadn't needed the written word, though, those months in the riad near Mohammed V, she had learned to speak business to the French. Souria was indeed *pretty pretty*, just the way Lahcen had said that first day in the royal gardens, and so the Frenchmen, in their khaki pants with tucked-in oxfords and leather belts, and the Saudis, in their snow-white thawbs and goatees, called Lahcen's mobile phone and asked for her when their planes touched down at Menara Airport. The Saudis called for her when they were in Marrakech, on their congresses, in a neighborhood the taxi drivers called Hivernage. She'd leave Yu back in the medina, at the riad off Derb Chaban, with Rashida, who had aged to a point where her clients were measured between months rather than between hours or days. Not one time had Yu been content to be left, and so many times, Souria closed the heavy door on the image of Rashida squashing Yu against her body as Yu squealed and tried to break free.

There came, finally, the day Yu landed a kick against Rashida's thigh, and Rashida grabbed Yu's soft, tiny face and squeezed her cheeks until her lips puckered and she could not make a sound. Tears ran down Yu's face, but Souria had to meet the Saudi at 4:00. Sharp, exactly on the hour, or he might leave the restaurant in embarrassed doubt, and Lahcen would punch her repeatedly on the meat of her arm, on the underside of her shoulder, where no one would mind the bruise. *Is that Yu crying?* she'd wonder, as she clicked down the alley in her whore's uniform—tight pants, knifepoint heels. Babies woke throughout the quarter that hour of the afternoon, all of them uttering their own strangled cries. But she knew. Babies were like birds in a garden, and of course you always knew which one was yours. On her way to meet the Saudi, though, she pretended that Yu's cry belonged to a different bird.

When her taxi got to its place on Rue Mohammed VI, Souria would shake her hair to its full, salon-cut volume, slide her feet back into her stilettos, exit the taxi, and stalk into Caruso's, where she would look for the recognition in a man's eyes. More often than not, the man would stand on her approach, kiss her on both cheeks as though they were old friends. He'd buy her dinner and make the small jokes of his language, appraising only in clandestine glances her pert breasts and smooth shoulders.

Every language had its own particular sense of comedy, and she had to learn to laugh wryly, for the benefit of the French.

How to laugh for old Moroccan grandfathers with their full bellies and moist eyes and their memories of Eliane d'Almeida.

How to laugh with the Saudis, who seemed at once frightening and frightened.

How to laugh when she wasn't quite sure what had been said.

How to laugh while wishing her daughter could also have couscous and freshly butchered lamb for dinner.

How to laugh while calculating what sort of bodily pain her client might inflict by gauging the hostility with which he held his fork against his knife while cutting meat.

How to laugh with the familiarity that would convince any undercover cop watching the table that she was niece to her dinner partner. How to hold her aura of whore's mystery while committing such a laugh.

It was always a relief when she got in the man's car, out of sight of the restaurant, and they could stop pretending.

The Frenchman took her to hotels and sometimes to their own apartments, and the Saudis took her in their big boxy cars to a settlement of vacation rentals called the Babylone. If they met her for lunch and took her in the afternoon, she leaned out their windows afterward as she dressed and watched the vacationing Moroccans playing in the pool, the mothers sometimes in the bathing costumes of the Europeans, sometimes covered head to toe in wetsuit burqinis; the babies in their thick plastic swim rings. She couldn't know what Yu was doing these afternoons, whether Rashida was screaming at her or brushing her curls.

The birth itself had taken forever, though through the gauzy sleep of its aftermath, Souria had heard Rashida tell Lahcen that it had taken only four hours. Those four hours had been a mountain of pain pressing down, and then had come the horror of the final minutes, when Rashida had held Souria's legs open so she could push. After Souria gave the final push that ended it, Rashida asked her, "What will you name this little one?"

"Hassan," she said. She wanted to die from the pain.

Rashida laughed. "No. It is a girl we have. Not a Hassan at all."

"Then. Yumna."

"What does that mean?"

"Good fortune. Success in this life."

"And so may she have," Rashida said. With one of the dirty rags Lahcen kept upstairs, she wiped Yumna down, placed her in Souria's arms with rivulets of blood still in the folds of her baby skin. Yu woke and took Souria's breast the very first hour, and Souria put her own finger into Yu's baby-sized grip. She raised Yu's hand, turning the tiny fist this way and that, marveling at the perfect little creases in her palms. She brought Yu close and smelled the place under her chin, already sweetly sour with the scent of sleep and milk. Yu had been blessed with dark curls, and Souria pecked her all over her little head, trying to kiss each ringlet. She couldn't remember the face of the tireseller from Zouérat, but she felt that if Yu had arrived looking at all as he did, his face would instantly have come back to her. It didn't. Yu did not smile for weeks, but whenever she lay face up on her pallet, she kept her round eyes fixed on the circle of Souria's face, waiting for her mother to tell her about love.

At Babylone, Souria would pray to Allah that Yu was well. When her client finished, she'd pull her silk maroon panties over her ass and lean into the matching bra to resnap herself. Slide into her tight jeans and tank top, redrape her unnecessary blue scarf and refasten the silver necklace that dangled the hand of Fatimah from its chain. She'd study the scattered pattern of her beaded bracelet as it lay on the man's coffee table, and try to divine whether she'd find Yu with mustardy French fries smeared across her chin, or with a welt on her backside where Rashida had lost her patience.

Back across three miles of Marrakech, on the quiet alley off Derb Chaban, Yu would come crawling across the foyer before the heavy riad door could even close against its threshold. Souria could never tell from Yu's face whether she'd been treated poorly, but often, Yu seemed so residually afraid of what had happened there in the riad, she wouldn't ask for Souria's breast. She'd close her eyes, this baby, and fall right to sleep. At last in her mother's arms.

Souria began a practice of asking for twenty dirham above what her clients gave Lahcen. A little something for eating on her way home, she'd tell them. Twenty was nothing to these French, these Saudis, these old Moroccan grandfathers, and in the taxi, she'd fold it into a square chunk and fit it in the back of her mouth, between her cheek and a molar. At home, in her tiny room, she'd stick it in the small crack where the wall missed the baseboard, a place no one would find save someone like her, who'd stared at the walls of the room for so very many silent hours.

There came the night, though, that the German got her drunk, so drunk, and she folded the chunk sloppily enough into her mouth that Lahcen asked what it was she was chewing. Before she could even arrive at the thought that swallowing the twenty might be a lesser loss than whatever was to come next, he was on her, his hand shoved in her mouth, his fingers probing. When he found it, he beat her, with his fist around a metal jar. The bruises on her face were such that she did not work for another week.

Once in two moons a Frenchman might want her for the weekend, as part of his own personal holiday at the beach, and it was in this way that she'd first seen Agadir, and then Essaouira. Essaouira was quiet, and cool like a desert evening, and when she'd seen the cluster of blue and white buildings coming ever closer to the Frenchman's windshield, she'd felt a small feeling of home.

"I have a house here," the Frenchman said brightly, as he'd noticed the sudden happiness of her face. "I think you'll like it."

It had been a small bungalow, with an open, brightly lit parlor. Sweet blue doors and traditional mosaic tile, on a cliff near the beach. She went out on the first night, looked out down the colline, and said a prayer for Yu. "May she have better fortune in this life," she said, as the waves, in slow, drumless time, beat the land. "May she live in a better world," she said. She closed her eyes and let the breeze cleanse her naked shoulders, and she didn't open her eyes again until the Frenchman had come outside.

"Where are you from, chérie?" he asked. He stood behind her. He seemed to enjoy simply watching her, as though she were a fish in a tank.

"La Mauritanie. Une petite village-là."

He came closer, pointed to the horizon. "Someone once told me," he said, "if you walk down the beach just that way, you can get all the way to Mauritania."

He was joking, she could tell. She ached, suddenly, for her brothers, but she laughed wryly for the Frenchman.

He treated her well. Took her on Friday night to a quiet, pretty restaurant with white tablecloths and swizzle-stemmed wineglasses, where he let her choose her own food. The restaurant was in a hotel, and above its lobby, up a precarious flight of wood stairs, was a library, where Souria went while he paid the bill and spoke with the reception. The loft had a low ceiling, and she had to duck, and eventually resorted to crawling on hands and knees, but when she got herself to the one low table, she found a book of photographs, a study of the town of Essaouira itself. She flipped through and found the fish hall, the port, the Amazigh of the countryside eating their celebrations, and she forgot herself, forgot the situation, forgot the Frenchman. She was back in the desert, even though she could smell the fish of the port. She was in her head with other people's family happinesses, which bloomed, momentarily, into her own.

That night, the Frenchman strung tiny brass bells under both bedrails as a joke. In all six sessions of that weekend, it was the only time he was rough with her: he fucked her from his knees; he fucked her so hard, she closed both her fists. But he kept at it, registering the bells as loudly as he could, until she heard the echo of them tinkling off the ceiling. The next morning, as he slept, she crawled alongside the bed, reached her hand under the mattress to untie the long ribbons. Her thighs were sore. As if she'd been running, in her dreams, over sand dunes.

When he woke, the Frenchman told her his name was Cyril and that she'd have to come back to his house some other weekend. Cyril was not his real name; she could tell by the way he said it.

In this way, with ten clients a week, she moved through a year that felt like molten liquid. Her clients' love caused so much fire along her insides that she flung herself out of reality; she thought of Yu, on the other side of the city, waiting, crying, waiting. Because she no longer collected the twenty dirham over, she had no thoughts of leaving. And no idea what she might make happen next, because running seemed only to take her sideways.

Her dreams of escape all seemed to require money, but in late March, when the Saudi gave her the two thousand dirham from atop his thick stack of bills, she felt fearful enough, almost, to refuse it. Still, there was one thing she might do. And that night, when Rashida handed her sleeping baby over, Souria slipped the two thousand right into Yu's diaper.

Then, upstairs, against the fear that wanted to swallow hope, she slipped the two thousand into her high-heeled boot.

Lahcen wasn't a stupid man. He never let Souria leave with Yu, not unless he was with them both, which happened on the very hot Thursday in April when he went to the écrivain. Like Souria, Lahcen saw the written word only as pictures. The three dots beneath the *tha*, the mark that made the belly of the *jeem*, and the tiny squiggle of the *tanwin*, they all laughed at him, and so he needed someone else to write his documents. Because of his handling so much money from the other five girls, who did not live in the riad, he often had to go to the bureau, which was lodged in a different corner of the medina. That April day, on their way through the winding alleys, Souria saw Adwan.

He was squatting in a small patch of sunlight near a snack counter, counting his change, readying to buy his roasted nuts. As she passed, he saw her. She saw him seeing her. Lahcen was holding Yu as limply as one might hold a small melon, yet as convincingly as if she were his own child, and Yu was instinctually not fussing in public but keeping a close eye on Souria, who was walking just beside them. She wondered if Adwan was mistaking them for some happy little Marrakchi family, out for a day of shopping.

For the shortest of seconds she smiled at him, and she'd regret later that she hadn't at least waved—what would it have hurt? She knew he recognized her, even in her black leather pants and t-shirt—after all, he'd seen her so many times with no clothes on at all. And yet she knew she was wearing the costume of a woman who'd fallen on higher times. She couldn't presume to know what he assumed, but he'd said nothing, even as her body began having its own memories of him. His face made no movements, even, of recognition.

"Hey," Lahcen said, breaking the spell. He pulled her back from the path of a passing motorcycle. She accidentally stepped on his foot with the high heel of her boot, and he rolled his eyes.

The écrivain was an open room where a man and a woman sat hunched over stacks of papers. Writing, typing, signing. "Wait here," Lahcen told her, and he went and slapped hands with the woman clerk, then commenced to explain his document to her in the rapid Dharija that Souria still had a hard time understanding. She wondered how he could be certain that this woman wasn't taking liberty with his documents, how he knew she wasn't simply a frustrated storyteller trapped in her dusty life of other people's papers. But she knew that Lahcen didn't take one full breath in his day without considering whether a woman in his life was cheating him, and she also knew that he had an exhaustive list of ways to punish a woman who was.

"Lahcen," she said. The écrivain had propped open the bureau door to let in the pretense of a breeze. "I'm going to sit out where it's cool."

Yu had just started toddling. She squirmed out of Lahcen's arms and wobbled over to Souria. The clerk lifted the spectacles on the chain around her neck and pushed them up her hooked nose, and she and Lahcen became sunk enough in conversation that he barely noticed when Souria walked to the open door.

"I'm going outside," she said again, more quietly.

"Outside," she said, but she said it silently, only moving her lips. Yu snuggled in her arms.

She moved slowly once she crossed the threshold, and inched over to stand with her back to the window glass. But she could feel when Lahcen looked at her—a certain heat would always flash electric across her scalp, the hair on her neck prickling with its own knowing. This week, she'd had a client who fucked her with his closed fist. Another, a Frenchman with a big house near Jardin Agdal, watched while she was licked, là-bas, by his freshly bathed German shepherd. She'd had to smile while being licked. And then be sick to discover that she herself found it half-funny.

She turned sideways so that she could keep Lahcen in her peripheral vision without his seeing her looking. The écrivain lay his stapled papers down on her desk, gestured at the stack of them, counted to three on her fingers, and threw up her hand to illustrate her point. Souria could hear the timbre of the argument through the window, but the noise of the alley drowned the words. She moved her head slightly to the left, saw in her peripheral vision a giant red truck with a company's logo painted on its side. It was the logo of the drinks in the cafés. Coca-Cola, they called it. It was brown, and it fizzed and burned your throat as it went down. This truck full of Coca-Cola, it was so wide that she walked easily behind it as it moved with considerable difficulty through the narrow alley.

"Zid qeddem wahede shwiya!" cart keepers yelled at the driver, slapping the back of his truck with their open palms. Others yelled at him to stop. "Reverse!" they yelled. "Tout droite! Sir nishan! Merde."

All around the truck's body, pedestrians streamed, heedless of the driver's intentions or their own personal safety. If the truck accidentally lurched even three feet ahead or behind its position, it would kill twenty people. She wouldn't look at Lahcen but she felt, in the freedom of her scalp and neck, his not looking at her. What she could see in the window of the écrivain, she knew, could also see her if it tried, and so she wedged herself farther behind the truck as it moved. She planted Yu firmly on her hip and ran, all the way to the arched doorway of the Bab Jdid, to the open space and the roadway beyond.

The CTM to Essaouira wound through the mountains that radiated to the rest of the kingdom, and Yu vomited the contents of her little stomach. Souria let the child vomit into her open palm, and wiped it on her own black t-shirt. She didn't want her daughter to dirty the Moroccans' bus. There was nothing terrible about this ride. Some people wanted freedom, she thought, and others wanted safety. She'd never find the two in the same place.

XV. Essaouira

Souria wants the cold to solidify her into an immovable statue, but she wants Yu to stay warm, for the rest of her life warm, and she's bundled her daughter through two Moroccan winters. Nasr has given her fabric remnants to wrap the child's ears against the wind that blows around this knot on the side of Africa. It's wind like no other on the planet: from November to February, it blows the sand on the beach straight up into their faces as they walk, trying in vain to see the cold ocean. Even in summer, the door to their flat knocks all day against its own frame. Still, Souria loves this town for being the ocean's echo to the desert; the wind kills all other sound. The boundless sea, stretching out as far as she can see, and the eternal roar of the waves. At night, she can see the moon out her window, ringed with a corona of ice that obscures the stars on either side. She sleeps under a warm quilt with bleached sheets, and has never known a bed so free of struggle.

They are conquerors, she and Yu. She makes sometimes seventy-five dirham a day, and they have a place of their own, inside a modern building with concrete walls and a sturdy roof, out of reach of pimps or johns or the vicious storms that roll up past the continental shelf. In late summer, when she has extra money, she takes three dirham and buys Yu a giant punch balloon from the Senegalese who sells them on the beach. She sits in the sand while Yu plays, watching the throngs of tourists. The Casablancais and the Saouiris, she can pick out—they're dressed in light jackets and sweatshirts, for coastal weather. The Frenchwomen lie topless on the beach, their breasts so age-ravaged as to be perfectly inoffensive. They're trying to have a vacation, but they'll go back to Paris with chest colds. This isn't a beach like a beach on the television.

Older boys swim in the harbor that fills on the days the tide keeps itself at sea, and other children, smaller ones, stand on the passenger bridge, leaning over the white railing that keeps them from falling in. They marvel at the spotted brown fish with their winglike fins, flying underwater like long, spotted birds. During the Festival Gnaoua, the little town fills, and is so happy, so filled with possibilities, that Souria almost feels that she, too, might one day live for nothing save smiling and fun. If she could find a righteous man of the Prophet (peace be upon him). A husband, with his own proper flat. If she could last long enough in this country, she could be a grandmother of many happy children.

When the town empties, Souria loses this faith. She begins again to believe that save for having to carry this small girl all the way, she might walk down the beach in the direction the Frenchman said would lead her back to Mauritania. She'd walk and walk until she left the scrubby Sahel and found the desert proper, the small stand of spirit trees within; her tribe, her family's tent, the cooking fire, her small, laughing brother. She'd take big steps. She'd skip. She'd get a good running start, and then strong wind would catch under the sleeves of her shirt and send her airborne.

Every year, she says to herself that she will find a way home.

Every day of every year, she does not have enough money even to think beyond what's for dinner.

She's seen it on a wall map, how far it is, how northern Mauritania is a shelf holding up the Western Sahara. Nasr has explained about the bus, how it is three days' ride that costs six hundred dirham. Nasr has also explained, hinting at her situation, that she needs papers to get through the gendarmes posted at the border. He hasn't asked why her Arabic is so poor, or why she doesn't know the names for the subtler colors of fabric, but he knows. He pays her daily, and he invites her to his family's Eid feasts. He knows.

She had gone, first, to the hotel where she and the Frenchman had eaten, to inquire after work. The manager had been a man the same olive color as Yu, with the tiniest childhood scar on the bridge of his nose. He pushed up his glasses and took in the vomit on her shirt, the fresh newness of her high-heeled boots. "Wait here," he'd said, then brought out a paper bag, which he'd handed to her. "Please," he gestured to the upstairs, where she'd found the book of photographs, "asseyez-vous."

A pool of grease had already formed, in a perfect circle, on the face of the bag, and within, she found grilled fish and pommes frites. Yu reached in and pulled out a fistful of frites in her chubby hand.

"Shukran bzef," Souria had said, touching her heart.

"Afwan," said the man. "It is nothing."

It had been low season, and the man had put her and Souria in a tiny room, where they slept as stones, on sheets with no troubles. The following morning, the manager took her to the medina. They wound through three long cobblestone streets, Yu running and stopping and running and stopping behind them, until they arrived at Nasr's shop. Nasr and the man kissed four times, both cheeks. "So you need work," Nasr said to Souria. "It is a happy thing. I need help."

Souria thanked the man again with a hand to her heart, and he left her there, in the middle of the medina, with Nasr. Yu ran back and forth in the street in front of the shop while Nasr taught Souria how to read the numbers on the measuring stick and haggle with buyers by mentioning the high quality. He told her which countries' people had the most money, and which countries' people would easily part with it. "The Japanese and Americans," he said. "Not so smart. They'll pay anything."

The foreigners were also willing to drop many dirham for kif, though Nasr had not explained this to her. She'd gathered truth for herself when she watched him take the Americans and the French into a back room of his shop with the petit guide who brought them; she watched the petit guide hang back and stand guard just outside the shop, where he could see the gendarmes if they approached. She knew these young men from her Marrakchi life, because she'd watched them hustle the tourists, shake down their desperation in exchange for money. The foreigners needed the kif, it seemed. She saw the relief on their faces as they left Nasr's shop, their sly smiles as they thanked the guide and headed off into the day. If they left Morocco without having kif, it seemed, it would be as though they'd never been to the kingdom.

Souria spent two more days living in the tiny hotel room, where she spent her evenings mending clothes that Nasr had found for Yu, and telling her daughter desert stories. The manager of the hotel was named Ghazi, and at the end of the two days, he took her in his old, boxy car, dropped her off at the little flat in Diabat, and explained to her that he'd paid the first month's rent. Again, she cried, but she had learned, finally, how to express gratitude in the new country. "Barak llahu fik," she said, and touched her heart.

Ghazi gave her upper arm one swift pat that said he was

embarrassed. "It is nothing," he said, and he waved goodbye and got in his old, boxy car.

The apartment was six kilometers out of the main town, an hour's walk away, but when she'd saved enough money, she and Yu could stand on the side of the main road and wait for the Lima Bus to come in from the country. It was a new life. One of small, surprising happiness.

She'd walk and walk until she found the desert proper, the small stand of spirit trees within. Her tribe, her family's tent, the cooking fire, her laughing brother.

But tall as she'd grown, they wouldn't know her, came the thought, when she saw the man with the curly hair, carrying the fiddle. His skin reminded her of the depth of sand. He had boarded the horse-drawn taxi she and Yu were riding; he didn't even let the horses stop, he just drifted onto the rolling carriage, liquidly, wedging the soles of his black shoes onto the runner board. He wore a black t-shirt under a black suit. With her new knowledge of fabrics, she could see that the suit was perfect, except for a small hole near his pocket. He held on to the carriage's dusty plastic roof for four blocks, smiling at Souria, holding her gaze every time she looked up from her lap, until the carriage driver asked for his fare and he drifted from the runnerboard, moving as though he were a bird on water. As he dropped onto the street, she wondered how much roof dust he had taken away on his hands. She turned to look after him, to see the direction in which he'd walk, and Yu almost slid off her lap. Souria let out a small cry and gathered Yu back onto her arms. "Next time," the fiddler yelled. She didn't know whether he was saying it to her or the driver.

She'd walk and walk until she found the desert proper, the small stand of spirit trees within. Her tribe, her family's tent, the cooking fire, her laughing brother.

But the trees might have passed into death, came the thought, when she saw the fiddler again, sitting on a bench in Orson Welles Square, fiddling to himself. The stand of spirit trees might be a stand of trees in the next world, she reminded herself, her family moved on to a more hospitable part of the desert. They might be moved south to the grand river by now, to a better place for crops, and she'd spend the rest of her life there in the dead place, scaling dunes, listening to the howling winds, waiting for them all to return.

He sat fiddling on his concrete bench, and none of the local people paused to listen. Tourists stopped, and some of them offered coins, but he waved them away. He wouldn't play a complete song: he seemed stuck on one strand of notes, which he played over and over again. A soccer game between a clot of young boys moved in front of his bench, and when the ball flew in his direction, he punched it deftly back into the square. The boys cheered, laughed, went running away toward the Scala and the fish market beyond. Souria was far enough across the square that he wouldn't see her watching him. It was so immodest. Gulls circled, hungry for the market fish that the humans kept from them. Souria took Yu's hand and hurried her through the medina entrance.

She'd walk and walk until she found the desert proper, she began the thought again, when the fiddler found her at a fruitseller's stand at Bab Doukkala. "May I walk with you?" he asked, and she decided she never wanted to walk anywhere else.

"You may walk with me," she said, "if you walk fast. It's cold. I've got to get this child back to her home."

This. Her. As if she were another woman, she heard herself lying.

Nasr's wife had passed on one of her old jackets when the previous winter had reached its most dead, profound point, and now Souria turned its ratty collar up around her ears.

The fiddler smiled. "Of course," he said. He removed his coat and put it around her shoulders.

"I have a jacket," she said, shrugging his off.

"No, really. Please. It's colder than you think." She was carrying. Yu, who was asleep, and when they came across the end-of-day crowd at a carrefour and had to stop, he put his palm on Yu's back. "She's beautiful. How old?"

"Two."

"And your husband?"

She shook her head. "No husband." *If I walk to the desert proper,* she thought. *But this man's face is as peaceful and eternal as any desert.*

She thought it so loud she was sure that he heard her, but he just looked straight ahead of himself and nodded, in the same self-satisfied way as the customers who felt they'd reached, with Nasr, some sort of heartfelt bargain.

The bottleneck of people evaporated once they got past the medina arch, and Souria picked up their pace. He was as tall as she was, but her legs were longer. "Tea?" he asked, when they came to a café.

"Okay," she said. She tried to say it hesitantly, as though it might tax her will to drink.

They sat at a dirty table whose plastic cloth was ripped in places and stained with coffee in others. It was late afternoon, and sunlight was disappearing behind the walls of the port. Yu hadn't napped all day, and she'd been rancorous for hours, screaming in front of the store, upsetting a table stacked with cloth, so that Souria had had to grab her by the wrist and slap her butt. She'd sat in the floor, sniffling tears, as Souria refolded and straightened. Hafiza, who sold soaps in the shop on the corner, had passed and seen Yu crying, said, "Come with me, little bird." She took Yu to her shop and told her the names of all the soaps, showed her the room in the back where the lye and oils cooled. Souria heard Yu giggling in front of the soap shop as Hafiza's husband, Driss, played hiding games with her, and at the end of three hours they'd brought Yu back, and asked Souria if she could come to the soap shop more often. They'd lost their only son, they said, and they missed the life of children. Now, Yu slept deeply, lying sideways in Souria's lap. She was tanned from the day playing outside.

The kitchen had made the tea so strong with sugar that it almost hurt Souria's teeth as she drank. "You're Saouiri?" she asked the man. "Like these here?"

"Yes. Born in Sidi Ifni but raised here. And yourself?"

"No. Not born here."

"Too pretty to be born here. Where?"

"La Mauritanie." She hadn't told anyone in the new town. The feeling of relief was like flying.

They finished their tea, and the fiddler insisted on carrying Yu as they wound their way back through the medina. Yu woke for the shortest of seconds and looked up to his chin, to the stubble there. Her eyes flittered back shut and she took the deep, hiccuping breath of a child fallen asleep crying, but then she fitted herself more snugly into the crook of the fiddler's chin and returned to sleeping. At last, they reached the arches of Bab Doukkala and crossed the street to the line for the Lima Bus. "Salaams," the fiddler said as he carefully handed Yu over. "I'll see you round again. I know it."

"Na'am," said Souria. "We'll see you."

155

She got on the bus and squeezed them into a window seat, past an old man who smelled so strongly of ink that Souria could taste him on her tongue. The bus passed through the town, down its main street of grand hotels and out into the country, where the passing scene went dark. Souria could see, in the window, the reflection of the sly, sideways smile she was giving herself.

The next day was a Monday, a day no one shopped in the morning, a day Nasr, in his own custom, asked Souria to stay home. "I trust you'll rest," he said Sundays when they closed the shop. It was a joke between them when she showed up at the shop on Tuesday and he asked her what she did with her Monday, and she'd tell him she cleaned, or did a big cooking for the week.

"I told you," he'd say, mocking disgust. "A day for resting. One day. You sleep, and let Mademoiselle do her coloring book. It's not good, you always hovering. She'll never know her own mind."

Nasr had raised three daughters; Souria never doubted his advice.

This Monday, the clouds were a veil, and rains tinkled on the roof until midmorning. Yu snored into the air above her face, and Souria lost all pragmatic thought in the balance between these steady noises—the rain and the sawing of breath. She turned her face into the mattress to smile and daydream about the fiddler: the fiddler in his hat, the fiddler grilling bread in a Western-style toaster, the fiddler boarding the carriage taxi, the fiddler with his shiny shoes. When finally sunlight showed through the window and the rain slowed to intermittent plinks on the roof, she woke and went to the kitchen, where she saw, through the window, her upstairs neighbor. He was in the courtyard, hanging wet laundry on his plastic line while his wife sat in the doorway giving directions. In and out of the already-hung sheets, their two small children played—hiding, finding, giggling. The wife went back up to their flat, and the children stayed outside playing while the man filled the rest of his line.

Souria baked shakshuka. After breakfast, she and Yu took the Lima Bus into town, where they found a beach barren of tourists. A few locals walked along the shore, and a group of older boys kicked a soccer ball in the sand, but mostly the beach was a long, empty stretch of sand. They left the bus at the edge of town, near the tourist restaurant where a few sunburned French sat on a large patio eating pizzas and drinking mint tea, and Souria and Yu walked the sand. The wind was too weak for kitesurfers, but three men were dragging a fishing boat out of the water. The men weren't in fishing clothes, and the boat was missing its seats, such that anyone at sea would have had to sit in its murky wet floor. Weather had busted its gunwales, and time had chipped its paint away to such a degree that there was more exposed brown wood than vibrant blue stain. It was less a boat than a carcass of a boat.

She looked into the men's faces and said salaams, but none of them was the fiddler. She and Yu walked farther down the beach. They found a Senegalese—not her usual Senegalese sending balloons but a different man, dressed in a print of bright orange mudcloth, selling polished wood giraffes. This day was like the boat, she thought—a carcass. No tourists, no locals— she couldn't imagine the Senegalese would sell one single thing. She imagined him waking that morning on the pallet he shared with however many other Senegalese, thinking that after all, this was his job in the new country, and he'd have to walk the beach on principle.

"Salaam alaikum," he called to her.

"Alaikum salaam," she said back.

He rubbed his beard and adjusted his beaded green kufi, and Yu walked up to him and inspected his bag, pulling its thick knotted drawstring. Souria was holding her other hand, and she tried to pull Yu away, but the man thrust a polished giraffe at both of them. Souria had learned to look at the eyes of men for evidence of their kindness. Hassan had had such a face, and Ghazi, and Nasr, and the fiddler. This Senegalese, with his gentle smile and the straw of souwk in his mouth, he had such eyes.

"Tu vois," he said to her, "solid ebony." He stroked the giraffe's two-dimensional neck. "Not just painted black—it's solid ebony. You can see here where it was cut."

Souria looked into the tiny nick the Senegalese indicated, but it was such a small cut on the joint that it, too, could have been painted over black. She'd been in Morocco long enough that Africans from other countries knew how to play her. "We're not tourists," she said.

"Of course not. I sell it to you sister price." He handed the giraffe over to Yu so that she might inspect it in her own child's way.

Souria laughed. "We don't have sister price. You'd have to give it to us mother price. Self price."

"Ah," the man said again. It seemed that he liked to fill space in his talking in this manner. "You're not tourists? Really? Your mama and your papa, they are born here?"

"I didn't say that."

"Well then, where?"

The sun had risen high enough that it winked on the surface of the sea, and when Souria turned her head to keep the sun from blowing in her face, the reflection in the water hurt her eyes. "Come on," she said, taking the giraffe out of Yu's hand and giving it back to the man. Yu whimpered.

"Hey," the man said. "There is no problem. You don't have to answer."

Good, she thought. *I won't.*

But she remembered the relief of telling the fiddler, and could not think of any reason not to extend it. Maybe every time she told someone, the feeling would build on itself, until her bones were filled with enough air to fly. "Je suis mauritanienne," she said.

"Ah." The beads on his kufi glinted in the sun. He had the smallest patch of gray in the part of his beard just under his bottom lip. "You came here to attend school."

"You already know that I did not."

"You came to work."

"I was in the desert. And I ended up here."

"And now you cannot go back?" said the man. "I know. It is the same for all the Blacks in this country."

"Before I was here, I never ate fish," she said, hurriedly. "Now, I have fish every day." She felt herself filling. More air. Soon, she'd be light enough to float all the way home.

The man narrowed his eyes into slits of calculation. He reached into his bag and brought out the tiniest whittled giraffe, unpainted, made of thuya wood. "Comme cadeau," he said, putting it in Yu's hand. The giraffe was so much tinier than the original, yet that meant it had been that much harder to whittle: as an offering, it seemed a misunderstanding of scale. The man picked Yu up and held her on his hip as if she were his own child. A worried bird fluttered in Souria's stomach, but Yu smiled as she handled her giraffe. "I'll tell you something," said the Senegalese. "I know someone who can get you back there. He lives right here in Essaouira. In El Borj."

He took his cell phone out of his pocket and dialed a number as she watched, then spoke in his own language, which she did not recognize. The air filled her so that tears welled in the corners of her eyes. In fact, she hated fish. She brought her sleeve to her face and held it there so the man wouldn't know.

He left off his call. "Allons-y," he said.

"I cannot," she said, taking Yu from his hip. There was but one way back, and she did not want to go. Not through the desert, where she'd been raped. Insulted. Stolen and bought and re-sold. "Salaams," she said, and she walked off the beach and onto the boardwalk.

But the tears held, like seeds in her eyes. The real part of life had been that small stand of trees. Her tribe. Her family's tent. Their cooking fire. Her laughing brother. She held her breath. She stopped hoping.

And then started hoping anew.

XVI. Louisville

In Vlad's backyard, far beyond the pool and its protective privacy fence, stood an endangered oak. The tree had no bottom—its exposed roots formed a bridge across a gully of washed-out soil, so that it was suspended over air, its trunk hovering over the creek that flowed beneath it after heavy rains. It was an ancient tree: cut through its middle, it would have shown Shannon a hundred, maybe two hundred rings. Its roots were so strong, she thought, they defy gravity in this way. Her roots weren't like that. They'd never grown.

A flash flood warning had chimed into her phone at six that morning, startling her awake, but the rains had cleared to chilly sunshine, and since Vlad was in Morocco, she'd left the back door of the fence open to listen to the water running down his gutters. She went outside, sat down, and lit a joint, draped her hair behind the chaise lounge. Watched an atoll of cloud pass behind the top of her tree.

From over the fence, she heard her neighbor's patio door slide open, then shut, and she instinctively dropped the hand with her cigarette to her side, though she knew she couldn't be seen through the fence. "Fuck," came the woman's voice into the putative silence. Shannon smirked to herself: Mrs. Ganes was no less than seventy years old. She never talked much, had never come over to introduce herself or bring zucchini or borrow an egg, but Shannon had seen her out in her sunhat and utility gloves, had heard her hoe as it dented the wood of her squash beds.

Shannon swirled her joint back to her mouth for a draw. Tried, silently, to lift herself from her chaise. But as she shifted her weight, the metal frame flipped, and the scraping noise it made as she righted it was loud enough to make Mrs. Ganes call out.

"Hello?" she asked, her voice shaking with its aged lack of modulation.

"Hi," Shannon said. She heard her own sheepishness.

"My apologies," said Mrs. Ganes, "for the profanity."

"Hey, it's your backyard. Where else to cuss?"

Shannon saw, through two slats of fence, that Mrs. Ganes was standing very still. She knew the woman could smell her weed, but would settle for silence—of course, it would feel better for her *not* to say anything. The same way it had hurt Shannon less to settle for Vlad as a spouse than to try to come up with impossible dreams for her own life. Following him around the world on his adventures in mechanical engineering, she'd forget that she hadn't managed to make a life of her own. Always, people neglected the critical things because they hurt more.

A harder wind came and rushed Shannon's ears. She might sit like this forever, she thought, with Mrs. Ganes saying nothing, and her cigarette burning down to its skunky end. But she knew, from a childhood with her mother, about the tiny air bubble in the level that could not be disturbed, the meditative balance of gardening that all women seemed to grow in their middle forties.

The spring she was failing fifth grade, she'd drawn out a list of games she and her mother might play on Fridays. She was just home from the hospital, and both parents seemed so happy she was alive. She thought she'd plow through, toss more confetti into the party. But it turned out she'd drawn the list at such a bad time, in April, when her mother wanted to be out in the evenings, seeding her roses, laying paths for her peonies. Shannon crossed off chess. She crossed off ludo. Pared her list down to checkers, which seemed a more reasonable ask.

"Can you play?" she asked twice, but the month of April passed without a yes.

The last Friday in May, Shannon put on a new dress before she came downstairs and asked. Her mother had bought it for her birthday; it was a tidy pink cotton A-line, with two red bows on each shoulder. The bows were sewn permanently closed, like military chevrons—Mrs. Cavanagh admired neatness. Shannon drew the dress's waist ribbon behind her, tied it into what she hoped was a tight overhand knot. "Can we play?" she asked.

Mrs. Cavanagh removed her leather gloves, carefully pulling them from their inside cuffs. Her hands were surprisingly muddy anyway, and she leaned over and pressed them into her skirt. "Mommy's had a long week. Checkers doesn't fit into Mommy's Friday." She pressed one of her hands into Shannon's forehead and smiled. Shannon felt the ghost of dirt there, even as she knew it hadn't been enough to leave a mark. Her mother walked away, down her rows of seeds.

Shannon never asked again. The rose stems grew thorns. The red blooms came. She put the game board under her bed. Freshman year of high school, while advancing her room décor toward womanhood, she took the checkers out to the skip.

And now, why bother Mrs. Ganes? Why ever bother anyone? "Well," Shannon said, "it's getting chilly." She snuffed her cigarette on Vlad's immaculate patio. He was gone for three weeks—it would rain, and he'd never know. "I think I'll go in," she called out over the fence, knowing Mrs. Ganes would likely neither hear nor care. Because out on this café-free land, eight miles past the sinkhole country where she'd grown up, she still had sinking conversations.

She still hadn't made Vlad a baby. "Let's make sure I'm not the problem," she'd said that day, ten months into her marriage.

This brought forth the confession that melted her wax enough for him to carve himself into her, when Vlad said, "I couldn't make Nastasia pregnant either."

"Was probably her," Shannon blurted. She kept her face low-key, though she felt the blood rising in her cheeks. "I mean, there are so many ways to go wrong in a female body. It's more complicated."

Vlad looked down into his cocktail. Said, "She's got two kids now. A girl and a boy."

"How do you even know this?"

"Larry." His boy Larry, the one he'd known all the way from college, Larry with the bum knee from the street ball accident. Why hadn't Larry kept Nastasia's reproductive information to himself? she wondered. Why pain Vlad? Just why?

She hugged him close to her, pressing his face into her neck. "It's not you, baby. It's me." She said it in a sterile fashion, without explanation. "I'm sure it's me."

Yet that wrinkle, that vulnerability about his testicles, made her slide an inch into his miasma despite herself. She'd never fit into anyone's life so neatly. No one had ever cared for her in this way, and here was this man, trying to make her fit.

Now, two years later, beyond the collection calls that have disappeared into some ether of negative GNP, she regretted the whole thing. The conversation. The tests. The shifting of that large burden onto her own sad uterus. She regretted their wedding at city hall, she regretted meeting Larry and Derek, Vlad's other roommate from college, who had served as second witness. Vlad thought it just one more mathematical proof of her laziness, that she wanted to adopt a kid and call it a day. He had money for IVF, he said, when she felt up to it. He wanted her to get on with the program of his swimming boys.

And she was going back to Morocco, maybe to make a baby, maybe not, because thanks to Vlad's soil consistency studies, his wind projections and 3D blueprints, Windsolver had won its bid. Along with a company from Denmark, it was in the first stages of the kingdom's second wind energy project, live and on-site. Vlad wanted her to see the real Morocco, he said, in the tiny town of Essaouira, the windiest spot in all of Africa. This curve of beach with its Portuguese ruins, he promised, was something she'd enjoy.

She had to be at the airport in three hours, so she showered and finished packing. Jumped in Vlad's old Beemer and drove down Shelbyville Road toward the Watterson. Just before she exited onto 264, she was cautioned by a yellow light, and she could have floored it but she didn't, because why proceed when you didn't have to? Why ever move forward without a gun to your head or a wolf at your back?

She stared at the light in its black casing above her, noticing for the first time how traffic lights weren't at all solid colors. The one above her glowed in a hundred little bright globes of red. It was a marvel.

XVII. The Atlantic

Embassy Messages—Alerts: June 16, 2019. Use increased caution when walking in isolated areas, especially at night. Do not physically resist any robbery attempt. Avoid walking on beaches after dark.

But whoever at State wrote this advisory has never sat on a pitch-black beach, in a dimple of wet sand, under a field of Moroccan stars. Does not know that this kind of heavenly affirmation is worth risking robbery, or kidnapping, or even the approach of the petit guides passing out their handwritten business cards. This army of stars, each one of them a massive helium god still transmitting its power from ten thousand years long passed. Each of them, perhaps, light long dead. But each of them now something Shannon might wish on: the head of Cygnus might give her a pregnancy; the bright, hot center of Lyra might take sacrifice in exchange for Vlad's unending devotion.

A wave rolls in so far that it drowns her toes with numbing cold; Shannon rolls some kif, lights it, and narrows her lips around the cigarette's neck. She's gone to such lengths in her life to stay supplied: she's sucked dick, she's worked hours of overtime, she's driven to a dealer thirty minutes across the city. Weed's the one thing that can scrape the edge off her feelings. To have not had a father—that's normal. But to never have had a real mother? She's like one of Harlow's monkeys, she thinks, rocking away under a marijuana cloud.

She takes her cell phone from her jacket pocket and looks at the time: 9:36. Well past the hour the State Department has envisioned an American encountering the miracle of the Atlantic Ocean.

She rises, brushes sand off the cheeks of her ass, thinks, *fuck the State Department.* She shakes her sandals from her feet and takes another hit, holds her breath. Her brain clears to nothing save the revelation of peace she'd find if she waded out to the darkness, stomped past the steep drop of continental shelf that even the fish can't now see, and started swimming. The riptide would pull her under with a quickness; current would snap her down the coast. The gendarmes might recover her body miles down the beach, her face beatifically swollen, beyond recognition of all the American torture she's lived. If she died here in Essaouira, she'd never have to have a baby, get a job, grow old.

Alerts: Ongoing. If you decide to travel to Morocco …
- *Be aware of your surroundings.*
- *Do not display signs of wealth, such as wearing expensive watches or jewelry.*
- *Be extra vigilant when visiting banks or ATMs.*

But whoever at State wrote this advisory does not know what it is to have your husband leave a small, Saran-wrapped packet of weed on your pillow before he leaves for work in the morning. Whoever wrote the advisory does not know what it feels like, either, when another woman is in your husband's eye, when you know she's there, but you have to act as if she isn't. Whoever wrote the advisory does not know that the shame of the situation is that it's not at all like a play: your performance must be stellar, but you won't win any awards.

When Shannon tries to open the packet, the plastic clings, stubbornly, and in frustration, she pries it open until it stretches to tearing. On the rose-covered pillowcase next to it is a note Vlad's written, directing her to the fabric shop next to the egg-cup seller. *I'm assured it's safe to buy in a beach town,* he says, *but be discreet.* Embarrassment rises in her chest. It's the first time he's acknowledged her level of habit, but here he's known it all along—the deepest, most amygdalic part of her reptile brain. She's thought, in hiding it, that she's protected his neuroses, the million fragile eggs of his legalistic personality. He's like a snail she found when she was a little girl and, thinking to protect it from bigger animals, took inside and named Sherman. She'd put Sherman in a glass jar and not told her mother, because she'd thought to protect the snail from her too. But when she woke the next day, she found Sherman, the desiccated sliver of him, shriveled to his premature death at the bottom of the jar. She'd gone and married a thing like Sherman. She'd never move Vlad from his mind.

Still, the excitement of finding a Moroccan weedman made her shame pass as quickly as might a cloud under the wing of an airplane. She tried to open the hotel window, thinking to clear out the skunk before the maid came, but the Hotel Atlas Asni did not have functional windows, she found. She dressed and went downstairs, hesitated in the revolving door. She couldn't tell what mechanism was cooling the inner sanctum of the door, but when she looked at the street beyond, she found the waves of radiating heat and felt that when she exited, she might be completely vaporized. Then thought, that wouldn't be such an undesirable death either.

She set out for the medina, crossing the sidewalk to the face of the Attijariwafa. Removed her card and put it in the slot. Once you'd had the fantasy of dying so far from home, she found, it wouldn't quite leave you. She punched in her PIN and thought how simple and clean it would be: her body, rotted to bones, transported back to the States in the cargo hold of a plane. Better yet, Vlad might have her cremated, so she could reenter the Old World as ash and dust.

It would be what they all deserved—Vlad, her parents, the fertility doctor. Vlad would have to tell the people from Denmark, when it happened, that he'd been wrong about his wife. They were all wrong. She was in no condition to be anyone's mother.

Alerts: Ongoing. The threat of kidnapping of Westerners by criminal or terrorist groups exists in the region of Western Sahara. Extortion and kidnapping for ransom are significant sources of financing for criminal traffickers of all kinds.

Share important documents, login information, and points of contact with loved ones so that they can manage your affairs if you are unable to return as planned to the United States.

Draft a will, and designate appropriate insurance beneficiaries and/or power of attorney.

But whoever at State wrote the advisory clearly had something to live for. Perhaps they had loving parents. A great career writing State Department travel advisories. Perhaps they had babies. And financial insulation enough not to understand that there were winners and losers in their country, just like there were winners and losers everywhere, people working for $11 an hour who ended up owing a $147,000 because they'd been in a car accident, people who'd wipe down tables in a diner for forty years, only to end up at the end of it with rotten molars.

She finds the eggcup house and the fabric store next door, but when she enters, she wonders if she's made a mistake.

"Bonjour," says a woman, supermodel tall, dark-skinned, her eyes blazing amber. Her pitch-black hair blends into the midnight blue of her djellaba. From under it, atop four-inch heels, fall black leather pants. She's breathtaking. Not a weedman at all. Shannon is so dumbstruck, she's almost unable to speak. She asks, weakly, "Kif?"

The woman points to the back of the store, where Shannon finds a fattish, balding man who looks an awful lot like her paternal grandfather. But she asks again—"Kif?"—and he produces, from under his measuring table, an eighth.

"C'est combien?" she asks.

"Five hundred dirham."

And for the first time in Morocco, she's so afraid of losing something, she refuses to bargain, though she knows that like every number in the country, his is a lie. She gives him the two 200 notes she's withdrawn at the Attijariwafa, then fingers her fanny pack for the dull, worn wallet she's kept in the event of theft. "L'argent americain aussi?" she asks.

He nods, and she peels off a twenty, ignoring Andrew Jackson's judgment. She takes the baggie and buries the eighth in her purse, beneath Kleenex and used boarding passes. She nods her thanks and rushes back out into the cooler, open air of the shop proper. "I'll be back for fabric!" she tells the supermodel, whose calm eyes follow her. "I'd like something purple."

The woman crosses her arms in amusement. Like Vlad, she knows.

But Shannon's so proud of herself for having sealed this international transaction. She's made nothing but wrong decisions in life, but this kif seems like a solid. It will enter her lungs and ease her pain, keep her alive another day.

She's thinking about the sweet relief of it when she sees her, the same little girl, in the same pink jacket as the day before. Her hair rising free of its braids, in a bush of curls around her head. She belongs to no one, this girl. She's been sent to Shannon as an emissary of possible adulthood, and why not? Why not believe that she, like anyone else, could go from not being a mother to being a mother, all in an instant? No one did it perfectly, she'd heard. You just rolled with the imperfection. She'd have to give up weed. She'd have to give up suicidal thoughts. But she could make it her kind of perfect, even if she received this blessing in such an imperfect way; she could be the mother she never had. She could save this abandoned girl from this cobblestone street.

She bends until she's eye level, and carefully uses the phrase she's absorbed over the course of two Moroccan visits: "As-salaam alaikum."

The girl clenches her fingers open and shut: a wave.

PART IV

LOW SEASON

XVIII. Essaouira

The hour Yu vanishes, the clouds break just enough to drop a seasoning of rain, and as Souria searches and calls throughout the medina, she finds herself damp rather than soaked. Her hair is wet only at its front edges; the hood of her djellaba keeps its length dry. Then the clouds break completely, pouring a torrential rain that washes away all the dirt of the souk, channeling it into muddy rivulets that run down the slopes of tin roofs and out of shop corners. It picks up gradually, until suddenly, as though Allah has pulled aside a curtain, it falls in windy sheets that bring the storekeepers outside cursing, packing away their pristine leatherworks and elaborate rugs. The rain flushes itself in streams down the cubed street grates and under the cobbled stones, through pipes under the medina, south to the collection pool and out to the Atlantic.

She's been sitting on the dry ground in front of the soap shop, waiting for a glimpse of her daughter so long that her hips have lost feeling. She's not far enough under the overhang to completely dodge the rainfall, and her sleeves start to stick to her arms. Her hair, woven into one long braid down her back, feels cold, weighted. Still, she appreciates the downpour; physical discomfort is the only thing that stanches the absurdity of her missing child.

Even before the rain picked up speed, she'd been nauseated, as she'd been so many times in the last three years—first, in the back of the tireseller's van, where he'd forced himself on her, and the thick smell of rubber in his hair worked its way up her nose and down into her stomach. She'd been nauseated while waiting for Yu, in those first months of pregnancy before she'd even understood there was another body inside of hers. There'd been other times when she and Yu had eaten spoiled food and vomited it up in hurting waves, and they'd been relieved to be free of what ailed them. One of those times, she'd happened upon a lemon grove, right in the middle of the city, and she'd peeled one half-naked to offer to Yu, who—inexplicably, wonderfully— giggled at its sourness. *You have the smile of a thousand lemons,* she'd told her daughter, and the girl again sucked and giggled, and it seemed she was forgiving Souria all the times her stomach had gone wanting.

Once, when they were living in Lahcen's riad, Yu had vomited her breakfast in loud coughs and then looked up to Souria and smiled through tears. If Souria could vomit like that now, she thinks, she might be able to cough up some of her terrible fear. But she can't. She doesn't dare dirty the Savons' sidewalk and step on Driss's welcome, for his shop is the last place she saw Yu. She closes her eyes against the gathering bile and thinks of the unmasted sailboats she saw strapped to the bed of a train car when she first crossed the Moroccan border.

She would also like to scream, so loudly that her voice might overpower the rain. She wants to draw her whole breath and scream until every person in every shop comes out to watch, until every man, woman, and child in the souk of Essaouira comes out of their houses to witness. One of them, she imagines, will have a three-year-old child on their hip, and that little bird will recognize its mother's screaming and come running. She'll gather Yu into her arms and press her face into her belly; she'll tally all the bad ways this country has treated her and find a way to leave it.

But she can't scream, because that would attract the gendarmes. Instead she whispers under her breath, a prayer she'd once been commanded to recite, when she was a slave in Bou Ctaila: Allah, make this a profitable downpour.

She sits a meter from the street grate and watches the rain flush through in such excess that it swells at the top and pools before disappearing. She can see, in the water, all the life the dirt has been—a piece of orange rind thrown out, or perhaps lost in the ecstasy of someone's eating; a chip of paint, faded to a sick red; a fist-sized ball of dust, loosened by the storm from an eighty-year-old roof. All the detritus of the souk, waiting for nature to move and transform it. She thinks she should be working, and that Nasr is wondering why she's so late. She needs to go to work so she can gather her pay: she is low because of the season, down to fifty dirham extra above rent. This poor child, with only one chance at having a mother, Souria thinks, and how unfair that Allah has given her such an inadequate one. She rises, loosing her hair from its braid while she waits for feeling to bleed back into her feet, and then she walks the winding paths to Nasr's shop.

"Where've you been?" he asks. He's on a ladder, folding bolts of cloth. He steps down, shakes his watch as if it's broken, and puts it to his ear. "We've had customers."

"Sorry," she says. She could tell him that Yu is gone. That she's been sitting outside in the rain looking for her daughter, who is all she's been able to accumulate in this life. Her hair is still soaked, but now full, falling down her back like a carapace of ice, and she could tell him that she no longer believes the day or the people in it are real, or that the air on the earth is still moving. She could tell him that cloth and long trousers and all other ideas of covering the body are ridiculous in the nakedness of loss. But Nasr shifts his wild, gray eyebrows from anger to inertia, as if he has too many problems to hold or remember just one, and she says nothing—what good would it do? Perhaps he would call round the medina. Involve the gendarmes. Who would send her away, and then she'd never find her daughter. She climbs up his ladder and begins folding the cloth herself, stopping only once to attend to an old country woman who has no teeth, top or bottom.

"La bes darim," Souria says to her, for her chin is tattooed with religious symbols in the habit of the Berber, but the woman ignores her. She paces around tables, looking at her own feet, and seems to have entered the shop only to escape the rain. She approaches the most beautiful bolt in the shop—indigo with gold braided through its stripes—and picks it up with one hand clamped to its cardboard core.

"Minshk aysker?" she asks.

"Four hundred for the meter."

The woman sucks on her gums. "Nuqs emik. I'll give you fifty."

"It is not possible. You come from the desert? Me too. I'll give you Berber price. Three seventy."

Again, the woman sucks on her gums. "I'll give you sixty," she says.

Souria takes the bolt from the woman's hands.

"Mal élevé," says the woman, and Nasr rises from his chair and shoos her into the wet alley.

But the old woman is the only customer they have all day, and for the distraction from her troubles, Souria feels she would have given her the entire shop for free. When she and Nasr have done all the folding and wiping and sweeping they can possibly do, and are simply sitting on stools, stealing bored glances at each other, Nasr tells her he's closing the shop for the day. The thought beats wildly in her head, that she can't leave until Yu returns, she needs to sleep in the shop if need be. But the thought is trapped there, like a bird under an eave, because she can't tell Nasr, embarrassed as she is to have lost her own child in a medina alley, afraid as she is of the power of the Sûreté Nationale.

Nasr ties both sides of the plastic door together at the middle with a thick cord. Together they reach to pull the steel gate down its track, until it meets the place where the track is lined with rust, and then it takes all the strength they have. Outside, Nasr pushes it the remaining difficult meter to the floor, and locks it. He gives Souria thirty dirham, generous for a day when she's sold nothing. He might have noticed that Yu hadn't been around all day, flitting in and out of the shop like a mosquito, but he hasn't asked. "You don't look so well," he tells Souria. "Look better tomorrow."

Free of the shop, she roams the medina in a grand circle, coming again and again to Savons Mogador, until almost all the shops are closed and the only people left are gendarmes, who've been roaming the medina in their sharp blue uniforms ever since the bombs went off in Casablanca. Sometimes they're not in full dress, but they're all men of a certain age, with new shoes and severe haircuts, so Souria knows exactly who they are. She can guess what questions they'd have for her. What papers they'd want that she could not turn up. They'd arrest her and send her away, so far that she could not come back in the morning and search for Yu. If she were a Moroccan citizen, she could linger. As it is, she has to go home.

She vomits on the sidewalk before the Lima Bus even comes. Since she's had only one glass of juice this whole day, it's hard coming—just a thin yellow stream that puddles cloudy on the wet street. The other riders murmur and step away to give themselves space, but over the sound of herself retching, she can't hear what any one of them is saying. A young student with a new back-pack nods to ask if she's okay, and she nods back, and gradually the crowd shifts back to its silence. When it finally does come, the bus fills with people, but no one takes the seat next to her. Down the main street and along the residential gates with their metal spires, she cries into her scarf, all the way to Diabat, where she gets off the bus and climbs the rocky hill to her little flat. She keys into the door and tries again to vomit into her little blue laundry pail, but nothing will come.

She feels things that are missing, like the stickiness of Yu's hand as she helps her up the hill, and the warmth of the water Yu asks for as soon as they open the door. Where Yu had been just twenty-four hours earlier, jumping on the old twin mattress they share, asking questions about how the moon works, there is now silence. Where Yu sang herself a daily anniversary— *Aeed milaad saeed*—there is now silence. When Souria blows her nose into a paper napkin, the sound of it makes an echo off the ceiling that she's never noticed, and she can't help it then— she screams. She screams, and then she screams prayers, and she screams a song from her own childhood; she screams for min-utes that feel like hours, and the mother and the father from the upstairs apartment bang on the ceiling for her to stop, but no one comes to find out what is the matter. She screams until her lungs ache, until she has no voice, and then she cries herself to a sleep so deep she forgets that Yu is gone. She wakes up in the middle of the night dreaming she has felt Yu's hand on her cheek, but when she turns over to empty space she remembers, and then she cries some more.

"My baby," she whispers. Between drifts of sleep the loss seems revocable, like losing a kite to the wind or losing a coin in a sand dune, and she half expects her little girl to come out from the corner of their tiny, useless balcony and say, "I was hiding here all along." But when Souria sits up and wakes completely, she finds that Yu isn't on the balcony or even in the building. She cries until she tastes her own tears, and then until she tastes Yu's, and then until she tastes her daughter's hair, her skin, her blood . . . she retches again, again yielding nothing, and she cries herself back to sleep.

The next day, the rains come again, harder even than the day before; it's a furious storm whose thunder makes the keepers of the souks bring in their wares and cower. The tourists again keep their money indoors; the only customers are Essaouiri women who've been kept from essentials by the previous day's rains. With the stronger rain comes a stronger wind, one that rips loose part of Nasr's roof. Souria hurries with him to put plastic covers over the tables and mannequins, and Nasr squinches his eyes and looks up to the corner of the ceiling through which rain now falls. He moves a bucket under the leak, mumbling something about calling someone, but mostly he seems unconcerned. In the crippling rain, no one needs cloth, so he sends Souria away,

"I can sit and do nothing all by myself," he tells her. He chuckles, expecting her to laugh with him, and she could tell him then—*my baby's gone, Monsieur, and I will not laugh until she comes back*—but Nasr's eyebrows fall slack, and she does not speak. Her voice is hoarse, in any case, and has come out of her throat all day in dry chirps—what good would it do to say anything? He gives her thirty dirham. She tells him shukran, and she leaves.

She wanders the old medina—looking, studying, guessing. She has avoided social knowledge of her fellow shopkeepers; the wages of this sin are that now she dare not ask. Wherever Yu is, Souria wants to believe that she is dry and warm and well-fed; the girl has sense enough not to stand outside getting drenched. She goes back to Driss's shop and asks has he seen her, but he says no. He holds her hand and cries with her, and his wife

Hafiza comes, embraces her, gives her the four kisses. She puts a hand over her heart and says she knows what it is to miss a child. Souria is welcome to sit outside his shop as long as she wishes, says Driss. The girl will come running up the lane at any moment, Hafiza says—they all know it.

Souria walks and walks some more in the alley, and though she doesn't want to draw attention to herself by asking the vendors, she does study their faces. Might she look into their eyes and see, written in their dark pupils, where Yu has gone? If someone in the souks has taken her, they would have been studying her all this time, charting arrivals and departures, waiting for the time when Driss and Hafiza were too busy in their shop to have a good eye out. Whoever it is, their eyes, when confronted with hers, will give them away.

But not one shopkeeper gives her such a look. She is dark-skinned, farafala, harratin, abid, so most won't so much as return her glance. She shudders in the cold and she keeps walking. Her daughter is somewhere in the medina—where else would she have gone? She's always shied away from the medina side of the beachfront, fearful as she's been of the high waves crashing against the rocks, the old lead cannons left by the Portuguese. Yu is here, somewhere, right under Souria's nose, and if she had help, if she could turn this maze of medina upside down and shake it out, she'd find her. But finding a lost child isn't, under her circumstance, a simple matter of going to the douane. Without papers, she must stay quiet, perfectly quiet.

Even when the rains aren't heavy the roofs of the souks spring leaks, and if you look up to follow the path of a bird, you can see pieces of blue sky showing through. Sometimes a bat is stuck, and the men chase it with a broom until it flies off to the city, to continue its life in some wiser fashion. She wonders what she was doing when Yu disappeared. Watching Nasr shout at the football match on the radio? Bargaining with a French woman? Selling a meter of silk brocade to a bride? The possibilities make her crazy. It's not like losing an apple or a key—losing a human, one you love, is impossible to live through. The bus is so delayed that people give up waiting, and Souria ends up hitching a ride to Diabat on a truck full of onions.

The rains have stopped, the heat kicking Morocco right back to cruelty, and the smell of the produce strafes her nostrils and smothers her lungs. After she's home and even long into the night, onions sting her eyes. She sits on her little patio for hours, unwilling to make the steps that will echo so loudly in her flat now that Yu doesn't fill it. When she finally goes inside to lie on the mattress, she finds that the return of the heat has thickened Yu's smell, and this makes her crazier still. It's the sweet smell of her sleeping child, the smell of spittle souring on the mattress, the smell of her own baby. Souria thinks of Yu singing the rest of her own anniversary—*le'aagouba limyat aam inshae'allah*—and she buries her head and cries. She dreads the day the smell will wear away. It will mark a point. If she hasn't found Yu by then, she will die.

The third day, when she wakes, the sunshine has already come, and that is worse. The chickens in the halal market are waking, clucking; the oil seller yells his refrain. Life proceeds all around her, as if no one knows. She hears a knot of teenagers playing soccer in the courtyard and is shocked to learn that joy still exists somewhere on the planet. When one of them laughs, it is a sound from a distant realm.

She eats breakfast alone on the little square of patio and drinks the persimmon juice Yu loves. She drinks it slowly, as if to communicate to her daughter, wherever she is, its sharp taste. Later, in Nasr's little storeroom, she moves aside a box of kif and finds the bag of things she's collected for Yu over the months. There are clothes that belonged to Hafiza's son before he died, and clothes Nasr had tailored out of material he allowed Souria to select for herself. There was a photograph of Yu that some German tourists had taken at the Scala. They'd had an old-fashioned camera, large as a box, with a slot to roll out its own photos, and they'd taken one of Yu for themselves and then, in lieu of offering her a coin, taken one to give to Souria. It had been just a couple of weeks after they'd come from Marrakech, and Yu had been so happy, sitting on a stone wall, her tiny arms thrown up toward the sky. In the box also was a toy, a stuffed bear, that Yu had brought to the shop in the days before she'd disappeared.

"What a happy bear! Who gave you that?" Souria had asked.

"An American lady. She smelled good."

Souria turned the bear in her hands, checked its goofy smile, which had been so simply discarded. She wondered if she'd one day have to give away Yu's belongings the same way Hafiza handed over her dead son's clothes. After her son died, Hafiza had lost weight and let her hair go completely gray. Souria sat outside her mind and wondered how her own grief might progress. She drew the string of the bag and put it in the corner of the storeroom. Yu would be back. She'd made sure of so many things, and she'd make sure of this. The bag, it needed to stay.

XIX. The Coast

Hafiza Belkacem

You didn't grieve your son's death, not for one full year, because you didn't realize he was dead. You went to the burial, you tucked your head into Driss's shoulder and wept, but it wasn't a weeping for the loss of your son, because at any moment your son was going to come running back through the front door of your house saying, *Mmi, I want a drink of water.* You were weeping because of the hysteria all around you; you were weeping because the wind cut so cold against your chest; you were weeping because the words of the imam sounded so crisp and insensitive against the wailing of your own mother. Or, more honestly, you didn't know why you were weeping. You found the tears there in your eyes, felt them brimming over until they were running down your cheeks, and once they fell, it was such a relief that you found you could not stop.

But you didn't understand *why* your son had died, and so you didn't understand *that* he had died, and you weren't bitter, not once in that year, because your arms still held the muscle memory of him, and for you, he was not gone. He'd just wandered off, quickly as his toddling legs would let him, and fallen off a ledge between houses. And you didn't know, either, how he'd even climbed up there, which made it improbable that the fall, and then the death, had actually happened. But in some other plane of existence he fell, and he made enough of a fuss that you went out to the side yard and scooped him up. He stopped crying as soon as you did so, and in any case there were no tears, but just to be safe you closed the front door and asked him to play in the living room. He bounced his little blue ball for half an hour, then you heard something fall, and you knew something terrible had just happened, but you finished scouring the pot anyway—he wasn't crying, after all—and by the time you got to the living room he was shaking in seizures, and then there was screaming telephoning hurrying pounding running shaking voices and more screaming, and then the emergency crew was carrying him away with a sheet over his sweet little angel's face, and they were telling you how sorry they were, but you were telling them that nothing had happened and they need not be sorry, you were screaming it at them, only it turned out you were only screaming it in your own head and no one was hearing, and they were all just looking at you lying on your own divan, a speechless woman whose high olive skin had blanched all the way to white.

And then, almost a year later, it happened to a man driving on the route from Marrakech: he hit a bump and his car flipped over, and though it was said that his face wasn't even bruised, he died of massive, invisible bleeding in the brain, such as apparently happened occasionally to people on the planet Earth. It was only then that you realized what had happened to your son, only then that you would shut yourself up in your bedroom for days when you heard news of another pregnancy in the neighborhood, only then that you would see small children walking with their mothers into Savons Mogador and have to look away. Driss would take their orders, their money, their credit cards while you retreated to the back of the shop and counted gift labels.

And then the young girl showed up one day at Nasr's shop

with a child exactly the same size as your son, who was frozen in time now at the age of twenty-seven months. The young woman showed up again the next day, and the day after that— she'd come there to work, and you thought it was Allah trying in his gentle way to either chide you or heal you, and you couldn't decide which, but you badly wanted the healing. And so when you noticed that the little girl alternated between two outfits all week, you gave this young mother your son's clothes. When you saw that the little girl seemed hungry and thirsty, you gave her food. Money to go buy orange juice. "Our shop's not so busy. I'll keep an eye out for her," you told the young mother, because Allah had already worked on your heart to such a degree that you wanted this young mother to have the happy ending you didn't, and when finally the fiddler started showing up at Nasr's shop to talk to this young mother and sometimes bring her a kebab and some chips, or a single rose from the flowerseller, you were overjoyed. The young mother had seen trouble, you could tell, and she deserved this.

And then the fiddler went off to gendarmerie school, is what Nasr told you and your husband, and though the young mother would come out to stand in front of Nasr's shop from time to time, looking from left to right as though she were lost, she kept the taller walk the fiddler had given her. She still crossed her arms nervously across her breasts, but now the arms seemed looser, more hopeful.

So when the American woman came and took the child down the alley—repeating her question of *la glace?*—you didn't think twice about it. The woman, with her big, boxy shoulders and her leather fanny pack, was so obviously American. She had a deep gash that something had riven on one side of her face, yet still was beautiful, with curly black hair and brown skin, and she seemed full of peace and light; delightful, like almost all of the

Black American women who came in your shop, wondering at the goat's milk soap and the argan oil, telling you they were seeing their Motherland for the first time. Strangely enough, the woman and the child so resembled each other it was as though they belonged to each other already. And the woman brought her right back to the alley the first time, and the child seemed so happy, and when you saw the sheer delight in the little girl's face, you wished that the woman could take the child for ice cream every hour of every day. So there was little question in your mind that she'd bring her back the second time: this American woman was just giving sadaqah, so that she could get back on her plane to the United States and feel that she'd really *done* something for her Mother.

But then, that second time, she didn't bring the girl back.

Or maybe the second time, the woman got lost in the winding medina, whose logic seemed to elude all Americans. The maze was so American-proof, perhaps, that the woman had simply left the girl in the wrong alley, and the girl was making her way, and would be back any day now. Or maybe the girl got so lost she ended up in another mother's home, or the child traffickers took her, or she fell off a ledge. Nasr had been selling the kif for so long—it was foolish to think that nothing terrible would ever come of such.

But what you really think, because now you know you're capable of thinking anything into reality, is that the American woman saw the sheer delight in the girl's face, and she decided that the child should indeed have ice cream every hour of every day, and so she took her back to the United States to make this happen.

And you convince yourself that this is the best way, that no matter what this little girl loses in the bargain, she will have escaped this bedraggled life in her mother's little flat in Diabat, and that the young mother will be free to marry her fiddler. And even if it is not that way, there is nothing you can do for the young mother by telling her what has happened to her child, and so you say nothing. You listen to the young mother's cries and the alarm of your husband and, later, of Nasr; you touch your heart and you cry with her, but you say nothing.

If you can turn over your son to Allah, this young woman who's too young to even be a mother can surely turn her daughter over to a rich American. It is niyya, it is obedience, it is the divine plan. To be unwritten by no human hand.

Mohammed Toufiq

You were counting the room charge receipts, but vacantly, because you'd already counted them three times—really you were thinking about your own aftershave and wondering if you'd put on too much, and whether your workmate Tisbeh could smell it, because she had neither husband nor boyfriend, and she had thick dark hair and straight white teeth, so you wanted to smell good in a way she'd notice, but not in a way that would cause her to know you were smelling good just for her.

So you were counting and hoping, and keeping these two forces simultaneously in your consciousness, when you saw the American woman ordering the elevator for herself and the little girl. When she turned to glance over her shoulder, you looked back down to your receipts so she'd think you were only counting—not noticing, though she'd caused a hiccup in your calculations that sent you straight back to one.

You'd seen the woman already, many times—she had one terrible scar down the left side of her face, and she'd been a week at the hotel already, with a man you assumed was her husband. He always left in the mornings right after the downstairs break-fast was served, and so you assumed he was here on some sort of business, but when this small girl suddenly appeared with his wife, you wondered just who these people were and what they were doing in your country. It didn't sit right in your gut, but anyway who were you, and what was a gut? You looked to Tisbeh, who was so much smarter than you and so much better educated, at University of Ifrane, even. You looked to her, but she just kept on with her typing, and so you told your gut to shut up and wait for dinner. Hassan would serve couscous tonight, because it was Friday, and you'd get to eat on the hotel's fancy plates with the fancy silver with the handles in the shape of fleurs-de-lis, the silver that made you feel like a king in your own country. The Americans and the Europeans often had their own strange business, and you'd learned in the last year and a half that it never profited to care. So you started over at one with your receipts, and you tucked your head slyly into your shoulder, gauging the power of your own aftershave.

Fouad Fassi

When they showed up in your consulate office, they seemed, actually, like decent people. Hopelessly naive, like all Americans, and overconcerned for their personal health and safety: the woman was drinking a bottled water, and when she asked you where she might buy another one, and you told her there was a water fountain down the hall, she shook her head and said she'd just wait until you were finished.

The man you'd seen the day before, skulking around outside the embassy. You remembered because he wasn't just American but rigid, Trump-era American, at the embassy in a suit at 5:30 in the evening. Dressed as he was, you'd thought it curious he wasn't coming inside for business, but standing there in the hot sun, consorting with security guards. But after all, even the most rigid Americans eventually got around to kif if they were in your country long enough, and somehow, comically, every American expat discovered that the embassy security crew, sitting for hours per day in its boredom, was a critical link in the chain.

Still, the couple seemed decent right up until the moment you refused them their papers. "I don't know where you found this child or who gave her to you," you said. "I will certify nothing." You raised your one eyebrow over your glasses, because you knew—you'd been told—that this gesture was intimidating to strangers, even though your own children found it wholly dismissible.

"Look—we are prepared to compensate you for your trouble," the man said, and he said *compensate* almost with a French accent, he'd been in the country miscommunicating that long. He handed you five thousand dirham. But this child, this small, clean, well-dressed girl who did not look like one of those Casablancan street urchins you didn't give one shit about, looked to you with pleading in her eyes.

"Is this your new mommy and daddy?" you asked her in your language, raising your eyebrow again, and she shook her head no.

"My mommy's at her store," she said, and she started crying, and you realized that anything you could buy with five thousand dirham would not last so long as the damnation you'd feel every time you came to work and caught your reflection in the overhead security mirror. You'd committed smaller sins for less money and felt it for months afterward—how long would selling a little girl last?

"Who is this child?" you said to them, viciously, but the woman narrowed her eyes and said to you, "Maybe her name is Peyton Clark."

And so you thought for a minute. And then that minute turned into two and then into three, and there was no noise in your office except for the little girl's quiet sniffling, and the woman hugging her to her bosom to shush her. And then you motioned for the five thousand back, and you counted and stuffed it into your bottom desk drawer, and you got out the blank certificate of birth, the I-600, and a passport waiver, because you and Peyton Clark were taking a flight to Paris next week, and your wife thought you were going to a congress. Indeed, you completed the certificates as fast as you could, and justified your speed by telling yourself that, after all, this thirsty American lady needed to go buy her water.

"Here you are," you said finally, standing up, shoving the certificate at the man. "Now get out. Vas-y."

You used the familiar *tu* because you hated them then, for making you feel as though an American economist with a shaved pussy and a neck covered in expensive Italian perfume was more important than a sniffling little girl. You hated them for offering you one-tenth of your annual salary, these people even darker than you, and you hated them because they probably could have offered you even more than they did.

And after they'd gone, the woman carrying the little girl to the elevator, the little girl looking at you over the woman's shoulder all the way down the hall, you wondered how they even knew about Peyton. And you thought about the other men at the embassy whom you'd told, the few you'd high-fived when you described Peyton's waxed Brazilian, and the way she took your penis all the way down her throat and made noises. You thought about Rafiq, who worked in the cultural affairs section and had his own string of women outside his marriage, and could thus not afford to talk. You thought of Lucien, the tall, brilliant head of security, whom you'd told in a moment of recklessness, when you'd just fucked Peyton and were feeling invincible. You thought of Muhsin, one of the night guards, who'd seen you and Peyton driving off at least ten times in her new Peugeot, and you thought

192

about what you'd heard about Muhsin—that he'd do anything at all for a brick of kif.

But then you decided almost as quickly not to think about it at all. Rafiq and Lucien were trustworthy. You didn't know Muhsin well, but these Americans—the husband in his juvenile khaki shorts and the woman with her nervous way of twisting her own hair—could not possibly know the night staff. You would say a quick prayer for this child the next time you went to the mosque, and you'd think that no one on earth was perfect save the Prophet himself (peace be upon him). You'd think about Paris, which you'd never seen, and you'd feel like the luckiest man in Morocco.

Fatoumata Larbi

You were thinking of your dead husband when you heard the child pleading to go back to her mother. You understood what she was saying, but the man and the woman sitting in the flight lounge with her did not, you saw, because the woman just kept smiling and patting her curls at the wrong moments of the child's words, and that just made the child cry harder. The man and the woman were not Moroccan—you determined this from the bulkiness of their bodies—and so you took your cleaning cart closer, to see if you might help the child translate.

"My mother will cry," she was saying, but it didn't make sense, because the way the woman was so calm when she took the girl on her lap and gave her a sip of juice, you figured she was some kind of relative, maybe an American auntie, taking her for the vacation of a lifetime.

A woman in niqab sat next to them, and she, too, had noticed—you could see, through the holes in her haik, her eyes shifting in suspicion. You always wondered what made those women take the extra step of wearing the haik, what terrible thing they'd done that made their men mistrust them, or what awful port wine stain they had on one cheek, what hooked kind of aggressive nose. You pushed your cleaning cart alongside a line of eight Jews readying to board. One was so pale and European that his side locks didn't curl, but hung sadly down to his shoulders: little tails. One was very cute, dark-skinned like a Moroccan, and you had the terrible urge to touch him as you passed, to brush your hip next to his so that he'd have to go wash your female off of himself, to maybe make him miss his flight so that he'd have to remain in this country with the so many people he resembled. But, if you thought about it, he belonged here, you were thinking, and well, if you really looked at them, so did the American man and woman. Definitely Moroccans by some degree of descent. At least their grandmothers, if not their parents.

And anyway your husband had died because you lived in the wall of Marrakech, in its very medina wall, with a tin roof and the brush of trees over your heads, and in the spring, when the rains came and the floor under your feet muddied, your husband caught a terrible something and could not stop shitting, until he was shitting blood, and in the next two days he'd simply died, his eyes facing your tin roof, sweat glistening on his forehead even as his hands grew cold. And you'd buried him there where you lived, not even twenty paces away, because really anyone could belong anywhere, and we all of us would belong back to the earth at the end.

And if anyone could belong anywhere, why was this little girl crying? She would go to America and she'd learn to belong, for however long her very nice auntie was keeping her there.

Vladimir Grenfell
She was unstable. You knew the minute you saw her, waiting for you with her cocktail at a little round table in Rudy's. Trouble:

you could see it in the way she let those jet-black curls tumble so wild and unruly over her shirt collar. Most of the Black girls you knew were still putting perms in their hair, or weaving tracks, or cutting it down close to their heads in teeny weeny Afros. But this girl was just letting her hair go all militant, all Angela Davis on the Afro pick.

You could see, too, by how dark her lipstick was—something almost black—that she wasn't like the women you met in your line of work. Those sensible women, those women who were square, but in that calculated way chicks have when you need a tissue and they have one in their purse: a perfect equation on either side of themselves. You'd struck out with all three lady engineers and that one girl with the MBA who was the financial controller. You'd even struck out with your first wife, and after Nasty left, you'd finally faced facts—you were almost forty, five-foot-nine and growing no taller, possibly starting to lose some hair on the back of your head, though without a woman in the house, you couldn't even be sure of that. You were just possibly going to have to settle for a wild one.

And did she turn out. Even after your second date, which came three months after the first date, after a car wreck that probably should have killed her, she was wild as a Pacific salmon. She used the word *fuck* as both expletive and conjunction. A windshield had cut into her face, but she never tried to hide it, discarded the Dermablend after a month. When she met you in restaurants, she came smelling of weed. When you walked her to her car, you found a blanket spread across the back seat. When finally you got her to your house one night, you found that she'd been commando all evening.

And by all this, you were bewitched. It was more fun than you'd dreamed. Your father had warned you when you left for college not to stick your dick in crazy. But anyway both your parents were dead and gone, and who were you not to tangle with this woman? She turned your world from black and white to Technicolor. The woman your mother warned you about turned out to be as essential as air.

She barely spoke to her own mother, though she didn't know that you knew this. She never mentioned it, and seemed as unfazed by her unemployment as by her chronic pain or anything else, and the way she chugged her life along, as if nothing bad had ever happened to it, was just fucking magic. When you asked her to marry you, you said *please*.

And then you got married, because you were in a hurry to make her yours, and she was in a hurry to have dental insurance, and everything was fine. Nothing changed.

Until it did.

It showed up first in shopping receipts. She didn't want the things the sensible squares would have wanted—no True Religion jeans, or shoes, or increasingly alt-rock lipsticks. She didn't even buy books, though you knew, from the number of consecutive coffees you saw on your AmEx, that she spent a good portion of each weekday at the Barnes & Noble in Broad Ripple. No—what she began to buy were documentaries. Two-hundred-fifty-dollar ones not marked for mass distribution. When you googled the titles, you found that their trailers were morbid, and sometimes vile. One on a drug gang that ran a favela. One on the closing of a toy factory in China. One about the plastic surgery acquired by Los Angeles prostitutes. You watched that one for five minutes, from behind her, in the next room. "Going to bed," you said, but you dared to glance back at her on your way upstairs, and what you saw, in that one second before she turned back to the television, was that she felt sorry for you.

And then you got it. Got. It. You were boring, and you always had been, even since the first grade, when you were trying to tell your friends the story of your Christmas Lego set and none of them would listen. And maybe you'd always be a bore; maybe you'd be boring on your deathbed even; maybe you'd be trying to describe the tunnel and the light, and your nurse would turn away and yawn. It was an incurable condition you had, and Nastasia and Shannon had married you because either you'd managed to initially do a good job of hiding it, or—more likely—they'd wanted your money. The next evening, when you got home from work and told Shannon a story about how Jitka Stehnova had saved Windsolver three million dollars by redesigning a series of circuits in the turbine casing, you heard it, her false "wow," the same sort of "wow" someone might give a sausage dog at a circus. She had no interest in or need of you beyond the fact that you'd increased the quality of her financial life by powers of ten, and she'd probably leave you just like Nasty left you, and this time, if this marriage lasted long enough, she might take half.

Half your money, but also half your hope. Half of this warm, vibrant chiaroscuro you'd gotten used to living since you met her.

And so when you saw her there in the hotel room with the girl, you felt the solution to a problem had just dropped right out of the sky. "This child has no parents," she told you, and she seemed so wrought about it that you didn't even ask how she knew. "Look at these," she said, taking the child's shitstained panties out of the hotel trash can to thrust them at you, and you said, "Don't show me those."

You'd been trying to get her pregnant for the whole two years you'd been married but nothing had happened, and bless her heart, out of some sort of fear about your psyche, she hadn't yet asked you to stop. You'd known, even before you offered to get motility testing, that it was her—it wasn't you. If it was you, then how could you have needed all those jimmies over the years? And every month, when she got her period and cried, you could feel the sadness and regret trying to stretch from her heart to yours, but your body was too hardened with fear for it to actually permeate, because every month she wasn't pregnant was one more month that she was free to leave you, to serve you with your second set of divorce papers, to turn your world back into a silent movie.

And so you called the team leader from Denmark and told him you guessed jet lag had finally caught up with you and you needed a long lunch break, and you sat in the hotel room watching the girl watch you while Shannon went to the Aswak Assalam and bought her five sets of new clothes. She had dresses still on the hangers and wrapped in plastic, shirts with ruffles on the sleeves, two pairs of patent leather shoes with hearts appliqued along the straps, and you wanted to ask, *wait—how long are we keeping this child?* but something told you not to.

And you went along with it, and you took them both downstairs to the hotel dinner that night, and then you called the home office in Louisville to tell them another lie, that your wife had come down with some sort of gastrointestinal mess and you needed a couple of days to take her to a better medical infrastructure, and you hustled her and the girl up to Rabat, to the American embassy, where you told more lies and shelled out five hundred American dollars in bribe money and showed the child to a doctor who signed off on her health. You got Shannon to offer her brick of weed to the security guard, who let you in the embassy without an appointment—she was that much of a dope fiend, you had to spell it out for her, how she could either take a child or a brick of weed back to the States, but not both; she was going to have to *make a choice here.* You paid five thousand dirham to the consular employee, who created a birth certificate saying your new daughter was born June 15, 2018 (an inside joke for you, the day Uruguay beat Egypt), and then you got her a temporary passport, and an IR-4 visa, and the next thing you knew you were back in Marrakech, at Menara Airport, waiting for your wife's plane.

Everything okay? came a text from Jitka while you were sitting on the hard bench at the airport, and you ignored it, not because you weren't on fire wanting to simply touch Jitka's naked hand by now, but because you needed time to think; every time Jitka opened her mouth to speak, little moths swam in your belly. When you returned to Essaouira, without your wife in the country, things might turn messy. You almost hoped they would.

And it shocked you, truly, how you could create another person's entire identity in the course of four days, and when you were sitting there in the airport the old fear came back, that this had all been too easy, and that somewhere in the chilly air between Africa and North America your wife would take on the vacant stare she'd been giving you lately, and she'd have six airborne hours to think about it, and you'd lose her anyway.

The fear was still there when the Royal Air Maroc clerk finally found your daughter's hastily booked plane ticket after thirteen minutes of trying, and the fear was there, palpable as an actual living thing, as you all three sat in the Menara Airport lobby for the requisite two hours before the flight. The fear was there when Shannon texted you to confess, as a joke, that the female security agent who'd screened her at the x-ray belt had squeezed her breasts while searching them, and she was on the plane still blushing, and she thought something had definitely happened between them—*haha*—and the fear was there when she texted to say they were still sitting on the runway, waiting for air traffic control to release them.

"We made it," she finally texted you when they did. "See you on the other side."

You imagined your new daughter, looking out the window in wonder. She and your wife would soon reach cruising altitude, 7.5 miles off the surface of the earth, 157.5 miles from space, 4.5 percent of the way there. You were a family now, and you might never end.

XX. North America

Outside me, beyond skull and muscle and a thin layer of skin, is a new land of clear air and lush, emerald grass. Sun, when it shines here, lends a different quality to light: it burns at once weaker yet more efficiently, infusing the soil with a power that will grow anything it wants. Apples and pears are so large and shiny that the people here don't dice and scrape them into harira or tajine. The American woman peels an unblemished apple and leaves it whole for my mouth; my mouth eats it. The juice hits the nerves in the tongue, changes their proteins, travels the old neural road to hit me. Apples are sweet and sugary. Plump. In the new land, I enjoy them.

What I refuse to let the body enjoy is sleep. Instead, I make the vocal cords scream all night, at a pitch that brings the American woman to tears. Her man paces around, rubbing his bald head, further worrying the sparse hair he has left. The frontal lobe is just beside me, but even when it begins to learn the man and woman's language, it screams all night, even when it can finally manage the words it has learned from their own vicious infighting: "I hate you."

When the woman picks the body up out of bed and says, "It's okay," I remember how she said those words over and over again on the plane, and I get the lungs to increase air and volume. The woman tries to hug the body to herself as it screams, tries to rub the back with a knuckle, the way someone has no doubt told her to do. But I press the eyes closed and I tell the back to arch, because I never meant for her to bring the body here, and now, there's no way to go back.

The synapses give me this code, which transmits into memory: a day in the cliffs of Diabat, where my mmi sits on a pocked boulder, watching me balance on the smaller rocks near the ocean. Wind assaults us both; it takes my mother's hair, tears it into shreds that fly high above her head. Just close enough for us both to hear, a very white woman in a fuchsia wetsuit falls off her surfboard. She flails and screams, though the code in the synapses says that the screams are of someone who knows she will be okay no matter what happens. Her instructor yells from the beach. "Go still," he says. "Be very still, and you'll get yourself to safety."

So I do this now, as the woman picks up the body—I make the body go stiff as a plank, because that's what might have prevented her from taking me in the first place. When I do that, the man and the woman they work together—one of them takes the ankles and the other holds the body from under its armpits, and they take the body outside because someone has clearly told them to do that also. They exhaust themselves handling the weight of me down the stairs, so once we're all outside, they have to leave me on the ground next to the pool. Still, I keep the body screaming. Once, I made the body roll right into the pool, pajamas and all. The woman dove in and hauled me out, but still I kept the body screaming. She knelt beside me, whispering, "It's okay it's okay it's okay shhhh," right in the ear, but that just made me tell the body to scream louder, because nothing was okay, not at all.

One night, when I was making the body scream, someone

next door came outside. The bones of the ear heard the patio door slide on its groove, but then they heard the person say nothing. This person, they live alone in a huge brick house with candles in all eight windows; the candles, they blaze all night. It is one more unbelievable thing about this land, how everyone lets everything burn, how light bulbs glow so softly under the frosty globes that the people here forget about them all night. The candles next door, I wondered at first how they didn't melt down to their wicks, why they were always standing at the same level of attention, but then one night, I climbed out of my room and made the body go downstairs and unlock the front door, just so I could go closer, stand in the bushes and explore. I'd been in the new land four months by then. I missed my mmi, the way she laughed with me and told me stories, and the skin missed the heat of the place it was born, and the vestibule of the ear, it missed the rhythm of the bus as it wound through the mountains.

The body needed to explore the new land, I knew, and the payoff was that there, in the bushes, the eye saw that the flames of the candles were actually currents running along drop-shaped electric filaments. The eye saw it, the cortex registered, but this is what I felt: that whoever lived in this big house, all alone, was every night afraid. Just like me.

But the American man, he saw me standing there in the bushes. He came off his front porch and grabbed me. Said something the cortex registered as "You trouble are a world." *World*, the cortex soaked up. *Trouble*. He grabbed the body and took it home, and then I made the lungs scream. I made them scream, scream, scream: "I hate you!"

Sometimes, when I make the lungs scream, I also make one of the hands wring the opposing wrist, to the point of burning the skin. The man and the woman, they hold the arms apart then, they look at each other knowingly and appear to think they're doing a great, gentle service, but I register it as a hurting, wrenching thing, a malevolence. They won't let me hurt the body even though the body belongs to me, and I can't figure out why, since they themselves have already hurt me so deeply.

Finally, the woman sings, in her language, which always makes the lungs stop screaming, despite my efforts. The woman, I can tell by the way her eyes relax then, thinks this means her voice is like the angels'. It is not. My mmi's voice is, and this woman's voice is nothing like my mother's. No. The frontal cortex stops the lungs screaming because the cortex has such deep interest in puzzling together the language. *You trouble are a world. You are world a trouble.* Once this puzzle is solved, the cortex tells me, the man and the woman might remove me on the plane. All I have to do is pass this test, of learning the language, and they will let the body back home.

And so I let it learn. I allow the frontal cortex to count to fifty; I let it absorb the words for *butterfly, cat,* and *frog.* One night, when the body is screaming, the man gets angry and tells the woman that this is all her fault, that she's made *one more shitty mistake.*

She tells him then. She tells him that the shittiest mistake she's ever made, in fact, was him. The man slaps her, but clumsily across the neck, where the frontal cortex thinks it probably didn't hurt. He screams at her that bringing me here was a *crime.* The frontal cortex then focuses on the word *crime,* and suddenly ding! ding! ding! understands that the man understands. *You are trouble world.*

The woman removes gluten and casein from the body's food in the daytime in order to make it sleep at night, but still, I don't let it. The man stops coming into the body's room at night to help the woman stop it screaming, and the frontal cortex tells me that maybe he's helping me instead, that he's plotting a way to get the body back on the plane and to home. In the daytime, the arm takes the bowl full of quinoa and flings it to the floor. The woman makes the body sleep under a purple blanket that has little weights sewn into its patches, but the body tosses it off and refuses to sleep. The body naps slyly, like a stray cat, all day long, when the man and the woman's routines of work and cleaning and television viewing do not allow them to sleep, so neither the man nor the woman ever truly goes to bed. "A vicious cycle," the woman tells the pediatrician in his office, but the cortex has to put that momentarily into the unsolved puzzle of the English language.

My name is Yumni, and though no one calls me it anymore, the whole of me knows this deeply all the way through the skin, through the skull, through the accordion folds of the cerebrum. The man and the woman, they call me Mardi. The cortex has the language to tell them otherwise, but it does not see the reward in doing so, so it doesn't. "Mardi," they say, "please eat your eggs." Or, "Mardi, please fold your washcloth. Good job, Mardi. Gooooooood job, baby."

One day, the woman comes upstairs looking sad, sadder than the eyes have seen her since the body got tired and gave up screaming. "Mrs. Ganes is going for a surgery," she says. And we've never met Mrs. Ganes, but the woman asks me to make her a card, and the body does this—it works together to draw a picture of sand and a beach, and brown people playing soccer ball while white people surf. But something has happened so that only I understand what the body has drawn a picture of—not the cortex or the cerebellum that helped draw it—and when the woman comes and takes the card, she takes in a sharp breath and puts her hand over her mouth, because she remembers sweet home too. She stares at me for one second. But then I feel the body smiling, and the cortex wanting the woman's approval, so when she smiles back, I remind the body and the cortex and the rest of the cerebrum of nothing.

And then, the woman is sad all the time. Mrs. Ganes dies, and someone else moves into the brick house. The new person, really people—five of a family plus a dog—leaves off the candle routine. The house is dark at night, so they can sleep, and I understand that they are less afraid than me and Mrs. Ganes. I understand they've never known what to be afraid of. They just do not know. The woman, whom I've begun to call *Mom*, as she's asked me to—she knows. She's sadder now. It's because she used to think she could control everything. But the cortex and I, we don't blame her, because everyone in the new land thinks this way. Everything here has a solution: the dirty dishes have a machine, the wet clothes have a big drying box. Food comes from a huge store that has clean food everywhere, no dust atop the pea tins. I want to tell *Mom* about eating out of a garbage bin, about wondering whether it might make me and my mmi sick after. I want to tell her about how it usually did. How we vomited in the sand, on the part of the beach the tourists never saw. I want to tell *Mom* about losing hope, how it's a process she'll get through.

But the body and I are older now, and *Mom* is too, and now the new sadness seems to have deepened into a pool she is swimming in with the man. I'm not entirely sure how *Mom* knows. I know because the man made the body go out with him and the other woman for la glace. Her name sounds like *Yitkeh*. The man loves her. I can tell because he looks at her like she is a fire. He listens to all her words, and when her hair falls into her ice cream, he pushes it behind her ear for her, as he might do if he were her father and not mine. She laughs at the way I mash ice cream in my mouth instead of eating it, and asks me whether I think there is this much time in the world, that we can wait for it to melt down my throat.

The woman talks funny like I do, in clicks, because she is from Poland, the man tells me in the car on the way home. She speaks Polish, just as he once did. She's teaching him Polish again, he tells me. *Mom* makes me call him *Dad.* The cortex tries to come up with a connection for this word, but cannot. *Mom* also makes me put on an actual dress before he comes home from work. She calls herself "encouraging hygiene," says, *Mardi, make sure you smell nice when your dad gets home.* She makes sure I've had a bath. The frontal cortex, the body, and I have all intuited that it's because of the woman. It makes me fall a bit in love with *Mom,* even as the body stays rigid when she comes in for a hug.

The folds of my surface develop, but there come these small hiccups in growth. Like this chink in the plan: the smell of my mmi. She smelled like makeup and argan oil, and the molecules of my mother would catch on the glomeruli (the cortex does not now know they are called that; one day it will). I have not managed to hold on to the memory of her face, but I do still have this—her hair. How the body would close in on an embrace when she came back to the riad at night, how the shiny pouf of her hair draped over the back of my neck and mingled with my own curls. How her hair was ripped apart by wind that day on the beach, though memory is a tricky code—you can reconstruct it any way you like. When it knows that I have to put my mother away, it dissolves her face into a vague blur of benevolence, the sun shining through her pouf of hair like a saint's halo. The background behind her changes as well—the sky shifts from a muted blue to a sharp gray; the cliffs that may have been sheer, they turn jagged. The synapses make determinations that protect themselves from harm—they decide what that day was, after all. The woman hugging her surfboard wears a suit that burns purple. In the reconstruction, she flails further, fearful, yet heedless of her own safety. The wind blows sand in my eyes. In this renovation of memory, it stings.

The synapses have stored the wax of my mother's lipstick, though impressions of my mmi stop other development in the cortex. The greasepaint she used as a base. Its smell. Its color. The faint outline of her lips, stamped on every used tissue in the wastebasket. Some nights she smelled so strongly of the after-dinner coffee she got in restaurants, but remembering doesn't make me feel good. The cortex knows neither how to articulate the feeling nor who it would articulate the feeling to, which makes it feel worse. It makes me feel so terrible, in fact, that it shows up as an ache in the body's throat. So as the folds deepen, they stuff this hiccup deep below; it's useless to remember.

When the cortex has absorbed eight rooms full of language, the woman takes the body to a place called *kindergarten*. The new land children are all around me. They don't understand everything I say, but in short order, now that it's motivated by people the body's same size, the cortex, it turns the word *cahk* into *cake*, it removes the khamsah from *kite* so that the inner pieces of the mouth are moving as might any other child's in the kindergarten. A year wears by, and the frontal cortex learns the numbers fifty to one hundred; it learns how to spool clay beads along a string; it learns how to color pages in the shades of the new land, how to decorate them with tractors and forests. It learns to give the farmer on the tractor two dots for eyes and a tiny parabola for a mouth. It learns how to imagine his shirt is flannel and color it bright red. It learns how to use a blue crayon for the trees when someone else has the green.

In May, the body walks across a stage in a blue hat perched on the head like a dish, and the body is surprised to find that it is finally one and the same with me and the cortex. The teacher hands me a paper she has called a *certificate*, and the mouth is delighted to find that it can repeat the word just as the other new land children. Later, in the car on the way home, while the man and the woman are sitting in glum silence, I read it. Not out loud, but in thinking the English language, the way I can do now. *Mardi Grenfell. Kindergarten. The J. Graham Brown School. On this 20th day of May, 2019.*

You are a world of trouble.

I can't remember my real name. I've gone through a tunnel. Inside, I lost it.

XXI. Louisville

In the five years she's been Mardi's mother, Shannon's never quite seen the girl make a proper dive. Mardi's jackknifed straight into the pool with her eyelids shut in delight, or she's cannonballed, yelping in anticipation of the cold water, her matchstick legs splayed out at angles like a frog's. Sometimes she leaned sideways into her eight-year-old consciousness and fell, her one arm held straight up in its own protest against gravity, the backs of her toes grazing the concrete as she went. Or she held her nose and yelled "Geronimo," abandoning all form whatsoever as she smacked her body onto the surface. But she never quite executed a dive, and Shannon felt slightly offended by her entrances into water.

Shannon herself rarely swam now, because of her cramps. Her bowels were sluggish; she moved them along in the mornings with coffee. The cramps were with her at all times, period or no—she hadn't visited a gynecologist since her last round of egg harvesting—but she intuited that the bone in her uterus had resolidified into a kind of crinoid fossil. It had grown heavier than the lining of the uterus itself; it was stabbing her there, in deepest womanhood, reminding her. She'd stolen another woman's child. She who had never before stolen so much as a drugstore mascara, she who had never been competitive or cloying or grasping? She'd made the ultimate id-driven choice.

She was having a pool party for Mardi's seventh birthday, but she didn't even know what that was. Her real mother, of course, would have known. The birth certificate, issued now from the state of Kentucky, offered June 15. But Vlad had chosen this at random, in his consular hurry. They'd never discussed it. They'd never between them determined, even, to tell Mardi that she wasn't theirs. "She'll wonder why she has no baby photos," Shannon had said one night in bed.

In early summer the sun set late, and at nine o'clock Vlad had been reading, studying specs by the remaining light of day. "She was screaming like a crack baby," he said. He slid his glasses down so she could see his eyes rather than the reflected sunset glare of his lenses. "You really think she's going to remember being adopted?"

But Shannon knew. There'd been nothing wrong with Mardi—the screaming had started after they were well in America. The little girl she'd hustled down the alley to the Dolce Freddo had been fine. Happy, even. Shannon just hadn't seen it. She hadn't seen it because she'd seen only herself, her own need. She'd settled her head into normalcy by erasing Mardi's Moroccan identity. On school forms, she checked the box for African American. Christmases and Easters, they all attended a Southern Baptist service. It was the new slave transport, Shannon thought. No one knew Mardi wasn't Black. Not even Mardi herself.

Mardi broke the water now, and a school of bubbles broke free of her braids to float to the surface. Mardi receded into the shadow of the trees' reflection and then swam the length of the pool. She smacked the tile wall with her palm and spun underwater once, then twice, just like a trick dolphin, turned a somersault at the five-foot mark before surfacing for breath. She launched onto her back and propelled herself. Again she broke the reflection of the trees, then swam past a skim of dead insects and floating leaves that Shannon hadn't bothered to net since the initial descent of autumn. It'd been weeks.

The lawyers had written into her divorce decree that Vlad would do all the yardwork until the house was sold. Vlad had insisted on this provision in order to preserve the curb appeal even though it was Shannon who mostly benefited, Shannon who could steep in her pain, smoking weed as Vlad meticulously pruned the bushes outside her living room window. Her mother, in all her divorce-veteran wisdom, had expressed delight: "I would have killed for a built-in yardboy," she said. "Marshall never would have done that."

In a fit of weed-inspired generosity, Shannon had broken the fourth wall and confessed all to her mother. She told her about Jitka Stehnova, and about the mountain of medical and student loan debt her lawyer had had to produce during discovery. She told her about Vlad's peculiarities, his bad temper, the flatulence she'd endured each day after he ate his brie. "It happens," her mother had said soothingly. "It's hard to live with another adult. Nothing to be ashamed of if you grow up and kill that."

Her mother offered to babysit Mardi the day of the prove up, when Shannon and Vlad stood before the judge, signing the final draft of the final document. Afterward, she repaired from the courthouse directly to her mother's house in St. Matthews, where she found Mardi in her mother's lap, crying, the both of them rocking in her grandmother's antique cherry glider.

"You hadn't told her?" her mother said. "I had to tell her. You weren't going to go on pretending she was something you *made*, were you? You weren't going to let her go on believing—"

She'd gathered Shannon's reddening face then, and stopped herself.

Let it go, said Shannon's gut. In the kitchen beyond, her mother had the television going, loud enough to compensate for her dwindling hearing. Jeffrey Epstein had been found swinging from the ceiling of his cell, a reporter was saying, and Shannon wanted to listen to the news and just let her mother's latest affront go, didn't she? They were getting along these days, weren't they? *Let it go let it go let it go,* her gut whispered, but when the whispering rose to the back of her throat, it came out as something else altogether.

"All those years," she said, "I never asked you to be my mother. And all those years you weren't. And now, you go and do this?"

Her mother dipped her head slightly, looked up with eyes gone crepey with age. "I was never your mom?" she asked, in a voice gone yarny and soft.

She looked like a wounded animal, and Shannon closed her eyes to remember her as a younger, harder woman in order to say it. "I'll tell you one thing—you don't get to be the same kind of shitty as a grandmother."

Shannon removed Mardi from her mother's arms, carried her out to the car, and fastened her in her booster seat. She was waiting for her mother to come out the front door, make a plaintive appeal in front of her neighbors, but that didn't happen. Shannon was both relieved and saddened when it didn't.

The season had made silkscreen of the sky, with indigo storm clouds mottling the arctic blue of the passing calm. The sun backlit this tableau, blanching the tree limbs white, and Shannon wished instantly that Vlad were there to see it. She'd loved him at some point, she supposed; of course she had. You didn't live in a house twenty-four hours a day with a man and not fall a bit in love with him, no matter how loudly he gargled saltwater or how carelessly he dripped coffee across the kitchen floor. You fell in love with the way he caulked holes in time, the way his gravity became a thing you could orbit around as you hurtled through space.

She wondered when she'd stop remembering him at all, when she'd get back to the point of wanting a storm front purely and only for herself, then thought how silly—she was the luckier of the two of them. "Mardi," she said, as she turned the engine, "look at the sky, baby." She'd share all the skies of this life with her daughter, who was, in any case, the only person who could perceive all their pure wonder. Her daughter, whom she thought she'd never meet. Shannon was 100 percent Mardi's, now that Vlad was gone. She didn't even have to share that.

Now, sitting at her own pool, she heard the loud European cylinders of Vlad's car turning into the driveway beyond the privacy fence. She left Mardi in the pool and went to watch her from just inside the open door; she stayed hidden behind the curtains of the kitchen that was now hers and hers alone. She watched as Vlad took shears out of the trunk of his car, then trimmed the hedges, which did not need trimming. Shannon listened to this futile snipping that went on for ten minutes, and then to the stilted conversation he had with Mardi about her math homework. When finally she heard his car gurgle back down the street, she rolled herself some weed and went back out to her pool.

He'd be back the following week for the same kind of maintenance, because she'd told him this half-truth, that the pain in her uterus had spread to her back, and she could barely move. He said he was happy to do her the favor, which was, she knew, also a certain kind of untruth. A cascade of lies between them, then. When the house was shown, people always wanted to walk through and see the pool. She began neglecting it out of a kind of scorched-earth malice.

When they'd first gotten back to the States that Sunday morning when Mardi was sleeping off the difference between GMT and Louisville, and Shannon was nervously stuffing crepes, Mardi had tiptoed downstairs and surprised her. Mardi had fallen asleep in the airport limo the night before. She'd struggled, because she'd wanted to see all the sights in the new country, the streetlamps and highways and skyscrapers, but when they hit the darkness of I-64, she'd given in to fatigue. Shannon had taken her upstairs and put her in their bed still in her street clothes—it wasn't as though she had children's pajamas, just waiting for the universe to produce a toddler who would fit them.

Mardi came downstairs that morning still wearing the green polyester dress Shannon had gotten her at a shop in the medina, still clutching the matching purse, which she'd opened and shut endlessly through layovers at Schiphol and JFK. In Schiphol, Shannon had bought her a lip gloss with the words I LOVE HOLLAND scripted on its side, just so she'd have something to look at when she opened the purse. Even when the stewardess brought dinner somewhere over Halifax, Mardi had held on to her purse strap, eating a buttered roll with her one free hand.

Shannon had drifted in and out of sleep on the flight, waking each time to find her legs doing their butterfly thing—*open shut open shut open*. She couldn't remember the last time. Maybe high school, maybe not even then. Bad things had happened, yes, but in all those years nothing had ever been this solidly her fault as to trip her central nervous system. The man in the seat next to her noticed. He gave her legs a particular kind of side-eye. Shannon assured herself, each time she fell back asleep, that Mardi had no living parents. Who had she stolen her from? No one but an alley. She'd done the best thing for all concerned. At long last, she'd taken a split second and made a fine decision with it.

In New York, after they'd passed through customs and had Mardi's passports stamped, Shannon felt, through the pain in her neck, how tensely she'd been holding her shoulders. Back in Louisville that morning after, she'd felt an undeniable release, and when finally Mardi came downstairs she stood there, staring through wet eyelashes as Shannon stirred batter. The air between the two of them seemed to stop circulating. Shannon was someone's mother now, no matter how it had been accomplished. It was the highest sign of American success, and she'd acquired it. A hundred forty-seven thousand dollars in medical debt, a student loan balance the size of a mortgage, but she'd jumped the gameboard spaces over *debt* and slid straight into the *parenthood* safe spot at the board's center. She was, at long last, an American adult.

"Viens," she said then, though she'd come to understand, in the procession of Moroccan hotels on their way out of the country, that the child knew no French whatsoever. "Crepes," she said. "Le petit déjeuner."

Mardi clung to her leg, muttering fearful Arabic.

"You'll be fine," she said. But she felt a smile stretch the skin around her eyes in a way that wasn't true.

The first year, Mardi never wanted to sleep alone. Mornings, after Vlad left for work, she snuggled with Shannon. Often during the first year, Mardi had the grippe, but still she wanted to sleep with her nose against Shannon's, breathing illness and 104-degree fevers into her mother's face for hours at a time. Shannon didn't mind. She felt it was her responsibility to contract whatever Mardi had. She'd have some small portion of how the child felt.

Yet Mardi would refuse to speak to either her or Vlad for days at a time; silently, she'd shovel cereal into her mouth while watching Sesame Street, and then, when the program ended, would rise from the couch to come over and look at Shannon. "I think Daniel Tiger's on next," Shannon would offer, but Mardi wouldn't return to the sofa. She couldn't stop staring at Shannon. Wouldn't stop staring at Shannon. Shannon would be garnishing dinner salad, and there Mardi would sit, in a chair behind the kitchen bar, watching. Just watching. Shannon would fix her a juice and stop to watch Mardi watching her, feeling a vague, incalculable misery for them both. Sometimes Shannon would fall to a midmorning nap on the couch, only to find Mardi hovering inches above her face when she woke.

Mardi was driven about it. When Shannon excused herself to the bathroom, Mardi would stand there, digging her toes into the carpet, watching her even as she closed and locked the door. When Shannon finished her business on the other side of the door and opened it, Mardi would be right there still, standing at attention, having never left her post. Her silence was like a scream. She knew that Shannon had made a terrible decision; she knew Shannon lived otherwise in a purgatory of inertia. She knew already that Shannon was a nonfunctioning adult, landed only at the mercy of this judgmental Rasputin with his oversized ears. With nothing of her own. Doing nothing of her own. Mardi didn't have to say it because she was staring it. Silently projecting it onto the whiteboard of Shannon's mind, her own personal horror movie.

Shannon played charades with Mardi, acting out language the girl didn't yet understand. She ordered an Arabic-language DVD to teach herself, but it was the wrong Arabic—classical.

Saudi Arabic, Vlad explained. Conqueror Arabic. Mardi never responded when Shannon pronounced the phrasings, so she gave up learning them.

When spoken to directly, Mardi would climb into the clothes dryer and shut the door on itself, as if its iron vent were portal to some other, better world. Her second Halloween in America, when Shannon was busy hemming the pants of her C3PO costume, Mardi climbed in the dryer and fastened the door; the machine, still set on its cycle, turned itself to spinning. Shannon heard a horrifying thud and knew they were all so lucky that she'd been just standing there sewing, pretending not to watch.

She pulled the door open and removed Mardi, who clung to her like a staticky sock, shrieking. What flashed through Shannon's mind then were all the awful moments that might have happened: Mardi's neck snapped at an irreparable angle, a telltale blue spot on her skull where the internal bleeding had already started. None of that had happened, mashallah. Mardi would get to live her little life. Grow up as Shannon's daughter. Maybe find out, through hypnotherapy or psychic hotline, that she'd been kidnapped. Maybe not.

After Vlad moved out of the house, there had cooked, slowly, a period of fondness between them: the child's eagerness to work through first-grade readers; the sweet smile she gave Shannon the day she learned to ride without training wheels. "I love you," Mardi said then, whooshing past, and Shannon wanted to believe the sentiment was real and not just a newly discovered linguistic outlet.

She lost her accent, and even constructed a fabulist history for herself—she'd come from a place called Birdyland, she said. She spoke regularly to the birdie mother when she played in her room, when she didn't know Shannon was standing just to the side of her open door, watching from the hall. *Daddy tried to give me an octopus at the restaurant*, she'd tell the mother bird, curling her hand around her mouth and turning her head at an angle, as if the animal were standing right beside her, *but I didn't want to hurt it, so I wouldn't eat it.* Shannon pictured a mother bird, a blue jay or a robin, an unarmored little animal who couldn't possibly have a real place in her daughter's heart.

When joint custody began, and the first time Vlad showed up for Mardi, he sent Jitka to the doorbell. "I want to introduce myself," Jitka said when Shannon answered. Shannon had thought she was a woman doing door-to-door sales.

She saw Vlad's new Mercedes in the distance, waved toward it. "Your green card's out there in the car," she said, closing the door on Jitka's look of shock. She sent Mardi out to the Mercedes alone.

When Mardi returned, she was wearing a new pair of jeggings and carrying a stuffed bear as big as her own body. Vlad had given her a speech at Applebee's, she said.

"Sweet Jesus. What did he say?"

"He said him and Yitkeh would take care of me now, 'cause you couldn't."

Shannon snatched the bear from Mardi's arms. She didn't intend to do anything; she just wanted to hold him while she spoke. The bear's head was lodged in the crook of her neck. He smelled like six pounds of solid formaldehyde. His fur made her chin itch. Shannon felt wild grains of rice swimming in her head.

"Some men aren't meant to be fathers," she said. She tried to give the bear back, but Mardi ran upstairs. Shannon rolled a joint and went out to the pool. She fell asleep in one of the chaises Vlad had left. She slept well. She slept until evening, and woke with sunburned cheeks.

"Watch me, Mom," Mardi said now, as she spun back over and breaststroked, seamlessly as a naval torpedo, back up the length of pool. The water reflected clouds, fluffy as new bread. Mardi swam through them. She popped her head through the water. "I love you the way I feel sorry for a monkey!" she said.

"A squirrel might be small, but if it's rabid, it kills you!" Shannon yelled back.

The nonsense of the game brought forth from Mardi a triumphant grin that she sunk back under water.

Shannon warned her, "It's almost supper." But she doubted her voice carried past the surface.

Vlad hadn't been by in a couple of weeks. He was off in Nicaragua building a viaduct, reveling with Sandinistas, spinning eggs from straw. Fucking Jitka while graphing papers curled on the bed beneath them—Shannon no longer cared. There in Louisville, she and her daughter were alone, magnificently alone, and it was another of those emptying nights when the shadows turned to dark, and the dark turned complete, and finally she switched on a fluorescent light and wondered, in terror, whether she was entertaining enough for a six-year-old.

Still, it beat being married. If ever she'd confessed fear to Vlad, he would have laughed at her. Used her paralysis for his own upper hand. *I told you so*, he would have said. *Why did you steal this kid?* From Shannon's upset, he never subtracted, only added. Like anyone good at operations and calculations, he continually increased the efficiency of his own closed system.

"Can we have pizza?" Mardi asked.

"Sure."

"With pineapples?"

"Why not."

Back in the kitchen, as she laid the pizza, Shannon saw Mardi through the patio door, topping the steel pool ladder, taking a few steps from the pool's edge, wrapping herself in a hot-pink Princess Tiana beach towel. Mardi had declared her own bed the week before, said seven was too old to be sleeping with a mommy. Now, when Shannon woke to the cold mattress and the growing pain in her groin, she figured it was exactly what she deserved. Her mother had told Mardi she was adopted, yes, but only Shannon knew the lasered truth of it; only she knew what had been undone and unraveled in a medina alley. The decision of revelation would always be hers, to keep shitty or clean.

Shannon diced canned pineapples into smaller pieces to cover the pizza, and pressed her abdomen into the counter in a bid to stanch the pain. Through the kitchen window, she watched Mardi drop her towel and jump into the pool again. But it was Shannon saying it, to her injured pineapples: "Geronimo."

XXII. Essaouira

The score was this, that people expected Souria to cover her sadness with anodyne, as if it were a fresh coat of paint. She knew people who'd loved Yu—Nasr, and Hafiza, and Driss—but they could not accept grief past the expiration date they'd marked for it. In small and large moments, they notified her: when she found herself gazing at the empty alley, Nasr would ask, in near whisper, whether she wanted to go home. When Souria asked Hafiza how often she cried for her son, whether the measure was weekly, daily, or hourly, Hafiza turned away and sorted her husband's soaps. When Souria handed the bus driver her six dirham, and he saw, anew, the tears brimming in her eyes, he waved her away rather than having to graze her cold fingers while handing over the ticket.

No one wanted to touch grief. Grief did not drop by to visit them at unappointed hours. But Souria would be walking the boardwalk and have to stop in her path, grief still held her that tightly. She'd be shuffling from one point of the souk to another, having forgotten not to look at children's clothing. She'd see a European couple in an open-air restaurant and hear them saying, in French, how très mignon was another small Moroccan child, skipping across the courtyard. Her grief was like sour candy, to be digested and redigested until it melted away.

Each night in her flat in Diabat was a year. There was an entire season in which she cooked herself the tiniest bit of dinner rice, another season in which she sat, astonished at both her inability to eat and her inability to starve. In a year's time, if she still hadn't found Yu, she would stop eating. She would cease meaning anything to anyone else. For now, she still had hunger, because she still had hope.

There was a third season those nights in Diabat, the hours she listened to the waves of the Atlantic not even a quarter of a mile beyond her window, of imagining her daughter stuffed into a shallow grave or drowned in the ocean, the hours she tried to press down that imagining. Then would come the fourth season of crying, sometimes so hard that she could not eat even one bite of the rice she'd plated for dinner. A fifth season of sleep that was not truly sleep so much as it was a release of sadness onto the dream realm. In her sleeping wakefulness each roar of the waves brought sorrow. When she woke in the middle of the night gasping, and looked out her window to the stars, she found that they were the same stars of the Sahara, but she no longer remembered them.

She knew, because grief told her as much between dreams, that she could not share her sadness with the fiddler. She wouldn't even try, because after a space of time he, too, would have refused to accept it, and a refusal from someone she was growing to love to such a degree would make the grief bigger in her hands, so unsizably big that she would no longer be able to carry it, and she had no imaginings of what would happen then.

She was relieved that Anass had already been gone when Yu disappeared, so he did not have to witness her disintegration. He'd taken his bus north to the gendarmerie school, leaving her with a mailing address on a scrap of paper and a chaste peck on the cheek. In the beginning he wrote her letters care of Nasr's shop address, because he didn't know she wasn't illiterate beyond the signing of her own name.

She mailed him back packages with cigarettes and freshly baked bread that would go stale and hard on its way to Zoumass. He understood in an instant, because there was no accompanying letter, that she could not absorb correspondence, and what he mailed her, after that, were photographs of his school and his friends, the other men at the gendarmerie. He mailed her a photo of shirts and underwear hanging on a line—laundry was a new experience for almost all the men, and he thought the photo might capture the novelty.

She began to understand the viewings of his letters as spaces that grief could not touch, squares that would let her move forward, let her live another day until Yu returned. She mailed him biscuits and candy, and he mailed her back photos of miners in Western Sahara, and her nights grew full. She'd look at his photos, studying them until she knew the colors and objects in every centimeter of each photograph; she'd tack them to the walls and imagine, if Anass was pictured, the name of the man who had taken the shot; she'd imagine what the weather smelled like, and whether Anass had taken the photo on a full stomach. When the wind off the Atlantic died down enough for houseflies, they would occasionally alight on the photos and fill her with an unexpected sense of peace.

In this way, she filled her evenings and her dreams. She'd played games in the sand as a child, and it was much the same: even after the sand blew away her marks, the pleasure came from the marks in her mind that remained.

When Anass finished the school and returned to Essaouira, when she bent her face into his neck and smelled his sweat and his aftershave, his bravado and his salary from the kingdom of Morocco, what had there been for her to say? In her excitement, the evening he returned, she'd cut her hand on the broken end of a glass bottle she brushed against on a wall in the souk, but a week later, the cut was healed. The world, she noted now, had spun something new. She'd not exhausted hope. Yu would come back—she'd always known that—but she had arrested the progression of her own grief. She'd even exhausted any language she had for it. She had nothing to tell anyone she loved about Yu beyond the day the child had disappeared. She had nothing to speak of a child who might then have turned twenty-eight, and then twenty-nine months, so she found nothing she wanted to say about the child at all.

"That small girl?" she told Anass the first day he went to work, in his new blue uniform with its crisp dark coat. "You misunderstood about her. She was my little cousin."

He hadn't asked further. Not even once did he ask further.

XXIII.Louisville

It's something she wondered about at times, in the car lane at the Brown School, whether the biological mothers all around her ever felt that they, too, had just happened on the surprise of parenthood. Whether it felt to them like the same kind of floaty happenstance, or if there were something that accompanied blood and DNA and fucking, a force that cemented as soon as the sperm hit the egg. A phylogeny that automatically taught them to pop their breasts into waiting mouths, let them smell the biochemistries of their infants' rotten moods before they edged into cries. She wondered whether she was the only one just making this all up as she went. Pulling it out of her adoptive mothering ass.

She wondered about these men and these women who seemed so damn *parental*. There was Bernadette Rachel, the mom of second-grade twin boys, whose shiny green minivan seemed freshly spat out of a car wash. Had Bernadette ever gotten drunk and gone home with a man she'd just met? Had the man discovered, when he got her back to his apartment and undressed her, just how much padding stick-thin Bernadette had in her bra? And had Bernadette laughed when he laughed, and fucked him anyway?

She wondered about Leslie Welch, the nervous, quiet mom

who sent her daughter to school in flowered headbands to match her dresses. Had Leslie ever been so broke that she'd had to scrape her remaining lipstick out of its cap? Marla had come over for a playdate once and, without asking, rummaged through Shannon's kitchen cabinets. She'd found a bottle of glue and some pink mylar confetti, which she'd squeezed and mixed together on a piece of paper until the glue soaked through to Shannon's dining room table. At pickup, Leslie apologized. Shannon told her no worries—the table had character now. But she wondered. If she hadn't miraculously found her child in an alley in an actual kingdom, if she'd had to squeeze Mardi down her own narrow birth canal, wouldn't she have seen the glue, simply, as a measure of damage?

She wondered about the men too—she wondered about Bill Montague, who, on parent volunteer day, always signed up to bring his leaf blower. She wondered whether Bill had ever gotten drunk and smashed a table at his fraternity house, whether he'd ever taken a baseball bat to one of his ex-girlfriend's mailboxes. Always, always, she wondered whether the biological parents felt, as she did, that parenthood was one big masquerade. A Halloween costume that might never fit.

She'd never quite seen through her own husband; she'd never been able to tell. Mardi's second week in America, Vlad came home and removed his weight bench from one of the upstairs bedrooms. He had a canopy bed delivered from John Kirk Furniture; he'd picked it out himself. Shannon was proud of him. She'd tossed Moroccan fabrics over the high rails in an attempt to make Mardi feel at home, though the girl still toddled down the hall sniffling tears every night, her blanket trailing dangerously between her feet. Shannon and Vlad would scoot apart to let her sleep in the middle.

In a bid to make her fall in love with her own room, Vlad

painted the walls using a shade of azure somewhere between sky and sea, a shade the sea might turn if it were sick with food poisoning. He'd picked that out himself too. Mardi hadn't loved the walls blue any more than she'd loved them white. She'd screamed, still, at night. She wanted to go back to Morocco, to the true, vivid, haunt-bleeding blue of Essaouira. Back to her parents, whomever they were.

Postdivorce weeknights, Mardi slept still in Shannon's bed. It was a queen-sized four-poster, and now that there were only the two of them, they could stretch out and rest well. Weekends were different. Vlad came to collect Mardi an hour early on Friday and brought her back three hours late on Sunday. At her first-grade play, he made a point of finding seats exactly one row closer than Shannon's, so she'd had to look at the backs of his and Jitka's heads. What she was learning, postdivorce, is that people never loved each other so much as they were waiting to reveal good or bad hands. Occasionally she cried, not for what had happened between them, but for all the months and years the thing had *not* happened. People always said you didn't love what you had until it was gone, but it seemed to Shannon that she'd pretended to love Vlad too much before he left.

Had she ever loved? She wasn't sure. Had she *been* loved? She remembered some boys and then some boys—the first boy she'd ever kissed, Bob Prin; seventh-grade Bobby who became ninth-grade Bobby and then lost-her-virginity-to-junior-year Bob. They fucked in Bob's basement on his dad's pool table, and then he passed her a note in Algebra II: *Hey, sexpot. See you on the green.* They were sixteen when she dumped him to go to prom with Les Guyton, a senior who drove his dad's handed-down Porsche. Bob had passed her his last note: *It is like you are turning a knife in my heart.* But that was just a song lyric. A line from an after-school special. It wasn't love.

And then there were boys and more boys, boys in college and boys in grad school, but it was no longer politically correct to call them *boys* or even *guys*, because the twenty tens had just turned and you were supposed to call them *men*, and so there was a man at the beginning of the end of her MA in comp lit, a man six years older than her and a concert pianist in the College of Fine Arts. Between fits of writing his dissertation on Chopin, he was an accompanist for the ballet classes, but even after being around all those tiny, limber ballerinas all afternoon, he wanted only to fuck Shannon, which she couldn't believe.

He proposed to her, so casually it might have been a joke, one warm spring evening while they were swinging in a city park. The sun had been setting, a flaming ball of fruit disappearing behind the budding trees, right over the edge of the earth they both faced while swinging through the warm air. *Shannon, will you marry me?* he'd asked, and she'd laughed.

Three planes flew overhead—the sun was that clear of clouds, she could see them—and exhaust trails jutted out behind them in three intersecting lines, orange with the sun's setting. *I'm serious,* he said, and when she just smiled at him, which was her way of more clearly saying no, he pumped his legs harder, swung his arc higher than hers. *Well have a nice life then,* he yelled down. One backandforth, two backandforths, three backandforths, and blammo, the sun disappeared, and they were swinging under a glistening Venus and she was hoping they could at least have sex afterward, anyway?

There was some fifth dimension of young, misguided love. Love's blistering, tangible manifestations filling a vortex that no one could see. Books purchased and inscribed to the wrong man, two-carat tennis bracelets engraved for the wrong girl. Lovebird suites booked and then canceled, minus the deposit, before the vacation could ever happen. If you pierced the veil that hung over this dimension and got close enough to brave the searing heat, what would happen?

You'd melt, she thought. And who the fuck wanted to melt?

She wanted a job. A job suitable for a bitter divorcée: challenging, but with enough flexibility to absorb her low moods. She had no idea what kind of career might be available to a thirty-five-year-old woman with half a comp lit degree and half a scarred face. She went to hock her wedding ring, but the ice-blond woman at the mall jewelry counter told her it was worth $293, not even half of her half of the half-hers mortgage. "Save it," the woman told her. "You say you have a daughter? Maybe one day she'll want it. She'll want to know her parents loved her enough to get married and make her." Shannon hadn't corrected her. Everyone presumed you'd proceeded through biology, and she never felt like correcting a single one of them.

She also did not sell the ring, though she hated having a diamond-studded keepsake of her miserable time as someone's wife. It seemed gaudy, like something you'd have after a weekend of throwing up buffet food in Vegas. But after all, it was a two-carat solitaire that had cost Vlad eight grand. The idea of romantic love was a capitalist construct, true, and she hated the concept of marriage, but she didn't hate it *that* much.

On Glassdoor she found a part-time job at the Lighthouse Guild, reading material to the blind. She was paid per client, by the hour, and she got to be in high demand because she read slowly and dramatically, delighting in each line of text. Under the spell of her voice, a light bill might sound as richly textured as a Broadway musical, and the consumers—as Lighthouse called them—quite often asked for her by name. She'd developed the habit as a child, living with parents who didn't much amuse her. Her bedroom had faced west, and winter afternoons, in search of the sun's heat, she'd line up her Barbies facing the window. She'd come to stand in front of this classroom of dolls, reading all her favorite books aloud, and now, all these years later, it was a vocation. The job paid almost nothing, but it was an item of pride.

The consumers often needed their mail read to them, or they might request an entire hour of a novel, or a biography. Once, she was asked to read a manual on vacuum cleaner assembly. The consumer, a retired professor in his late sixties, had apologized. "I'm so sorry, young lady," he said. "I know you will find this interminably dull." But she'd glanced up from her reading long enough to assess the professor's facial expressions, and found him emoting a happiness more complete than any she herself remembered feeling. She drove home with the diagram still in her mind, the verve of each sentence of technical instruction infusing her own intact optic nerve. *Rotating brush!* she thought. *Fan! Exhaust port!*

About a month into her work, the Lighthouse had a small gala so that its readers and consumers could mingle with staff, and it was at this party that she met Brandt. He was lanky and quiet, with a long face like the Pennsylvania Dutch, and marbled blond hair that fell to his shoulders. Under the party's low lights, his corduroy coat looked inauthentically aged; like so many hipsters in downtown Louisville, he was a rich boy playing poor man. "Enchantée," he said when they shook hands. "Alice tells me you read French."

"I'll leave you two," said Alice, tapping her cane twice, as she always unconsciously did when she was ready to walk away. Shannon had noticed that those who'd been blind since birth lacked the self-consciousness of ever having seen their faces in a mirror, and she read Alice's smile: she was satisfied to have engineered this meeting. Brandt was single, then. Alice was nosy. Of course, she'd have asked him.

Shannon took a breath, dove in. "Tu parles français aussi?" she asked.

To his credit, she'd think later, he refused this as icebreaker. "Do you live near here?" he'd asked, instead. "Downtown? The Highlands?"

He'd gotten right to the point then, and they left the gala and ended up at dinner at Telio. Just after they were seated, Brandt excused himself to the men's room, and Shannon texted her mother.

Hey ma. Kinda tired actually. Can Mardi just stay the night?

There had lain a terrible fermata of digital silence during which her mother had not responded.

Ma, Shannon texted. *Please. This one time.*

Ice clinked in glasses. Undecipherable bits of conversation settled on the air. Somewhere in the kitchen, a waiter dropped what sounded like a stack of trays. They clattered. She imagined chips of plastic everywhere.

No toothbrush, her mother finally texted back. *No pajamas, no nothing.*

She can sleep in her clothes. One night won't kill her teeth.

Shannon this is not how I raised you.

Brandt was returning from the washroom, walking quickly through the tables and around the potted trees, a tiger in a jungle. She turned the phone facedown on the table, ignored the insistent buzzing that rattled its top.

"Dolmas?" he asked, and she nodded yes, but when they came they were too oily. They did not taste like food of the gods. Just leaves and rice. She smiled as she chewed, so as to seem good-natured and pliable. Dinner would be a tyranny.

Brandt seemed delighted. "Aren't these awesome?" he said around his chewing.

"Mmm," she said, because *mmm* wasn't a lie. Still, the phone

232

buzzed. It hadn't stopped. She neither flipped it back to its face nor tucked it politely away in her purse. Men liked intrigue. She remembered this from the time before she'd met Vlad. You were supposed to let them wonder.

After dinner, they went to his apartment three blocks north, where they ended up sleeping together while the TARC buses sighed outside his window. It was a one bedroom in a three-story walkup, and it faced not only the bus stop but a main entry to Cherokee Park, and the next morning, when she woke, she looked down through his open window at the people scurrying about, adjusting the angles of their backpacks, transacting their Saturday business on cell phones. She felt Brandt tracing an undiagnosable pattern on her back. She had grown accustomed to catching people's eyes roving down her face to the scar on her left cheek, but in all these hours, Brandt had not once looked. "Eggs," he asked her now. "Will you eat eggs?"

"If that's all you have," she said. But at the sky beyond the treeline, she smiled, languidly.

She fixed her face into neutrality before she met him in the kitchen. He was from Bangor, Maine, he'd told her over dinner, but he'd moved to Louisville to work on a friend's congressional campaign. It was a third-party run. The Greens. In the parking lot, she'd found all the right bumper stickers on the back of his car: IMPEACHMENT IS PATRIOTIC. JESUS WAS A SOCIALIST JEW. MY OTHER CAR IS A BICYCLE. She'd watched his face over dinner. From the blankness he returned each time she offered a smile, she intuited that he wasn't the kind of person who accepted them.

A two-seat kayak hung from a ceiling hook in the apartment's one other room, and as she ate her eggs she studied it, wondering if the second seat were a revolving door of sorts, reserved for whichever woman Brandt had offered breakfast and no additional information to on any given Saturday morning. They sat at a card table with two folding chairs, and when she bit into her egg, she felt tiny pieces of shell crunching between her molars. Brandt smeared Nutella on his toast. "You boat often?" she asked.

He shrugged his shoulders. "Pretty much every weekend. I'm just one more stereotypical Mainer in a line of stereotypical Mainers."

"Your dad? He boats?"

"*Boated*, past tense. He's dead."

"I'm so sorry."

"He killed himself."

"My God."

"I'm okay," Brandt said. And for the first time since she'd met him, he smiled. It was sincere, she felt. You could trust an unhappy person the way you could trust no one else. "Am I the first White guy you've ever slept with?" he asked.

She patted her head, as if there might be a thought bubble hovering above it, betraying her. "Yeah," she said, giggling to make the lie sound like the truth. She'd slept with plenty of White guys, but none of them had had Green Party bumper stickers. It seemed important, somehow, to give Brandt the answer he wanted. "Your dad—did he leave a note?"

"People do that in the movies. In real life, only a minority of people do. Which is okay too. It's not like Dad's mind was an algebra problem."

"It really didn't bother you, not to know?"

"The truth wouldn't have been in the note. My dad didn't care, not about anything or anyone. That was his deepest truth. I didn't need his honesty, because I already had my own."

They had this in common then, that they knew lack of relationship didn't mean lack. Having had an unconditionally loving parent would have been like having an eleventh finger, Shannon thought: she'd never had one, so how could she be hurt that she only had ten? The attachment other people had found in their parents, Shannon had found in sixteen bars from the Violent Femmes. She'd found it in her favorite Banana Republic sweater. She'd found it in weed. The projection of love she thought she should have might have hurt her, as might have love that was seriously flawed. But indifference? Absence? You simply couldn't miss something you'd never known.

She dressed to go back to the Lighthouse: she'd had a Friday afternoon cancellation that was now the 8:00 a.m. appointment she had to attend before she picked up Mardi. She was grateful that no other staff would be there on a Saturday—only the security guard who would admit her into the building—and that her consumer, a regular, was visually impaired enough he wouldn't notice she was wearing the same clothes she'd worn to the gala. At the street-level door to Brandt's building, he kissed her on the cheek. "Have a good time," he said.

She was retreating, in long strides, backward down the sidewalk toward her car. "Is it a good time?" she asked.

"Okay," he said. "What I mean is, enjoy yourself."

She was far enough away she had to yell it: "It's not about that either."

"Okay then," he yelled back. He smiled. It was the second of his she'd seen. "Have yourself some kind of time at work."

She waited in the paneled hall of the Brown School for her end-of-term parent-teacher conference. She thought of Brandt's father, dead of drowning or carbon monoxide or a gunshot wound— she hadn't thought it polite to ask—now mere bones under soil.

Simple people decried suicide as selfishness, viewed is an un-imaginable thing to do to one's children. Yet being a parent required so much extra fortitude in a life, so much courage that could just eventually run out, like gas. She herself fought the urge on an order of once a month. When she accidentally stabbed her eyelid with the mascara wand, or closed her finger in the silver drawer and felt the sharpness of that sudden pinch as a relief against the chronic pain at the base of her skull, she wondered why she lingered on. It was only when she remembered Mardi's frightened tears at the sight of a circus clown, or her sadness over a terrible classmate, that she knew she had to stay. No one needed her but her daughter, but her daughter needed her in totality. Who else but someone's mother would care about the parent-teacher conference?

She'd signed them up for Wednesday, the last day before Christmas break, in the last available slot. Just behind Edwin Rao's parents, whom she hated for being school pets, and just ahead of Penelope Tudor's parents—Ruth Tudor, who brought cookies for the class parties, and Derek Tudor, who manned the Crayola arts booth at Fall Festival. She forgave them both. The Tudors, at least, always smiled and said hello.

Mrs. Lin-Wood was behind schedule, so Shannon stood in the hall with Ruth and Derek, in a nuclear parent pileup. Vlad stood a good ten feet away, far enough to signal that he and Shannon were no longer friends but close enough, on the other side of the Tudors, to sandwich them between the damage. The Tudors felt the tension. Shannon knew it because neither of them spoke. At this shadow of silence, she threw a pebble: "What are you doing for the break?"

"China," Ruth said. She rocked happily on her heels.

Vlad turned his shoulder into the cinder-block wall so he could face them. "Work or fun?" he asked.

"Both," said Derek. "Exploratory trip for work, but also—it's our big day. We're adopting another girl."

"Whoa," Shannon said. She tried to arrange her face in a congratulatory grin. But she felt ruined on the inside. She couldn't put a finger on the emotion, so she stamped it down like a loose tissue in a trash can. "That's the trip of a lifetime. Will Penelope go too?"

"We're taking her," Derek said. "All the experts say to take the biological child. We want to, you know, do procedure."

Procedure, Shannon thought, that black licorice of words. "So she'll be here in time for Santa," she said.

"Yes, but we're not giving her presents this year," said Ruth, "because we want her to understand the real meaning of love. We want her first Christmas in America to be all about Jesus."

Shannon looked at Vlad and found a speck of light in his eyes that she'd never seen before, a hollow pocket of shine pooling in the brown of his iris. She wondered if he had some sort of growing cataract, or an undiagnosed retinal cancer.

"Mardi's adopted," he told the Tudors. As a rule, she and Vlad had never told anyone. Since Mardi was Black, no one ever asked.

"Yeah, it sucked," Shannon said, "but Vlad's boys couldn't swim."

Derek and Ruth excused themselves to a place halfway down the hall, where they pretended to study the classroom drawings. They pretended to concentrate, as if fifteen primitive sketches on a wall might hold the secrets against entropy.

After the conference, Shannon walked to the parking lot without putting on her coat, letting late December come in for its terrible hug. She drove through East Louisville, past the treacherous spot on the hill near her house, past the deflated Santa Claus in the yard that was being decorated only in stages. Santa lay, still dead to the fun, while inflated Rudolph pulled a plastic sleigh through strung lights. The night before, on her way home from Keva's, she'd approached the same winding hill and found the red and blue lights of police cruisers flashing in the frozen snow, reflecting themselves off tree trunks. The ice on the road, too, held the effect, the roadway showing up as one long colored disco ball. It was a terrible wreck: she saw the burned-out hull of a sedan, and an officer taking a statement. The emergency vehicle blockage had been such that she'd backed into a driveway and turned, seeking an alternate route. That night, post-conference, traffic flowed easily in both directions. Her daughter was doing fine in school. She was a wizard at math, just like her father. And the road had been plowed and salted clean. But some other person, some stranger, had been paralyzed, perhaps killed, mowed down only because time hadn't waited these intervening eighteen hours.

She pulled into her half-hers driveway, closed the half-Vlad's garage door behind her. Mardi was at his house for the weekend, and Shannon could smoke anywhere she wanted. But she waited before she took out her herb, breathed in the scent of the seven-foot Douglas fir she'd bought for Christmas. It smelled heavenly and pure, like primeval forests and marauding Vikings. It smelled almost good enough to save her.

"Balloon Adventure!" she called, when Mardi flipped over her card, and Mardi enacted the phrase, puffing her cheeks and floating around the living room with her two arms flung straight out at her sides to balance her soaring. She'd been sledding all morning, and now the cuffs on the sleeves of her wool sweater had dried and tightened enough that Shannon could see it was too small, how the lonely wrists jutted out too far.

Mardi came to land at her spot on the fireplace, then flipped over her own card. "Dancing Dolphins!" she read.

Shannon jumped up and pretended to bob in water, fused her legs shut as she shook her ass, so that she looked like a poorly shimmying dolphin, which made Mardi giggle. "Sorry, love, but it's about time we go," she said when she sat back down. "You've got to change clothes."

"It's just Grandma's."

"Yeah, but she sees you in wet clothes, she'll blow a gasket."

Mardi ran upstairs while Shannon put the deck of Wai Lana's Daydream back in order. When Vlad first moved out, they'd spend their Saturday afternoons at the movies, but he'd cut her down to the exact amount of child support, which made twenty-five dollars in movie tickets and popcorn seem frivolous.

Piggy Bear. She found the card's match.

Bubbles. She searched.

Vlad had plenty of money to share. But he was a joyless person who, out of hubris, was requiring her to be joyless also.

She put away the last of the matches—*Silly Seals*—and went upstairs to her bathroom, where she spread a liberal dose of foundation over her face. She lined her eyes with shadow instead of liner—no need to scare Brandt on a Saturday afternoon—and brushed on mascara. She blotted her lip gloss: for this boating Mainer, she'd be as conservative as Nancy Reagan. She turned to profile and smiled at herself, then relaxed her mouth into a pout. She found a frown line forming at one corner of her lips, where no laugh lines ran. It meant she'd laughed less than she'd been worried, angry, or sad, she guessed, though she remembered her life up to the point of Vlad having been more satisfying than that.

Flying Kite, they'd played. *Floaty Flowers.* Mardi was her hostage. She had to play cards. *Snorkeling. Banana Battle. Double Rainbow.*

In a month, Brandt had taken her kayaking on Lake Cumberland, and then to a jazz concert downtown, and to a salsa dancing class at the Y. Now, on a Sàturday morning, he showed her all the secret trails in Cherokee Park, the small ones that branched off from the big ones. She was afraid of snakes, even if she knew it was irrational in the winter. She didn't tell him. He grabbed her wrist when she seemed unwilling to follow. It was harder for her to walk then, with her body wedged at the angle he needed to make purchase on her thick coat sleeve, but she would not pull away, would not break this physical closeness.

"Can you vary your appointments?" he asked when they finished the trail. There'd been an ice cream stand open, it was so unseasonably warm for February, and they'd gone to the window and bought cones. Hers was blue and his was red, but she knew they were the same flavor: sugar. Together, they sat on one of the city's green benches, watching other hikers. Women with strollers. Kids on Rollerblades, stripping out of their jackets. "If we both read on Wednesdays," he said, "we could make that a regular night out afterward."

She thought about it. She watched a girl with purple hair make a pirouette on the front wheels of her skates. "If I don't read on Saturdays, I'll never get to read to Alice. And I like reading the French. Je l'adore."

"Vanity project?"

"What if it is?"

"Well then," he said. He smiled. It had been a month now that they'd shared between them, and whichever this smile was, it wouldn't have gotten her past her second hand of counting fingers. "Whatever gets you there."

She didn't know what *there* meant, whether he meant "to the Lighthouse" there or "to other people's aid and assistance" there,

240

but she saw then that he wasn't an angel whose wings she wanted to stroke. She saw that he was enjoying his cheap ice cream in a way she couldn't. His father hadn't loved him enough, yet he wanted to save the whole world, all of it, all the people eighty stories above in their skyscrapers, all the rabbits eighty depths below in their warrens. Her parents hadn't loved her enough, and she could barely save herself. His world was so big, she'd fall off its edge before she could even know it. No room in it for someone whose soul was as small as hers.

"Where've you been?" Mardi asked, when Shannon picked her up. "You look tired." She was still clean and dry, in a pink sweater Shannon's mother must have bought her.

"Just out with a friend."

"A boy friend?"

"A friend."

"Will you get married again?"

"Why would you want that? Don't I seem happier now?"

Mardi played with the window button. She undid her own child protective lock and rolled it down, then up again. "I want to go to your wedding," she said. "I want to wear a long, pink princess gown."

"Why don't you keep the window down," Shannon said. "It's nice out." The sunset was blue fading to orange, like a mix of her and Brandt's ice creams. "And there won't be a wedding." *Finger Painting. Sea Voyage.* "Know why?"

"Why?"

"You are my love, and I will share you with no one."

She put Mardi to bed. She bunched the down comforter under her chin until she could see only the little brown head poking out of the bedding, then kissed Mardi on her nose. "No weddings, okay?" she said.

241

"Okay," said Mardi. She closed her eyes and smiled. Shannon plugged in her nightlight, switched off the overhead. Went downstairs to watch a movie.

Bedtime.

Sleepyhead.

XXIV. It Might as Well Be the Moon

Ms. Lin-Wood says I'm good at graphing equations, and maybe will be an engineer when I grow up, which is one way I know that the woman who calls herself my mom isn't my real mom. She can't put anything together without asking for help, not even the vacuum cleaner she bought at Target. And she can't count. The man she was married to, the man who calls himself my dad, comes less and less frequently to pick me up. It's simple subtraction, yet still, every Friday morning before school, the mom cutout reminds me to pack my weekend bag.

The first year, when the dad cutout was still looking at Jitka like she was a snack, he'd actually show up on Fridays. I'd have my bag ready but I'd stay upstairs, just standing there, long enough so he'd give up and sit on the porch. I'd tiptoe downstairs to look through the door glass at his back, hunched over still in its work suit, looking like it had lost a fight. He could have been listening to the birds, I guessed—not hearing them, never hearing them, neither the mom nor the dad cutouts ever hear a thing. I'd stay there while looking at his back, because I wanted to remember it, the feeling that he was losing a game even to me.

But then I'd finally pull the door open and say, "Hi, Dad," and he'd turn around like anyone's regular father, and we'd go have a weekend. He'd send me home with a roll of six twenties and half a dozen square photographs with rounded edges that he took of us on his little Fujifilm Instax. *It's like magic,* the dad said, *but that's not how things work. Nothing's magic, Mardi. There's a liquid concentrate inside the camera that reads the light and then prints out an image on a piece of paper. Just a connection of chemicals and their consequences. This whole planet and everything on it are just chemicals and their consequences.*

The first time the dad cutout missed a Friday, he mailed a photograph of himself on a beach at dusk, smiling like he was thinking about puppies. The photo included the whole of his body, his shiny black shoes soft in the sand and his black silk shirt rippled by the wind; an open can of something called *Mayabe* in his hand. Neither I nor the mom cutout wondered out loud who took the photo, but we were both thinking *her.* The dad cutout had moved on so far and so fast. Even I saw it, in the three open buttons of his shirt. There were things one just did not enclose in an envelope aimed at one's daughter, but that was him—never really a dad.

Not yet, anyway, because now he had another shot.

Yesterday, he told me some critical things at the trampoline park. It's a big building with high, cinder-block ceilings that are made I guess to keep the place cool and fresh, but it's bad for acoustics, and I could barely hear the dad cutout, let alone the Doja Cat coming out of the speakers, and he asked me to stop jumping and listen, that it was serious, but I yelled, "I can hear you fine!" and then he got this look on his face, like probably it was a good thing I couldn't hear him, and he kept talking,

When I bounced high, I heard nothing. But then his face, and the earth all around it, would rebound back up my sightline, and I'd hear him in dips of decibel. "You're.

To be.   Big sister.

                                      Jitka.

Baby."

244~

He didn't want to say all this in front of everyone at the trampoline park, I could tell from the way his eyes went kind of googly whenever he looked around and took in the general public, all its greedy ears. But I wasn't giving him a choice. The frown line down the center of his forehead deepened into a crevice. It was fun to watch the dad cutout trying to be so serious, turning this regular silly thing of Jitka into a big ceremony. *A trampoline is nylon stretched across a frame, anchored with coiled springs. It feels like magic, but it is not. It's tubing and galvanized metal, assembled so you can fly.*

The dad cutout ran his hand down the tiny blue diamonds on his tie, and the skin just under his face got red. He spoke again:

"Another   Your mother   Wasn't
Found yo   Passport

                                    Kidnapped   Right thing

Should know now

Old enough."

I refused to hear. The dad cutout wasn't my real dad. The grandmother cutout had already told me, years ago. He was just trying to hurt the mom cutout now, but I knew her already too. I'd known her for a long time, and I still didn't hate her.

True, she can help me with nothing. She's not like my real mom, because she worries about everything. She worries about the scar on her face, and thinks I don't catch her looking at it in her car's vanity mirror. She worries about money, and thinks I don't notice. She worries she's not doing enough for the world, and thinks no one can see. She worries I'll catch her smoking, and doesn't understand that she smokes so much because she's so worried. She worries that she is nobody, and she's right.

But the mom cutout has a heart where the dad cutout has

nothing. He bought a new car after he moved out, and it has leather seats that smell just like the rest of his life. They smell like success. Determination. A lifetime of math and graduate schooling and things he thinks I ought to do with my life too. I used to imagine layers in his head because I did not want to believe the dad was dull-witted, but really, he is not a complicated system. He points in one direction, always.

The mom even said it one day: "Your father's simple, Mardi."

I was doing homework. She reached across the table and shoved her hand into my curls.

"I always know what he's thinking," she said. "You, baby? Your mind, to open it up and look inside, I'd have to have a jagged little key."

It's because you're not my real mom, I wanted to say, but I didn't. I stayed quiet.

I give them Silent Treatment often, and they hate it. The mom cutout will ask me something, like how is my day at school or what do I want for dinner, and I become outraged by the nature of the question, so I stay quiet, and her smile will freeze there in its uncomfortable groove, but she won't ask me anything else; she knows when to stop. The dad cutout is like a train with no brakes. He'll ask me don't I like Jitka, or why don't I want to do Girls in Science this summer, and I say nothing, but then he gets angry. He'll say something vicious, like how did he raise a child so rude she can't respond to questions, but still, I'll stay quiet. Ms. Lin-Wood has been teaching us about sensory perception, about the difference between perceiving and actually registering sensation. The mom and the dad cutout are angry because they can never figure out whether I've perceived or registered. They don't understand there's a world so far beyond their talking or my listening that I can't even breathe with them in it.

I'm not like them, because I'm in love. I'm in love with every damn thing, connected and unconnected. When the dad drives to the bank, I'll watch the vacuum tube suck up the canister with the dad's transaction slip and count how long it has taken to travel to the teller window. I'll be ecstatic when my estimate hits, but the dad cutout, he'll just be listening to NPR. On windy days, when a gust rolls through my hair, something happens in my brain, like I've been plugged into a socket, and I stop walking to close my eyes and smell for the ocean, but the mom and the dad, they just plod on ahead of me, oblivious to the electricity in the air. On my way to sleep, I run my hand along the notched rings on each bed post, but the mom cutout will just be asleep. They can't live in my world. They can't perceive it or register it. They just cannot.

The dad will have a new family now, and he'll stop coming. I've seen it in after-school specials how it will happen, two new households blooming out of the rotten one. He came to get me the first of December, and then again the week before Christmas, and then for Martin Luther King's weekend, and then four Thursdays later—yesterday—when he showed up to take me to the trampoline park. At first, I thought of the gaps as simple subtraction problems, and then as fractional expressions of a year's worth of fatherhood. Finally, when Ms. Lin-Wood taught us the Fibonacci sequence, I saw that's what it was—the gaps in visitation would double in time until I was twenty-five, waiting for the dad cutout to text from his deathbed that he couldn't make it.

The less he picks me up, the less dreamy Mom gets. She used to lie on the couch all the time, claiming she was in pain, but she'd have her hair spilled all over her face so I could see how real the pain might be. Now, she wears it in a ponytail, tied with the kind of rubber band you'd find holding a bunch of asparagus. When I get home from school she sets the oven timer for an hour, sits me down at the kitchen table, and helps me with homework. She's lost weight around her middle, and she wears lower-cut necklines, but I don't think she means to be sexy. It's more like an intermittent Morse-code signal she's giving: *I'm still alive.*

And there was the dad at the trampoline park, saying all those words. I put them all together in my mind, then thought about not having the whole picture, the way Ms. Lin-Wood always says it's a good thing to consider that no one ever does. But then I thought about how that means Ms. Lin-Wood's judgy voice in my head doesn't have the full picture either. I know more about this situation than her morality does, because I've known it in my bones this whole time. *Kidnapped.* My mom's mother suggested it. The dad cutout confirmed.

That was yesterday, but this morning, the mom reminded me to pack my suitcase.

"I just saw Dad yesterday," I told her.

"Well, you never know," she yelled back upstairs.

So I packed my Hello Kitty, just to make her happy. But then I thought, maybe I should make *me* happy. So when she got in the shower, I bolted. And thank God that even though it's still February, it's what Ms. Lin-Wood would call *unseasonably warm.* She's been saying it all winter, and it's been true. I'm lying now on a long rectangle of concrete, one joint of a curved sidewalk, and it's so hot out that a honeybee keeps dotting over my pant legs. I came to Cherokee Park, which is where we ended up a lot of those days when the mom would note we had not seen one Black person all week. She'd hustle us into her car and drive us west on I-65 like she was going to settle the matter once and for all. Sometimes she'd get it right: she'd take the Roy Wilkins exit and drive us deep into West Louisville, where all the Black people at the park would ignore us anyway, and we'd end up at Jay's, eating yams sweeted up with orange juice and macaroni weighted down with cheese. The Black people there, the waiters and cashiers, they were paid to act like they were your relatives, and the mom would be happy with herself.

But usually, what happened was that the mom half-assed it at the exit for Grinstead, and we ended up in Cherokee Park with a bunch of White people. We'd merge onto the scenic route that wound through thick forest; we'd park in a lot about a half mile in and stroll down to the twisty slides and crossbar swings. That's where I'm lying now, but it's like I'm here for the first time. Looking at the moon, either already up there for the day or leftover there from last night, the porcelain blue all around it. I've never seen the moon in the daytime before. Maybe my real mom sent it, to tell me she's still somewhere out there, alive.

Hello Kitty's safe under a park bench, so I close my eyes. I breathe the smell of pine and my own winning, the concrete warms my back all the way through to my insides, and the bird-song weaves an auditory blanket. I hear heavy trucks making the main drag of Grinstead; I listen so hard I can hear the catch of their gears change. *In heavy vehicles, the brake pedal lets air into the chamber, and the pressure twists the cam shaft that turns the S-cam that presses the brake shoes into the drum. It's all connected.* The cutout mom had protected me from reality. She'd erased my ability to perceive, to analyze. The world is more beautiful now I'm free.

I hear muffled giggles, and when I sit up and look, there's a car that's parked, inconveniently, on the street, so other cars are having to veer into the opposite lane of traffic to get around it. It's an old car from the nineties, its blue paint faded along the bottom where road salt's eaten it through so many winters. Two huge, ragged pillows are lodged in the back window, so I can't tell how many people are sitting inside, but I perceive and see someone's dirty feet resting on the dashboard. "Shit," I hear a woman say from inside the car. Her voice is lain in a bed of gravel. "Shit, shit, fuckitall," she says. But it's a soft *fuckitall*, like she can't commit to being angry.

When Dad spilled all the tea, I felt shaky. True, I was on a trampoline. But the ground underneath had never been solid. Both the mom and the dad cutouts were shifting tectonic plates, always. When the dad let me out in front of the house, he said, "Have a great day, kiddo," but I did Silent Treatment. I slammed the door closed and didn't even look back at him when I walked up the driveway. I heard his car idling as he waited to make sure I got in the house okay, but I didn't turn around and wave. The dad cutout was using me. He was the one doing the wrong thing, telling on the mom. But the thing the mom did is unthinkable, which is worse than wrong. And I already knew that too. It would be nice to say that I'd ever thought of them as Mom and Dad, *my loving parents*, but that would be a lie. The ground under my feet has always been full of holes. I remember nothing, but my bones know.

There are five changes of clothes in my Hello Kitty. My iPad, its charger, Mom's entire carton of Kind bars, and the school library's copy of *President of the Whole Fifth Grade*. I'm not sure how I'll get the book back to the school, but it's not due for another two weeks, so. This morning, before I left, I stuffed a bunch of my dad's twenties into my little owl purse, fastened on the silver wristwatch the grandmother got me for my birthday, and wheeled my suitcase down the ten minutes of Innisbrook Drive and out to the main road. I didn't look at anyone in the passing cars, and I hoped they weren't looking at me. No one lowered their window to ask; no one even so much as slowed. It was eight o'clock on a Friday. People were too busy trying to get to work.

I knew the TARC bus stopped there on Highway 68 because

I'd seen the sign. I'd never seen anyone get on or off the bus, but I had sense enough to know that a body could, and so I stood under the plastic shelter and waited. After a few minutes, I saw the mom pass in her old black BMW. I held my breath and turned my head into my shoulder, but she didn't stop. If she was any kind of real mom whatsoever, she would have doubled back and looked through the tree that partially obscured the view, because she would have sensed me there, running away from her. It would have been like how Darth Vader knows when Luke Skywalker's on the Death Star. But she's not, so it wasn't.

The bus came whining along on its brakes, and I bumped my suitcase up the steps. I gave the driver a twenty, and he had to reach into his back pocket for his personal stash of ones. "You're lucky it's so early in the morning, young lady," he said. *The bills are printed with magnetic ink, read by magnetic scanner.*

"Thank you," I said, inserting them into the fare reader, and I rolled my suitcase, instinctually, to the back of the bus, where I spread myself across two seats. Fear tingled the soles of my feet. Would the driver ask where I was going? Would he call the police on the sly? His rearview mirror was long enough, I could see his shoulders and his face. I decided to keep an eye on him.

Everyone boarded the bus, and no one tried to talk to me. No one even looked. People got on, on their way to work—a woman with a crooked wig, a teenaged boy in a Panera Bread uniform, an elderly man with an old leather briefcase. We passed the turnoff to Henry's Ark and I saw the wild peacocks behind the fence, and it made me think about Claire and Sophia, who'd been going to the Ark with me since kindergarten. I'd never told them I was adopted. I've never told anyone. No one ever asks, because I'm Black like my parents, and White people rarely find subtlety. They can't see that my skin is toned red where the mom's is toned yellow. They can't see that I look great in blue, and the mom does not. They can't see how I'm almost as tall as my parents even though I'm only eight years old, and how that shouldn't, genetically, be the case. My real mother would be able to tell me what colors to wear. She'd tell me how to dress for her height. I'm a girl descended from giants. I bet they know everything about conquering.

Claire's and Sophia's moms let them have Instagram accounts too, but it won't be safe to message them until I've been on my own a couple of months, until I've established myself on the streets. And then they'll be sad for themselves but happy that I've escaped fourth grade, because we've all been dreading it. There are kids I'll never see again—stupid, high-strung Amelia; whiny, entitled Dyani; arrogant, lying Erin, who uses her lisp to gain sympathy. The boy I like, Colin? Sandy-haired, green-eyed Colin who, up close, isn't that cute but ignores me anyway? He'll marvel that I've escaped. He drew me one day in math class and gave me the drawing. He'd made me into a superhero with a red cape and platform heels. In the drawing I was superpretty, and he'd worked hard, with two or three colored pencils, to get the green of my eyes exact, but he hasn't spoken to me since. If I could find my real mother, she would help solve the puzzle of Colin; she'd have advice. She'd tell me whether it's because I'm so much taller than him. When I find her, she'll help me so much. She won't help me to be good at being like her. She'll help me to be good at being a Mardi.

I rethink Colin's face, when he finds out I'm not coming back to school. It might still be blank. It'll be too big for him; he won't be able to wrap his mind around caring. I'll be a legend among all the girls, though, and even among their parents. The news'll get around. This day in Cherokee Park is just the start of it. My mind is blown free of anything it's ever thought before. The petals of my brain are like a flower's, open and bent into a hundred little blossoming curlicues. I'm a Who, living on one little speck of Horton's clover, one girl in one park in one section of the one city of Louisville. I'm less important, now that I've run away from everything that knows me, but I'm more important to myself. And that matters more.

The blue car's door opens, squeaking along the rust of its hinges, and then I hear it slam closed, and then I sense—or maybe perceive—a presence, but I don't open my eyes until I feel someone tickling my stomach, and it cuts me: I didn't know my shirt had ridden up my belly. "Hey!" I say. I push myself up on my elbows.

"Hey, girl," says the woman with the sandpaper voice. I perceived her coming, but I hadn't heard her because she is barefoot. She hadn't made a sound, walking across the damp mud, dirtying her feet even more. "Hey, girl," she says again. "You live here in this park?"

"No," I say, though technically, at this very moment, I do.

"Then what's with the suitcase?"

"I'm waiting for someone."

She backs off a step. "Well, listen. While you're waiting, we want you to look at something." She walks toward the car, looking back at me as if she expects me to follow. "Come on," she says, over her shoulder. "We ain't gonna bite." She gets in and closes the door. "See? We ain't tryna steal ya." She rolls the window down, actually rolling it with an old-fashioned crank. "Come on, girl," she says. "You got to see this."

I don't want to come off as a scared little girl, so I get up and walk to the edge of the road, until I'm standing about my body's length from the car. This way, they couldn't steal me even if they tried—they'd have to reach out an entire girl away from their own bodies. It turns out there's only one other person with the woman, even though they've been making all that noise. It's a man in his early twenties. He sits behind the steering wheel in tiny rectangular glasses, bopping his head in time to music in his earbuds. I can't hear his beat, but when he notices me at the window he looks out and taps the windshield in time.

"I promise, little girlfriend, you're going to want to see this," the woman says. "Come on."

I feel my face freezing. If this were a movie, I know I'd look terrified—I can feel it. And that's the last thing I need right now, to look like one of the kids who should be climbing the kiddie slide instead of a young woman living in the park independently, so I step closer.

"This car still plays CDs," the woman says, handing me one. "You ever seen a CD, girlie?"

"Yeah," I say, even though I haven't. I take the plastic case. *Everlast*, it says. *Songs of the Ungrateful Living*. There's a silver skull on the cover. I hand it back.

"You like Everlast?"

"Sure." I've never heard of them.

"Well, you might like this one," the woman says, turning toward her boyfriend to dig for something wedged between the seat and the gear shift. I can see from where I'm standing how dirty the inside of their car is, the way pollen has spread a golden carpet on the dashboard. Photos hang off shoestrings they've wrapped around the stem of their rearview mirror. She hands me another plastic case—*Staind: The Illusion of Progress*. On its cover, a man sits in a chair on an ice-covered road. I flip over to its list of songs, then look up at the woman.

"Oh, you can't keep them, girlie," she says. "Hand them back to Noah."

I sense, then, some trickery. The woman I've been calling mom did not raise a fool. I won't reach into their car, won't lean over. I've been kidnapped once, and wholly forgotten it. This time, it would hurt.

I walk around to Noah's side and keep some distance still, enough that I can run if I need. I'm half their age but almost as tall, taller than anyone else in my class, and I especially could outrun a barefoot woman. I'd run across rocks, turn back to laugh when she had to slow down.

Noah sticks his hand out and wriggles his fingers to signal to me to hand him the CDs. As I do, I look back into Noah's sunglasses, but all I can see over his grin is my own reflection.

The woman produces another giggle full of pebbles, Noah starts the car, and they cruise away. I breathe the exhaust from their car. In the distance, I hear thunder break; in the sky, I can see a dark line of storm rolling over the skyline. I go back to the bench, get my suitcase, and roll it to the shelter. I take a transfer downtown, thinking to kill more of a day.

When the 29 makes its turn onto Bardstown Road and everything begins to look familiar, I dare myself to get off at a corner not even two blocks from the cutout dad's new condo. I wheel my suitcase into a nearby coffee shop and order a large chai with almond milk, just like the mom always buys me. I peel off one of my twenties, take my change, and sit to read my book, just like any young woman in a coffee shop. I sip in what I hope is an elegant fashion, quiet sips that let in polite drabbles of tea. The cup and saucer are lined with tiny blue fleurs-de-lis, whose pattern I never would have noticed if I were with the cutout mom. The track lights on the ceiling glint off the china's gilt edge. The spice of the chai warms the back of my tongue and I swish it around. I toss my hair, dog-ear a page I haven't read. No one here knows I'm eight years old.

A few pages past my bookmark, I close my eyes and press my

forehead down to my book. I don't mean to fall asleep, but just to rest my eyes. Soft jazz falls on my ears, and I can hear every skip of the bass, I can feel every squeak of the guitarist's hands moving along his frets. I'm right under the dad's nose, but he can't feel me here either; this isn't the bridge on the Death Star, and he's not my real dad. Rain pours down outside in sheets, perfect and beautiful.

When I wake, the mom is standing next to me, crying, looking high. "Mardi," she says. "Mardi. Your *fucking* father." Two police officers stand near the door of the café, the female of the pair looking down at her own shoes, embarrassed for the scene.

"That's her?" says the male.

"Yes," says my mother. The woman I used to believe was my mother.

"Okay," he says. "Listen, ma'am, we're not filing a report on this."

"Thank you," the mom whispers. She touches her heart in a move both terribly phony and frighteningly real. "Thank you." The officers leave the coffee shop, and the mom stares at me. "Come," she says. "Your suitcase is already in the car."

Outside I get into her BMW, but I have nothing to say, and the mom lets Silent Treatment go unchecked, and I find myself falling asleep again, miserable from the stress of the day. I'm glad the mom came at the same time I hate her for coming. The sharp, concrete world I'd discovered begins to disappear, bit by bit. The rain on the hood of Mom's car just sounds like rain. There's nothing to see in the puddles save water. All that's been sharp is now falling in fine with everything dull and unnamable. I can't tell my own feelings right now, even; nothing holds in this life. Nothing ever has. The third grade is going to be one more long riddle, connected to nothing else.

.

PART V

CANICULE

XXV. Louisville

A poltergeist rustled her patio blinds. She hadn't yet slid them open to sun, but an invisible presence now rifled down the panels, turning each slat so that it momentarily reflected daylight. It could have been air-conditioning, kicking on through a vent. Or it might have been the collecting haunting of all the fauna that she'd been slaughtering there, near the sliding door. She'd been found out by her daughter for a criminal, and now she was compelled to take her back to find her real mother. She'd taken out all her frustrations on the houseflies and mosquitoes that dared to spring to life so early in the year. She swatted them so hard, she often found their little insect bodies snapped right in two— here, on the wall, a thorax with its legs sticking out; there, still stuck on the grid of the flyswatter, a many-eyed head.

A robin had flown into the glass the day Mardi ran away, and Shannon had left it on the patio because she couldn't fathom the thought of discarding it. She couldn't bear the thought of its tiny wing bones in her hand, not atop all else swirling the tornado of her life. She feared the crunch its damaged little skull would give if she made contact, even through gloves. She left it to the ants to do their job, which they did—so fast. What came next were the maggots, writing through, making the bird twist and dance as if it had come back to life. She brought Mardi to the window to show her the progress. It was humbling, she figured, something a kid should see. Living was the painful part—there was, first off, all the money for living that had to be got somehow. And then all the meals one had to prepare, all the painful, struggling shits. All the moral decisions that could go wrong, so fitfully wrong. Death was the easy part. The ants, the maggots: they took care of everything.

Brandt had texted her early that morning, at dawn. No words: just a selfie. He'd been smiling there in the twilight, though not with his eyes—Brandt never smiled with his eyes, because he couldn't truly smile. Still, he was handsome. A man a scarred woman might not have hoped to sleep with. She'd looked at his selfie six times already, clicking on it between rowing through Facebook news and sipping cold coffee. She wasn't in love. It hit her each time she clicked on his face, the intense green of his eyes like a stuck traffic light.

She hadn't switched on the kitchen chandelier because she wasn't quite prepared for whatever was next, the onerous day of underemployment ahead of her. She no longer cared to sit outside, beside the pool that was still half hers but half Vlad's too, and therefore only half a pleasure. She hadn't covered it, not all winter. The leaves had continued to blow, and she'd continued to let them, and when finally she switched on the pump the day after Christmas, it had clogged. She called Vlad and left him a message, but he never stopped by. He was busy now, not only at work but at home, preparing for fatherhood, all that life of adventure dashed against the rocks. His boys, they'd swum Olympic-sized laps.

And she'd heard it from Mardi, how he'd turned into Florence Nightingale, bringing Epsom salts for Jitka's swollen feet and a heating pad for her back, which she claimed hurt constantly. Vlad took Jitka's food upstairs to the bedroom before returning downstairs to eat in silence with Mardi; after a hurried few bites, Mardi reported, he would excuse himself to go back upstairs, leaving her alone at the table. Vlad made Mardi sit in the front seat of the car, even though it was against legal guidelines, so Jitka could stretch out in the back seat. Vlad enjoyed damaged women—Shannon knew this from her own time married to him. What was hard to gauge here was Jitka's level of performance. Four beds in the house, but Jitka had taken over the daybed in Mardi's room. Mardi was sleeping on the couch, with the glare of the wall television as nightlight.

Shannon's door buzzer came: *brrrrzt*. When they were married, she'd tried to convince Vlad that they deserved a more elegant doorbell, one that played chimes, or the opening bars of Beethoven. He'd never relented, and now she was stuck with *brrrrzt* until they sold the house, just as she was stuck with the granite countertops with their spotted pattern of orange and dark brown, low notes from the eighties.

"Who is it?" she yelled, but the buzzer came again. It was him, then. Vlad. He heard her through the door, no doubt, but he wouldn't answer. Voice-to-voice communication with him was like a knife fight.

"Hey," he said flatly when she opened the door. "Can I come in?"

She looked down to her feet and bit back a smirk. In the spring heat she had on no pants—just a maroon tank top and a pair of panties. Jitka was six months in now, so Vlad probably hadn't seen the flat of a woman's stomach in three—whyever he'd come now, this was a tactical advantage. "Well it is still your house," she said. "At least half of it is, anyway." She pulled the door back and stepped aside. Cut the air horizontally with her arm. "Come in."

The darkness of the kitchen seemed to her advantage too, but as soon as Vlad sat, he was up again to open the blinds. He took some small way of reminding her, every time he came, that it was still his (half-his) house: For weeks after she'd filed for divorce, until she'd explicitly asked him to stop, he would enter without knocking. Several times, he'd reached behind the hallway bookshelf to adjust her half-hers thermostat. Looked in the kitchen drawer for a pack of her (hers-alone!) gum. He'd brought mail in from the end of the driveway; she'd rented a PO box. Now, he opened the blinds and sat again, at his kitchen table, the one he'd owned before she even met him, the one he didn't take because he and Jitka no doubt had a nicer one in their condo.

The small square of pool that wasn't choked with leaves reflected the morning and threw it back through the patio door at them. He was on his way to work and in his engineer's uniform: dark suit, silk tie, the Malcolm X frames that were so popular with men now. He'd brought his travel mug full of coffee inside—he intended this to be a long conversation. His tie was tight as a sailor's knot. He dropped his face to his mug to sip coffee, as if he were in prison. He looked like a trap.

"What now?" she said.

He pinched his entire face into a wince. "Can't you put on some pants?"

"Do you find nudity emasculating?"

"Please, Shannon."

"I live here. I'm in my own home."

"Fine," he said. He rolled his eyes to the ceiling and leaned over to reach in his back pocket, grimacing as if this small motion were causing him pain, and she wondered if Jitka had done him in in the bedroom somehow, if sex from Poland approached some outer reaches of athleticism. He took out a paper that had been folded so small it was a missile, and he threw it at her.

She flinched, even as it hit her in the shoulder and bounced to the floor. "What is *that*?" she asked. She scooped it off the tile and unfolded the cube of paper—he'd folded it over twelve times— but when finally she got it unpinched, she saw that it was Mardi's passport application. Her own notarized signature, ruined by an uneven crease.

"I'm not signing that," he said, his arms folded across his chest. He looked like a chimp.

"Why not? I told you. I won't take her without your approval. I promise."

He laughed. "Where are you going, with no money? That's not what this is about. I'm not signing, just on principle. You want to steal a kid from another country, fine. But then at least keep her in this one."

"That's ridiculous. So she's never supposed to travel?"

"Not on my signature she won't."

"Yet you leave the country weekly. You don't want the same for your kid?" Shannon stood up, turned her back to him. In the flash it took her to turn just as angrily back, she caught him look-ing at her ass, then the flicker of his turning his eyes to the stairs. "You are so fucked up," she said. "I didn't steal her."

"What would you call what you did?"

She narrowed her eyes until they were slits. "What *we* did," she said.

He snorted a bitter chuff of laughter. Sipped more coffee. Said, "Semantics."

Shannon banged the flat of her palm on the table in front of him, and he jumped. "Why are you giving me such a hard time now? Now that I'm trying to do the right thing?" She heard the whine in her voice, but she knew she couldn't stop it; it was like a train. "And why are you so angry at me? You're the one who needed a third wife. You got your Latvian. Your Black. Your Moroccan kid. You'll have your Polish baby. You've got the

United Colors of Benetton all in one harem, but you can't stop plaguing *me*. What is it, Vlad? What did I ever do to you?"

Vlad's eyes went watery, as if he'd been stabbed. He said something she couldn't hear.

"What?" she yelled.

"You used me," he whispered. He was standing up, rising from beneath her line of vision to somewhere just above it.

"Why would you say that? We were married, for fuck's sake. How is that—"

"You never loved me. You needed *things*. Like all women. You needed things."

"Vlad. Don't say that. I'm not that."

"So you find some sorry dork who'll follow you around like a puppy with its tongue hanging out, and you get all the things, and then *poof*, it's not enough."

"Vlad. When did I ever say I wasn't—"

But he got up and strode out of his half-his house, slamming the door behind him. She could have called him on the phone, continued her protestations. But it would have been like removing a piece of glass from her foot, only to throw it back in the same place on the floor.

"Sonofabitch," she said, to no one.

Brandt's name popped up on her phone screen, but she ignored it. Another gorgeous dawn cracked into ruin.

She looked around the kitchen at all the things that were Vlad's, the things he didn't now want. The cappuccino maker she couldn't now afford to replace; the printer without drivers, sitting on its side next to the kitchen island, waiting for her to take it to the e-cycling. She looked round at all the things that were hers and hers alone, the worthless things, like the pair of old-fashioned stereo speakers, and the framed print of Rico

Fonseca's Big Apple. She looked through the open floor plan she'd always hated, to the living room and the things that were now half. The bookshelves she bought after she moved in with him. The wine racks and their bottles collecting dust. The leather sofa, tanned blood red somewhere in Italy. She and Vlad could put one of their asses on each end cushion and have someone saw it right in half. Have someone wheel them apart and away on the plastic castors.

But Mardi? On a fulcrum between the two of them, she was 100 percent Shannon's. She hadn't held Mardi in her body, nor had she pushed her out in a sweaty, bloody surge of bone-bending pain. But she'd found a child when Vlad hadn't even had the smarts to look for one. He'd gone along for the ride, sure— he'd gone to piano recitals and baked corn dogs and given her ineffective baths. But that didn't make Mardi his. The proof was in this anti-Solomonic decision he'd made: If he really loved his daughter, he'd want her to have a passport. He'd want her to be able to fly to Morocco and answer the unanswerable.

This was no moral dilemma, then. They'd gotten her citizenship years ago, then just gotten sunk in parenting and never left the country as a family. She got a pen out of the stationery drawer Vlad had always insisted on keeping in the kitchen. She took the application into his half-his home office and she found, on the half-hers IKEA desk they'd assembled together, the file with his signatures all over every family court ruling.

She turned on the half-his desk lamp she rarely used because it was too bright; for the task at hand, it was perfect. She lay the application over a court document and slowly, painfully traced his signature, carefully filling in the date of the original notarization. And because she loved Mardi *that* much, she decided the first stamp would be from passport control in Marrakech.

Shannon would hire a car and take them back to Essaouira, to that same alley where she first met Mardi. If she was the mother she hoped to be, she owed Mardi this much, to set her free.

Only she hoped—in fact prayed—to a vague, Charlton Hestonesque God she rarely communicated with, that Mardi would love her enough to fly right back.

XXVI. Louisville

"Mom, can I bring Tweety?"

Tweety was a giant, body-sized pillow, with a face on one end like Tweety Bird's, but a knockoff Tweety Bird, with no eyelashes and a flattened beak. Vlad had won it for Mardi at the state fair, and she'd slept with it every night since—if it was to be cleaned, Shannon had to sneak it out of Mardi's bed while she was at school. Shannon imagined Mardi trying to bump the giant pillow through airport security. With horror, she imagined the TSA confiscating it—who knew what liquid explosive the Tweety Bird might harbor within? Or maybe, horrifyingly, they *wouldn't* take it, and Shannon would have to watch Mardi drag the pillow across the airport concourse, dust sticking to its trailing end. She'd take it down the dirty aisle of the plane, under the shoes of those already seated. She'd spill Sprite on it when the stewardess came with dinner.

"It's a long trip, baby. We change planes three times. Do you think your pillow will want to go through all that? What if we lose it in Morocco? What if we leave it in a hotel by accident?"

"Mom, Tweety can't sleep without me."

Since her day as a runaway, Mardi had insisted on doing her own hair. That morning she'd tied it into two ponytails, fastening a love-in-Tokyo around the root of each one. They were sloppy, with curls buckling between the elastic bands, but Shannon said nothing. Now that she was a flight risk, Mardi was a little terrorist who got whatever she wanted.

"Okay," Shannon said. "I guess they'll x-ray it at security. See there's nothing in it." She didn't say the rest of what she was thinking, that if they didn't find Mardi's real mother, she'd have to fly home hugging the pillow as stand-in.

The date on their return tickets allowed for three weeks of searching, but she knew that was a conservative estimate: how long did it take to find a mother? But it was what she could afford: three weeks of parking fees at O'Hare. Vlad had paid for the tickets and the hotel, and Brandt had offered to take them to the airport. He loved helping others, she figured. Why get in his way?

Too, it was her way of saying goodbye to him in the most sanitary way possible. He might not understand for a long, mysterious time afterward, but when they'd last seen each other, she'd already decided. They were out on the lake, in his kayak, her uterus killing her from within. Together, they'd paddled out to the dam and just sat there. From the shore, a family of deer munched leaves and watched them, but Shannon couldn't be sure Brandt saw, because his eyes were closed. He'd turned around in the boat to face her, and then closed his eyes. He breathed deeply, meditating, focusing on something deep within himself.

Shannon tried to close her own eyes, but when she did, she saw pain in actual colors, big, blocky blue spots under her eyelids. The pain had grown so large it buckled her spine, crunched her thoughts into a tangle of mesh. The motion of paddling had eased it at the same time it had brought nausea, and she felt stickiness between her legs. When they got back to the dock and she rose from her seat, she saw she'd left a smear of blood on the seat of Brandt's kayak, in the shape of the space between her buttocks. A bloody, inverted smile.

"No worries," Brandt said. He was looking at it. Focusing. "We'll go back to my place. Get you cleaned up."

"I can't go back to your place. Obviously. There's no point."

Brandt raised his head suddenly, as if he'd been knifed. "My point in hanging out with you isn't just *that*," he said. "That's a little insulting, if you think that's all I want."

Shannon closed her eyes. Focused to the count of four. Pictured something deep inside Brandt, a small wax curlicue of falseness. "Hard to know what anyone ever wants of someone else, isn't it?"

Brandt had dish soap in his car. It was a natural soap, yet it smelled like the inside of a hospital. "Here," he said, handing her a wadded t-shirt.

"You sure?" she said. She shook it out. A polar bear stood next to a man in a yellow hard hat. The text read, *Let's drill the Arctic together!*

"It's old," Brandt said. "Who cares?"

How to make him know, it wasn't just blood. It was her womanhood, dripped out all over creation just to show how eternally useless it was. He didn't know Mardi wasn't hers by birth. She'd never told him because she knew he'd turn her confession into a political event. He'd misunderstand entirely; he'd talk about international infrastructure, and female infanticide, and humanitarian intervention, and he'd never understand why she'd just plain stolen a child. She had to give Vlad credit, at least, for sneaking around in the thievery with her. He'd joined in on the forbidden. Accepted his role as coconspirator. Brandt, on the other hand, would just exhaust her with his overlay of morality. And someone like Brandt wouldn't want a barren woman, no matter how much of a feminist he thought he was.

"You'll be back the eighteenth?" he said now, driving them up to Departing Flights.

"I get to skip two weeks of school!" Mardi blurted.

"Yup," Shannon said. "We just needed a break."

There'd been something else she'd seen in those four beats of focus, something in Brandt's soul: he'd never change. He'd always be that hipster in the corduroy jacket, looking for Black women as novelty. She, on the other hand, was genuinely becoming a better person. She didn't need it on a t-shirt. She'd weep for that crumb of wickedness, that leftover DNA of her past, but she'd set it afire and watch it burn nonetheless. "Everyone needs a break," she said, to the car.

Brandt got out and untrunked their suitcase, gave Mardi and Tweety a prim, loose hug.

He came to stand before Shannon, said, "Well, I'll see you on the other end." But the way he looked at her when he said it. The green of his eyes was a permanent stop. He knew, then. "Au revoir," he said. He kissed her on the lips. A shallow meeting, his lips matching exactly the outline of hers.

Au revoir. Literally: *to the re-see.* A man could be so much more hopeful in French.

XXVII. Essaouira

Muharram 1439 had finally come and with it Ashura, and in Souria's quarter of town the children ran free in their masks and capes, knocking on doors to ask for coins, running in the street like wild animals. They ruined one another with water guns, and used kitchen matches and newspaper to set fires on the sidewalk, tiny surprises of flame that reflected off the sides of parked cars. They ran away laughing from their own danger. They tossed eggs at wrapped-up old ladies on their way to the souk. Souria had wanted to stay home, up in their second-floor flat, to avoid the mayhem, to boil the three of them soup and cuddle with Aamer. Aamer was twenty-five months old, the age Yu had been when she vanished, and she kept him always within a three-foot radius, a spoke to her wheel.

She put on her winter jacket and grabbed him up in her arms, carrying him around the living room like a log. "As-salaama, habibi," she said. "Mommy is leaving now."

In the living room, Anass watched a soccer match on the small black television they'd bought for the holiday, with money mingled from the sale of his violin and the proceeds that had poured into Nasr's shop during high season. There was the jumble of German coming out of the set, but Anass followed the game without language, in his pure way of absorbing goals and penalties.

Just as Anass had never asked about Yu, he hadn't, either, asked about Souria's family, not even when she found herself pregnant and they went to the civil bureau next to the Aswak Assalam. At the bureau he heard her lie, in a softer voice than her own, telling the judge that she had no birth certificate because she'd been born in a stone house in the middle of the desert near Dakhla. Anass hadn't even blinked as she told this story. He knew that the most essential thing about her was that she was unknowable, that the minute he started looking for answers would be the minute she began to uncleave herself from him.

Knowing nothing, he thought her overprotective. She never let Aamer out in the street to play ball, and she strapped him into his winter coat even in late June. When Anass took their son out, she smothered him with cautions. Now, as he sat with his attentions glued to his football match, she marched around the room with the child close to her bosom, kissing him until he turned his little bothered face away from her. She let him down then, and he ran across the main room of the flat, all the way into the bedroom. He'd gotten old enough that he knew how to slam the door against her, which made her laugh despite herself. She knew that one day, when Aamer was five or six or twelve or sixteen, she'd have to let him off on his own to places she wouldn't even know—the school with all its unknown teachers, the sweet shop with all its strange faces. The alley, where anything could and did happen. Right then, though, Ashura 1439, she could control it, whether anything bad would befall her son.

"Au revoir," she told Anass, who nodded without moving his eyes from his match. She was going out in the cold on this first day of the new year to visit Nasr, kind old Nasr, who'd saved her life, who, they all believed, was now dying. She'd blamed him, for a time, for selling the kif that had brought whichever drug-addled foreigner had walked off with her child. But the years

272

filled in spaces of grief, and each square of caulk brought for-giveness. He'd tailored her wedding dress out of the finest white silk in the store, as he would have for a daughter. He and his wife had been Aamer's first visitors. He'd held the baby close to smell his hair, and she understood that he saw her as one of his own. Forgiveness had been a process of remembering, rather than forgetting.

Nasr had fallen into illness suddenly. One week, he'd been fine—upright and ambulatory, lucid in his affairs and running his shop. But then that Saturday, he hadn't shown. Souria had sat on the stoop in the alley until Hafiza came with the grate key and told her she'd need to run the shop. Nasr was in bed, she said, leveled with low-grade fever, dizzy and wheezing.

"He said it's like trying to breathe through plastic wrap," Hafiza told her. She said it without worry. But then the Saturday turned into the Sunday, and the Sunday turned into the Monday, and on Tuesday, Nasr was no longer able to speak, and they se-cured him a bed at Sidi Mohamed, the public hospital.

Souria locked her own front door and took one of the horse-drawn taxis to Bab Doukkala, where she walked the few min-utes through the blowing gravel to Sidi Mohamed. Outside the locked gate people lined the street, waiting for the opening of visiting hours. Souria took her place along the gate next to a man whose eyes were half-closed, as if he were trying to sleep on his feet. He had a strong nose, long and hooked. You wouldn't mind kissing the mouth under that kind of nose, she thought, but you wouldn't want to pass such a nose on to your children. The man kept his eyes half-closed even as the wind blew dust from the street into his hair, even as noisy children passed him, and Souria decided that he must have a talent for so solidly shutting himself off from the world. When the orderly came to open the gates, and the man shuffled along in front of her with his eyes

still half-closed, she decided that he was trying to prevent anyone from seeing into his soul.

She signed the hospital registry and made her way down the
long, gleaming hall with its variety of offensive smells. In Nasr's
room, his wife was the only visitor yet come, and she'd scooted
a metal chair to the side of his bed, where she sat with her head
bowed into his hand, which she'd joined with her own. "As-
salaam alaikum," Souria said.

Amina jumped. She'd been lost in prayer. "Alaikum salaam."

Souria went to the older woman and kissed her, cheek to
cheek, four times. "How is he today?" she asked.

"No better."

Snaking from a bedside oxygen pump was a tube that branched
over Nasr's mustache and into both nostrils. His chest rose and
fell with great force; she could hear his labored inhalations. His
face had gone three shades lighter.

"Will you take the key again today?" Amina asked her.

"Yes."

Souria took Nasr's cold, dry hand in hers, bent down to kiss
it. After Amina dug the key out of her purse, Souria kissed her
atop the headscarf, and she went back down the hall, now noisy
with visitors. Out the hospital gates and into the cold, windy
day. A block from the hospital, in front of the Ocean Vagabond
hotel, she found an empty Fanta can, which she began to kick
in front of her. Zigzagging to its landing points, she let the
can lead the way. At the corner of the main road, it rolled off
into the street and narrowly missed being flattened by a passing taxi. She went out into the street and kicked it so hard it
went airborne. She didn't care who had seen. She kicked it all
the way through the arch at Bab Sbaa and past the old woman
in her wheelchair begging tourists for dirham. Every kick and
every crunch satisfied the crying thing inside of her, and she

didn't leave off her kicking until she happened upon the alley of her employment.

A blue taxi sat parked in front of Savons Mogador, but she barely noticed it. Occasionally, tourists were lazy; they wanted to find a shop but didn't want to do the legwork of retracing their steps, so they'd pay a taxi four times the normal rate to risk a circulation ticket, taking them through the archways of the medina. She thought nothing of the car. She turned the key in the grate lock and pushed. Without Nasr, she'd found, she had to put the whole of her body into the push, just to move the grate a few small inches.

Hubayshah, the wife at the ceramics shop, came running out of her shop door. "Souria," she cried. "Souria, I'm sorry. Your child is back. She is here."

Souria felt her insides harden, thinking Hubayshah had to be wrong, it could never happen, but then a foreign woman was stepping out the front door of the Savons, with a scar on her face and eyes as grim and empty as a plastic doll's. A girl came out after her, and her little eyebrows were terribly lost in confusion, but she had the clearest dimple in her chin, and curly hair left free in the wind, and—

"Yumni?"

The girl gave off a smile full of nerves. But it was also the smile of a thousand lemons. "My mother," she said, in English.

Souria stepped one foot toward this dream that was unfolding right in front of the soap shop. The day might be an old friend arrived to care for her, or a cruel stranger, arrived to tease her with perverse illusion. She hadn't understood why Hubayshah was apologizing, but now she did—Hubayshah, too, understood how unreal was hope.

"Yumni?" Souria asked again. She felt her own hand on her forehead, and realized that she hadn't, for the previous minute, breathed. "Yu," she said, more to herself than to her daughter. She closed her eyes. A breath rose from deep within and traveled to her windpipe until it escaped as a sob. "Yumni, Yumni. Habibi. You came home."

She felt all of them staring at her—Hubayshah, with her apology, the foreign woman with her shame, her own bewildered daughter. She heard a stranger call out salaams as he passed, and she tried to fix on the remark as some point of reality, but it was Berber spoken too fast for her to hold it. She heard a soft shuffling and felt Hubayshah's hand on her shoulder; she felt the woman embrace her. Allah had relented, then, to her sadness. Or perhaps this had been the divine plan all along, that her little bird fly away, only to return with both wings intact. But Souria had so little faith in the moment, she could not move.

The night of his marriage to Souria, there was no wedding feast, no parade with four men carrying her atop an amariya. Anass had no money and she had no family, and so the headache of hosting a wedding seemed like some other couple's problem. Souria was an anthill of secrets, and Anass was a man who deeply respected the anthill's sanctity. And so, on their way home from the mairie, what he did was to call his widowed mother long-distance in Sidi Ifni. He stood next to Souria with his arm circling his new bride's swollen waist, but he looked intently to the ground, as though she were a mere distraction. In his free ear the wind blew, and his mother's voice came into his listening ear as if from the other end of a long, twisted pipe. He told her what he'd done. Heard her exclaim, "Eh!"

She was surprised, yes. But Anass was the youngest of seven children, and so his mother's middle age had sprung full of surprises already. She ended the call not by asking about his new wife, what was her name or what city held her family, but by saying, "God be with you, my son." He wondered when she might meet his wife, and he thought that when this finally happened, his mother might be upset by the darkness of Souria's skin, but after the phone call ended, he realized that his mother was too old, with too little space left in her mind, to care. He'd seen the narrowing path of her affections as his four sisters and two brothers married and produced their own children, so he knew that when his own child was born, his mother would barely remember its name.

He walked Souria back to their quarter and upstairs to their flat, where she'd already moved in by joining her little chair and her zellij table to the big wrought iron bed he'd had passed down to him from an older brother gone rich in Casablanca. He closed the front door to the cold December wind and he pushed Souria against it with the force of a kiss. She smiled while he was kissing her, and he felt it; her lips were always so perfectly soft, and for the wedding, she'd tinted them with color. He unwrapped her face from its bright white hijab, which Nasr had beaded especially for the marriage day. She'd dressed prettily but warmly, and so he had to unzip her turtleneck sweater and peel it over her hair. He raised each cup of her bra over each breast and kissed both nipples, buried his face in her neck. "I am the luckiest man in this whole kingdom," he said. He took her to his bedroom, where he made love to her in a manner that didn't last as long as he'd wished.

He hadn't asked if she was happy, but if he had, she would have told him yes, infinitely so. She no longer practiced her fantasies of home, of the small strand of trees or her laughing brother; they had drifted away from her as if they were shadows of cloud blowing over the sand of the desert. He was her family now, and she'd have papers, and a passport. Like a village griot, she'd start a new line of family stories. Anass was the first man who'd ever loved her apart from her body. He loved her laughter and her soft disdain, it seemed, and he loved all the corners of her mind—even the parts she wasn't offering.

When she went deep into herself and remembered her lost daughter, he left her to listen to his radio matches, or he went up to the roof of their building to smoke a cigarette. Even if she were still curled on the floor, intent in grief, he never forced her to talk, never made her give herself to him. There'd been small night hours when she woke up thinking she heard Yu crying from a neighboring apartment; she'd sob, softly, and Anass would simply hold her. In the market, she'd once held a bag of potatoes and judged it to be the exact same weight as Yumni. She stood there in the middle of the route, with people passing all around her, the potato sack held close to her throat and her own hand thrown over her eyes. Anass took the bag out of her hand and paid for it at the counter.

There were all the times she didn't come home from Nasr's shop on time because she'd walked the Orson Welles Square looking for a little sandal that might have been sitting under a city bench, neglected all these five years. She'd wander to the CD shop Yu had loved so much and look for her daughter, still dancing in the shopkeeper's doorway. She'd wind through the medina, searching, and she was sometimes so late in getting home that Anass would have to make cheese sandwiches for his own dinner. But he never asked.

He never made inquiries, either, about why she had already known sex, or why small scars crisscrossed her stomach, or why she threw the plastic measuring cup into the sink in an unprovoked rage. Why she sometimes punched the bag of flour so hard with her knife that it exploded into the air above her head.

When Anass put another child inside of her, and when, after the fifteen hours of labor that stretched from Fajr to Maghrib, she heard Aamer's first cry, she'd fallen into a kind of forgetfulness. She still loved Yumni, still looked for her face on the head of every eight-year-old girl she saw. But now there was a son, someone to drive her attentions back to the world that was real. Aamer needed her songs and her swaddling and her breast. He kept her out of the Orson Welles Square and home in the evenings. Anass took over the shopping. He was terrible at picking fruits, and she'd get unripe melons and cherries rotted all the way to their pits. But she was so happy for this help, which she'd never had with her first baby.

"She looks like she might drop him," Anass says now, in Arabic, of her Yu, her Yumni-turned-Mardi, holding Aamer as he sleeps. Yumni flashes Anass a look; she's smart enough to know he's talking about her even if she can't understand what's been said. But it's true—even as she turns her face back down to Aamer's, she holds him stiffly, at a slight distance, as if at any moment he might wake up and bite her. She looks uncomfortable and pleased, all at the same time, the way she had as a baby watching the acrobats in the Djmaa-el-Fna.

Aamer and Yu are one half-each of Souria, but they look nothing like brother and sister. There's tall, bulky Yu, in her tight American blue jeans and sweatshirt, her big bush of unbraided hair. She's come back even darker than Souria remembered her, looking like a Senegalese or a Liberian, like a visitor to this country. Aamer, nuzzled in her arms, has taken his half of Souria and drowned it. He's taken his father's slick hair and light skin; he's as Moroccan as the king himself.

"So you take him," Souria tells Anass, in Arabic. She's tired of the suggestions he makes now in the night, that she kept Yumni a secret because she is tricky and distasteful, and what they've done in bed has been rougher in the four days that Yumni has been with them.

"Al-jaar qabit al-dar," Souria tells him. "She might not be mine at all. This child could be an angel of the Prophet, and then how will you have treated her?"

But he cannot let go of the thought that she and Yumni are agents of ruination for him and his son, and he has drawn the boy away from his mother so that the household, when Mardi and Souria sit in the living room watching cartoons, feels hewn in half. He asks unanswerable questions of the girl in Dharija *and* French, used as extra proof that the child has no language save English and is therefore too simple to belong in their home. The first day, Yumni had to be shown how to squat over the latrine, and afterward, Souria had to pour water from the plastic jug to clean her spray. On the couch, Anass shook his head, mopping his eyes as he smirked. Yu hasn't used the latrine since. The visits last hours. Souria knows she is holding her water. When Souria changed the propane for cooking, Yu stood back, too frightened to enter the kitchen.

The worst, though, is that Souria can no longer reach her daughter through words. She tries to teach her Dharija, but she runs into the wall of the girl's English, and Yumni, understanding her own limitations, resists learning. They've not gotten much further than "la basilik," and why should they? She has an easy American life now, this Prophet's (peace be upon him) angel, no need to cobble together communication. She has no concept of wudu. She sits on the divan watching as they prepare their mats and answer the call to prayer. She hasn't spent any of the four nights of her visit in their home; each evening after dinner, she asks Souria, in the plugged and halting French she is losing, to walk with her back to the American woman's hotel.

The American woman has a scar on her face that made Souria wonder, at first, what kind of terrible person she was in her country. But she's brought her daughter back as a person as free as the ocean, which is nothing Souria had ever been able to promise. In all the years Yu's been gone, Souria had imagined her fallen off a rocky cliff, run over by a taxi, mangled by the fists of abusers. It has been the will of Allah that her child has known, instead, such safety. Souria knows she will have to work hard not to undo it.

Anass goes over to take his son, and he's smiling at her, but Yumni knows better than to trust his face—she sees through it, to him. She hands her brother over before Anass can even ask, and as he puts his sleeping son in her lap, Souria feels a gallop of her beating heart, that the two halves of herself might never make a whole family.

"À l'hôtel, s'il vous plaît," Yu says to Anass, without looking at him.

"Attends," Souria says, and she puts Aamer gently down on the couch, so he stays asleep. She runs to the kitchen, scoops tajine in a plastic tub from the hypermarché. "Afwan," she says, but Yu is Mardi now, and understands neither the language nor the gesture. Her little eyes are moist, on the verge of tears. Souria kisses her and puts a hand over her own heart. *I love you*, she thinks. *You don't understand anymore, but I am your mother.*

She goes for her own jacket, but Yu says, "Non." She looks to Anass. "Le monsieur," she says. She wants him to walk her back.

And Souria is so afraid of what this means, whether it means Yumni will go back to the hotel and tell the American woman that this is all a mistake, that she doesn't want to come back and be Moroccan. Souria had always assumed that sadness was whispering terrible things in her ears, the things that had happened to Mardi. But here her child has been, all these years, across an ocean, in a new life with a French name and thick sweaters and enough, always, to eat. Returned now with a complete misunderstanding of herself, yet no need for the understanding. There were no magical powers, after all, to having the same blood. Yu had been in Essaouira two days before the American woman brought her to Savons Mogador, and Souria hadn't felt a thing, not even one tiny molecule of relief blown across her soul. She hadn't heard her own daughter as a whisper across space, even that little of it.

Anass isn't the first person to own his old motorcycle, or even the second. It's been handed over many times, passed down through men who've loved it, and though Souria doesn't know what year the machine came into being, she does understand that he has to kick the pedal sometimes twenty times before the gas pumps itself up the line. She's heard him complain that rust is eating the metal under his seat, and when the three of them ride, Souria on the seat behind Anass, Aamer snugly ensconced between her chest and his back, she can hear the springs screech as he leans into his turns. She watches him now, out their second-floor window, kicking his pedal, and she feels stirred at the sight of him in his blue gendarme's uniform. It would have been enough to belong to any struggling man in this country, but she belongs to an agent of the king himself.

Anass has told her, though, that there is talk. Reshufflings in the country's gendarmerie. There simply are not that many positions in a place like Essaouira, and it's a post that so many men want, in this tourist town with its petty problems. "We have to be cautious with money," he's told her. "I could be moved or I could lose my post completely, if someone higher than me wants to be here. We have no crystal ball. Mind how much meat you take from the butcher."

He's spoken of it only in the days since Yu has been back, but it may not be manipulation so much as coincidence: if Anass says he's heard talk, Souria will just have to believe him. There's nothing to do but trust him, as she's been doing since the day she left the little flat in Diabat. *Keep your head*, her landlord's wife had said, as she helped her downstairs with a table. *No one wants to marry a girl with no family.* But Anass has turned out to be a good man, just like the men of her village. He wants only her happiness, and he keeps making her happiness happen.

And so, when the American woman comes with Yu on the sixth day of their visit and says she wants to talk about what might happen next, about passports and certificates and aide financière, Anass says to Souria, *you know what you need to do,* and she knows that the heaviest day of her life has come.

She knows that she cannot bring a Mardi back and turn her into a Yumni. She has begun to doubt the will of Allah, but she knows that will get her nowhere. The wishes of one thin slave are nothing against Al-Khaliq, Al-Wahhab, Al-Qadir, or any of the other ninety-nine names of Allah. She could push back against the Timeless, the One, or the Perceiver, but it would be like pushing against the hard side of a mountain. Senseless.

She believes, too, that if she says the wrong thing, if the American woman becomes angry and runs off to the main road that leads to all the power of her three-story, landscaped hotel, she will never see her own daughter again. She knows that the second, final time of Yu disappearing would be worse than the first; the second time would kill her. The American woman has brought someone from the hotel to help her translate, and there is this small atom of hope, because why should Souria give up her daughter for a fiddler she met under the arch at Bab Doukkala? But the translator has a cream linen suit and perfectly straightened teeth, and she speaks perfect French, English as clipped and clean as a steel box. This old life would be too much of a new life for Yu: the smile of a thousand lemons has faded in the six days to a look of weariness. One of the days, she sat on the sofa in the living room scribbling figures onto graphing paper, and the sight of it kicked a pump in Souria's mind. They could never send her to

283

school here—they could barely afford to send Aamer, and he was a son; of course he would be the one to go. All those lovely mathematics in her daughter's brain would be gone to ruin. Yu would not wish for this new, old life. Yu isn't, now, even her daughter's name.

A pain comes twisting Souria's heart, and she packs it down with the light, airy laughter of the American people on her new television. She turned on the light and watched her own brown face in the mirror that morning, noted the way the lines were beginning across her forehead, the way her chapped pores told her that time could never be reclaimed. The world moved past a point; you lost that point. You had to move on with the world. She thinks of Anass, how he put the five fingers of the khamsah on her son's bald head the month of his birth. And this is the only thing that keeps her sitting still as the American woman begins speaking her Yumni's same English, and Yumni sits by the American woman, holding her hand.

Insh'allah doesn't always mean yes. Allah's will is a call, not an answer.

XXVIII. The Maghreb

Shannon had felt, her entire time in Essaouira, that she'd put her head in the deep, war-rutted groove of a guillotine, and each evening Mardi came back was one more day the blade had missed its mark. Their third day in the hotel, Shannon discovered a Hello Kitty sticker Mardi had fixed to the window. She tried, with her thumbnail, to remove it, but it had become one with the glass. She spent an hour rubbing and scraping, first with a rag and then with a razor, and then sunk onto the bed in a defeated sag. That night, when Mardi returned with a long, clinging hug, Shannon put herself in the shower and started the running water so her daughter couldn't hear her sob with relief. The following day, she knew, the crowd in her mind would reassemble. Mardi would go back to her real mother's house, and the executioner would don his little black hood. She'd line her head in the groove anew.

The fourth day she dropped Mardi off, she got directly into one of the shared taxis that roved Souria's quarter, but before she could fully close the door, a man reached through the window and grabbed the strap of the little black purse that held her passport and spending money. He couldn't possibly have known what was inside, but once the driver took off, he ran alongside, dodging traffic, his hand still clutching her purse strap. The taxi revved up to its five and then ten miles per hour, and an approaching car passed so close that the running man was almost gored by its rearview mirror. Everyone in the taxi screamed in their language to tell him what a fool he was, yet still he held on, until the taxi got fast enough to lose him. Shannon turned back to see him standing in the exact middle of the street, still dodging traffic. He waved an arm at her, furious. She had enough money in her purse to buy herself lunch. He'd had so little to lose in life as that.

If the world were a house, Shannon realized, Morocco was one of its tiniest upstairs rooms, one with frosted stained glass on its windows but chunks of plaster falling from its ceiling. Vlad had come to this economy to exploit its ten dirham to the dollar, and she'd come and stolen a child. In their twenties, her friends had gotten great jobs, married nice people, started 401(k)s. She'd watched them while smoking a blunt. Adulthood had passed her by, so she'd come to the cantilevered room and stolen a child. She'd told herself she'd rescued Mardi from the street, but there'd been nothing noble about it. Mardi's real, biological mother had been here the whole time—in the room, in this country, waiting.

Souria was taller than Shannon, statelier and more regal, and it should have blunted her pity, but each time she took in the woman's rake-thin shoulders under her djellaba, she felt wicked to her core.

Souria had waited two days before asking. "Why you took her?" she said.

Shannon responded in French first. "J'ai pensais qu'elle était perdue."

"Lost?" Souria had asked. "Lost?" she asked again, the starch rising to her voice.

"Okay, I was the one who was lost," Shannon said, in English.

"Al'negliziya," Souria said, her hands flying in frustration, like birds attempting flight, her way of reminding Shannon she didn't speak English.

"I just—" Shannon began again, in English, before finding that French was just as good for untruth. "Dans notre pays, les enfants ne courent pas dans les ruelles."

She'd wanted to wound Souria, chide her for leaving her bicycle lying around the neighborhood. But Souria backed off. Nodded once, then twice, as if settling a balance. "I had no other way to work," she said. There were years of sadness in her eyes. Shannon couldn't believe she hadn't noticed. Some open-handed part of her wanted to turn Mardi over directly, leave the country, and go back to America to die.

Still, Mardi was all Shannon had. Each time her daughter's stay in Souria's apartment stretched out to its fifth or sixth hour, Shannon was felled by how close her generosity felt to stupidity. Mardi would fall in love with her own mother—why wouldn't she? If she fell in love, too, with her stepfather and baby brother, if she fell for couscous and tajine and guembri and high winds, if she realized, even at eight years old, that blood was thicker than water and that she'd been stolen like any common slave, then she'd want to stay. If Shannon had raised Mardi to have any sense and decency at all, she'd want to stay. And Shannon would let her. No fighting. No begging. She would at last in this life do a right thing.

She'd been relieved, on the first day, to find that Souria seemed to be afraid of something. She'd refused to involve the authorities, and had confessed, between kisses on the back of Mardi's neck, that she had no Moroccan papers. *But she's her biological daughter*, Shannon thought, *and she'll do whatever it takes*. If Shannon raised a stink, Souria would simply take Mardi and run away, disappear into all that sand. There'd be no more evening laughter, no games with dream cards, no school pickup lanes or birthday parties. Size ten would be Shannon's last and final season of children's clothes. She'd live in a world where happy and meaningful things were dead. It would be a world without nouns, just verbs. *Lose. Cry. Regret.*

She'd melted, she knew then. For this one little person on Earth, she'd let herself melt. She hadn't even known it was happening, but she'd become, deeply and irrevocably, Mardi's mother. And because she was her mother, she would do the right thing. Smooth the fondant of her child's rage. Salve her hurt. Return her to her rightful mother. Because she had melted, she'd have to melt further—that's how it worked.

The right thing never felt like the good thing. She forgave herself. She hadn't known.

XXIX. Forever

My American mother has a story about what happened in the alley that day, and my Moroccan mother has a whole different story. My American mother says love fell on her like a piece of Skylab the first time she saw me, that it was like having a near-fatal car wreck all over again, but a good one, one that fixed her instead of breaking her. My Moroccan mother says she thought I was safe there in her little corner of the medina, that Driss and Hafiza were watching me like a daughter. She'd met with such good fortune, she thought, Allah having finally placed the fruit of her life on a vine that would produce more sweetness.

Both their stories smother me like a wet blanket. Neither story is mine. My mothers' feelings are so large, it's possible there is no room for my story. I just know that the pain of me is double for having known both of them. The pain of me is having two names and two points of origin. I'm split like an injured tree, forever waiting for someone to graft me back together with wax.

My sixth day in Morocco, I said goodbye to the woman who carried me in her body. She spent much of that morning on her prayer rug, and her misbaha broke while she was saying dhikr. She said it the twenty-third time—*inna lillahe wa inna ilaihe rajiooon*—and the string snapped, midsupplication, the thirty-three blue pearls scattering across the floor in their beautiful disorder. She looked at me like she'd gotten the message then: even a real, actual mother of blood and milk and skin could not tamper with divine plans.

I'll give her this—she did not cry. She made me one final breakfast of khobz. She folded her best red djellaba into a paper sack and gave it to me, made gifts of two oranges she'd bought at the souk. She walked me into the big French hotel and told my American mother to take very good care of me. She said it in the lobby, en français, to her own soft feet, then turned without saying goodbye. Neither I nor my American mother moved. It had all been like a dream that leaves you sweaty, but without fear. The woman who carried me in her body disappeared out the door and down the boardwalk in one long, brown line of hijab.

Both my mother and I watched my mmi as she walked smaller and smaller, her head drooped increasingly lower in private misery, until she reached the place where the sidewalk met a cross street, and her man stepped out of time to join her. Wind blew the tail of her skirt just high enough that I saw her knobby ankles and her thin calves, and I looked away toward the ocean to keep from igniting sadness. At the sight of the ocean my mind went a bit sozzled, as if someone had shaken my brain around in my skull: there came the fuzzy lines of another day on the beach; my mmi's hair blowing; a woman swimming, in trouble. Not a real memory but a shadowy onion skin of the present, I thought, something Ms. Lin-Wood might have called perception.

I looked back for my mmi to find her husband holding on to her waist as she fit her head into the crook of his neck. Together they hobbled down the street toward their quarter. They were a family again, sans intrusion.

But she'd said it, my mmi had. *Take very good care of her. One day, she will come back.*

And the next day we got on the plane, with its cavernous metal insides, its cramped leathery seats and small, humpbacked windows. On the way to Madrid, I rested my head on my mother's arm and looked out the window at the curve of the earth, the layer of atmosphere we were traversing, the slice of thin oxygen that lay above the bed of clouds but below the solid, dark line of ozone. Occasionally, I looked up at Mom's sad eyes and thought of my other mom's sad eyes, and knew that neither of them had won.

And I rarely tell people that I'm adopted—it's none of their business—but when I do, sometimes, someone who knows nothing will say, oh, you must be so grateful. But they're confusing love with gratitude. I don't need to be grateful. And I'm fifteen now, which, according to an article I found open on Mom's laptop screen, means I can be as ungrateful as I want. It's my new job. When I was thirteen, Mom got up the money to take us back to Morocco, but the woman who carried me, her distance was even farther by then. My half-brother, little as he was, was ashamed of my dark skin; he and his friends laughed, said things in Arabic when I walked past them outdoors. My stepfather the policeman (what else to call him?) asked me for two thousand dirham when my mother was in the kitchen and couldn't hear him.

In Dad's house, it is much the same. Dad (what else to call him?) plays ball outside with my half-brother the way he never did with me. Jitka asks me why don't I blow my hair straight, *how pretty that would be*, and when am I going to stop listening to that *gangster boogie*? I am the tallest, blackest, straightest spine in both my families, and only in Mom's house is that perfect. But Mom wants me to make straight As and hang all my clothes. She wants me to wear more deodorant and take my earbuds out when she speaks to me. I may be perfect, but not entirely.

My fifth day in Morocco, the day before I said goodbye to the woman who carried me, she took me to visit her friend Amina, whose husband had just died. Amina was more educated than my Moroccan mother. She spoke English in fits and starts, like the cantor of a horse. Listening hard, I pieced together that when her husband was dying, when he got to the very end, he started speaking to his mother. "It was the middle of night," she said, "and his mother talked back, I promise you, then next thing, he was gone. His mother, she was dead forty years." And then she told me that the nurses said they'd seen it so many times, that patients always asked for their mothers at the end. They talked to their mothers all the way across life to death, as if their mothers had just come to ferry them onward.

And I think about this a lot. It's a small and manageable planet, and Morocco is only eleven hours of flight time away. But even if Mom can never afford it again, even if the woman who carried me is lost to me for this lifetime, a life might not be such a long time. When I start calling out to my mother to come get me? I'll be lucky. I'll be talking to them both.

Acknowledgments

First and foremost, I'd like to thank my children, who have long inspired me to see the rich world beyond the visible one. I'd like to thank my friend James Bernard Short, who helped me keep the faith in every incarnation of this story. I am eternally grateful to Anni Liu, Fiona McCrae, and everyone else at Graywolf who brilliantly saw all the narrative possibilities I did not in this novel. I'd like to thank my translator, Abedelali En Nasry, for orthographic assistance in both Dharija and Hassaniya, and I'd like to thank the editors of *Generations Literary Journal*, *Germ Magazine*, and *Pluck! The Journal of Affrilachian Arts and Culture*, for publishing early chapters. A very special thank you to Charles Rowell at *Callaloo*, who celebrated and published so much of this novel as it went through its incarnations.

I'd like also to thank Al Jazeera for publishing the article on Mauritanian slavery that was the germ of this novel way back when, and especially Boubacar Ould and Salimata Lam of SOS Esclaves and Brahim Abeid of IRA-Mauritania, all of whom hosted me in Nouakchott during what would become the most powerful journey I've ever taken. This book would never have come to be without my experiences in Morocco and Mauritania, and none of that would ever have come to be without my Fulbright in Côte d'Ivoire—may Congress always fund the Fulbright Program. I offer gratitude to the Kingdom of Morocco for being a place where my children and I have grown up almost every summer for the last twenty years, and, for directing my travels in that realm and all others, Alhamdu lillahi rabbi alamin.

JACINDA TOWNSEND is the author of *Saint Monkey* (Norton, 2014), which is set in 1950s eastern Kentucky and won the Janet Heidinger Kafka Prize for best fiction written by a woman and the James Fenimore Cooper Prize for historical fiction. *Saint Monkey* was also the 2015 Honor Book of the Black Caucus of the American Library Association. Townsend is a graduate of the Iowa Writers' Workshop and teaches in the MFA program at the University of Michigan.

The text of *Mother Country* is set in Haarlemmer.
Book design by Rachel Holscher.
Composition by Bookmobile Design and Digital
Publisher Services, Minneapolis, Minnesota.
Manufactured by McNaughton & Gunn on acid-free,
100 percent postconsumer wastepaper.